WHO BY
WATER

A DAME POLARA MYSTERY

WHO BY WATER

GREG RHYNO

CORMORANT
BOOKS

Copyright © 2025 Greg Rhyno
This edition copyright © 2025 Cormorant Books Inc.
This is a first edition.

No part of this publication may be reproduced, stored in a retrieval system or transmitted, in any form or by any means, without the prior written consent of the publisher or a licence from The Canadian Copyright Licensing Agency (Access Copyright). For an Access Copyright licence, visit www.accesscopyright.ca or call toll free 1.800.893.5777.

The publisher and the author expressly forbid the use of this book in any manner for the purpose of training so-called artificial intelligence systems or technologies, and reserve this title from the text and data mining exception in accordance with the European Parliament directive.

   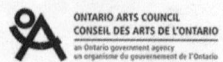 

We acknowledge financial support for our publishing activities: the Government of Canada, through the Canada Book Fund and The Canada Council for the Arts; the Government of Ontario, through the Ontario Arts Council, Ontario Creates, and the Ontario Book Publishing Tax Credit.

LIBRARY AND ARCHIVES CANADA CATALOGUING IN PUBLICATION

Title: Who by water / Greg Rhyno.
Names: Rhyno, Greg, 1976- author.
Description: Series statement: A Dame Polara mystery ; 2
Identifiers: Canadiana (print) 20240457560 | Canadiana (ebook) 20240457579 | ISBN 9781770867871 (softcover) | ISBN 9781770867888 (EPUB)
Subjects: LCGFT: Detective and mystery fiction. | LCGFT: Novels.
Classification: LCC PS8635.H97 W57 2025 | DDC C813/.6—dc23

United States Library of Congress Control Number: 2024944660

Cover and interior text design: Marijke Friesen
Manufactured by Houghton Boston in Saskatoon,
Saskatchewan in February, 2025.

Printed using paper from a responsible and sustainable resource, including a mix of virgin fibres and recycled materials.

Printed and bound in Canada.

EU RP eucomply OÜ
Pärnu mnt 139b-14, 11317 Tallinn, Estonia
hello@eucompliancepartner.com, +3375690241

CORMORANT BOOKS INC.
260 ISHPADINAA (SPADINA) AVENUE, SUITE 502,
TKARONTO (TORONTO), ON M5T 2E4

SUITE 110, 7068 PORTAL WAY, FERNDALE, WA 98248, USA
info@cormorantbooks.com / www.cormorantbooks.com

For Mark, Kityan, Frankie & Nico

A little water clears us of this deed.
— Lady Macbeth, from *Macbeth*

CHAPTER ONE

DAME DOTTED HER day-old pizza with sriracha sauce. Fresh from the microwave, the crust had the consistency and taste of damp cardboard. Still, to enjoy a few minutes on her own in the dingy break room — without tiny hands reaching for her, or a tiny mouth howling at her — Dame could have been eating lobster thermidor on the Champs-Élysées. Two years of motherhood had taught Dame that sometimes you had to go back to work to get a break.

When she returned to City Hall's Heritage Planning office, Lewis was staring at his computer screen and popping cashews into his mouth, one at a time. Beside him was a Costco-sized tub of assorted nuts.

"You've already worked your way through the pecans?"

Lewis nodded and stuffed another cashew into his mouth.

"Aren't you going to eat any of the almonds? They're good for you."

"Almonds are garbage nuts," he said. "Only Meera eats almonds."

Dame grabbed the chair from her desk and rolled it over to his cubicle. She sat down beside him.

"Any word about the Merc?"

Lewis shook his head. "They've been at it for a long time."

For months now, their team had been working to protect an old Ossington storefront called the Mercantile. Not only did the place feature art deco stone carvings that dated back to the 1920s, but in the past decade, the Merc had been reimagined as a cultural hub, a profitable gallery space combined with an ant colony of studio spaces shared by over forty local artists. This, of course, hadn't stopped the new owners from applying for immediate and total demolition. They wanted to break ground for a new high-rise by September. Dame had seen the rendering at the last city council meeting. Forty storeys of glass and steel. Three-hundred-square-foot starter units going for $800K. Commercial space below for a Chipotle or a Panda Express or a KFC. They were branding it as an innovative cultural centre for Trinity-Bellwoods: Bespoke Lofts.

Dame stretched out her legs. "You worried?"

Lewis ran a hand over his thinning hair. "I don't know," he said. "Maybe? It's Meera's biggest hearing since she got — you know — Peggy's job."

At the mention of their old boss, there was a sudden, quiet pressure in the room, like the feeling you get on an airplane just before your ears pop. Three years had passed since Dame had discovered that Peggy Beckers was behind one of the biggest arson conspiracies in Toronto's history. Three years since Dame had discovered that Peggy Beckers was responsible for her mother's death.

No one had seen Peggy since then. And no one really liked to say her name out loud.

"Okay, listen," Dame said. "When you guys drove in today, was Meera's hair up in a bun or was it down around her shoulders?"

Lewis shrugged. "I don't know. Why?"

"Think about it. Up or down?"

He stared into the middle distance. "Down. Her hair was down this morning."

"Well, there you go. Nothing to worry about."

"How do you know?"

"When she's stressed out, she puts her hair up in a bun. When she's got things under control, she wears it down."

Lewis frowned. "She does?"

Dame reached over and stole a few cashews. "How have you guys been married for, like, a gazillion years, and you've never noticed that?"

"I don't know. Maybe because I wasn't raised by the West End's answer to Sam Spade."

"Speaking of Dodge" — Dame stood up — "I better get going."

She stuffed her laptop into her backpack and started heading toward the door.

"Aren't you going to stick around and find out what happens?" Lewis asked.

"Don't need to," Dame said. "We won."

"And you're basing this entirely on Meera's hair?"

"Well, that" — she waggled her phone — "and the fact that she called ten minutes ago and told me so."

Dame dodged an airborne almond and made her way down the hallway to the elevator.

IT WAS HOT outside, and the hard blue of early August stretched itself out behind the skyline. Dame caught the streetcar on King, and as it trundled toward her neighbourhood, she caught glimpses of the city as it passed by. The sturdy Beaux-Arts beauty of the Union Building. The thousand light bulbs of the Royal Alex. And of course, the condos. So many condos. M5V, Six50, the Clock Tower, CitySphere. Glass and steel behemoths shouldering their way into every neighbourhood and levelling everything that came before.

Eventually, Dame managed to doze a little, but a sudden buzzing against her hip startled her awake. She dug her phone out of her pocket and adjusted her glasses.

The message itself wasn't unusual — *Could I give you a call?* — but the sender's name fired an unwelcome thrill of adrenaline through Dame's body. *Rachel Suarez.* Why was *she* texting her? It had to be a mistake. A slip of the thumb. Like the time she was in a fitting room and needed Meera's opinion on a pair of jeans but accidentally sent the picture to her aging father. Thankfully, he never replied to the photo she sent, or the question she asked: *Does my butt look good in these?*

It was best just to let it go. She settled back into her seat and tried to ignore the bad vibes mosquitoing around her brain.

"WELL, HELLO!"

Fatima, her father's former Homecare worker and current girlfriend, greeted her at the door and pulled her into a hug. "Come on in."

Dame followed the woman into the kitchen.

"Tea? Cookies?" she offered. "I have some of those Peek Freans you like, but your father ate all the chocolate ones."

"That's okay, Fatima. I'll just take one exhausting two-year-old, please."

A high-pitched wail erupted from the bedroom.

"To go," Dame added.

"Oh, let them play." Fatima sat down and patted the table. "Come sit with me."

Dame took a seat and looked around. The little apartment seemed more cheerful since Fatima moved in. Gone were the stacks of mouldering crime novels and serial killer biographies. Instead, there were books on the shelf like *More Than Words Can*

Say: A No-Nonsense Guide to Living with Aphasia and *Silent Partner: Romance Beyond Language*.

"She's quite a charmer, your daughter."

"Yeah," Dame sighed. "That's one word for her."

"She and your father have been building something in the spare bedroom for hours. Every time I go in there, they kick me out. It's like the two of them speak their own private language."

"Well, they essentially have the same vocabulary."

Just then, Dame's daughter blasted out of the bedroom, weaving like a first year on reading week.

"Mama!" she bellowed. "Mama up!"

The little girl clamped onto her mother's knee and Dame hoisted her up on her lap.

"Hey, partner," she said. "You two having fun?"

"Dodge!" She pointed at the bedroom as the old man lumbered out, sporting the ancient purple scars that a hotel fire had left all over his body.

There was a growling in the back of his throat, as if the words trapped in there were building momentum. A shushing sound came out of his lips, and finally, a word.

"*Shit.*"

Dame and Fatima looked at each other. Rosie eyed Dodge with what looked like suspicion.

He tried again. "*Shi-tuh—*"

As it always had since the old man's stroke, Dame's internal search engine started autocompleting:

shiitake

shih tzu

Schitt's Creek

But before Dame could offer a suggestion ("*Did you mean: Rosie shit herself?*"), Fatima held up her hand like a stop sign.

"Let him do it. He's getting so much better."

Dodge wrestled with the words and, eventually, managed to drag them out of his mouth. "*S-she takes*," he said, "*after Grandpa.*"

Rosie slid off her mother's lap. "Bad guy in jay-yo."

"Bad guy?" Dame raised an eyebrow.

"Mama come." Her tiny hands gripped Dame by the wrist.

At Rosie's insistence, Dame followed the little girl into the bedroom. There, she and her grandfather had constructed an elaborate crime scene that cobbled together most of the toys in the apartment. A Playmobil police officer stood guard outside a makeshift Lego squad car. A road of repurposed Jenga blocks wound past a Fisher-Price family farm and stopped at a cardboard prison. Inside, one of Dame's old My Little Ponies was behind Tinkertoy bars.

"Bad guy." Rosie pointed at a particularly guilty-looking Princess Moondust. "Bad guy in jay-yo."

Dame frowned at Dodge. In return, he offered an innocent grin.

"You know I still have to tell her about her father," Dame said.

Dodge shrugged.

"I just don't want her to get the wrong idea."

Rosie gave them both a quizzical look and then busied herself with drumming on a bankers box. When Dame took a closer look at the kid's makeshift bongos, she noticed dates scrawled across the side in magic marker: "*1990–1996.*"

"Are those old case files?" She pushed the bridge of her glasses up her nose. "Come on, Dodge. We talked about this."

The old man reached into the closet and pulled out a blue plastic bag. It was full of crumpled papers and file folders.

"Good. You should've tossed it all years ago." Dame crouched down and eased the top off the box. Rosie wandered across the room and started inspecting the closet. "Jesus, look at all this stuff. The Lawrence Park Larcenies? The Hoggs Hollow Horse Ransom?" She unearthed one heavy, battered folder, held together with a withered elastic band and marked with a "*J.W.*"

"This is the Weatherhead Case, right?"

Dodge nodded.

"Must've been over twenty-five years ago." She flipped through the pages. "This was a weird one."

The old man nodded again.

"What was that kid's name again? Spencer something? God, what a piece of work."

Dodge gestured for her to take the file folder.

"Happy to. I'll throw it right into the recycling bin." She looked at Rosie, who was trying to chuck a sheaf of paper across the room. "It's time we put all this junk behind us."

CHAPTER TWO

IT WAS ONLY after she muscled through the nightly whirlwind of convincing food into Rosie, reading to Rosie, singing to Rosie, and waiting for Rosie to say goodnight to her many, many stuffed animals, that Dame was able to enjoy a few precious moments alone in her apartment. It was a smallish two-bedroom unit in an old bay-and-gable on O'Hara Avenue. The floorboards were creaky and the walls were water-damaged, but the rent was holding steady, thanks to a landlord that owed her a couple favours. Compared to the tidy charm of Dodge's apartment, her place was a clutter of toys and laundry and Tupperware. All of it smelled a little like sour milk and urine.

Dame went to the living room and collapsed on the couch. In the old days, Thursday nights were close enough to the weekend to be packed with possibility. But now, the gravitational pull of comfortable furniture was irresistible. Even the television's remote control seemed out of reach. Staying still and closing her eyes was probably the most practical course of action. But just as she could feel exhaustion cement her into place, her phone started buzzing and wouldn't stop.

One of the things Dame appreciated about being a thirty-nine-year-old newish mom was that nobody actually called her anymore. Especially after nine o'clock. With that in mind, Dame anticipated a very ignorable telemarketer, but when she looked at her phone, she remembered the text she got earlier that day. *Could I give you a call?* It seemed like its sender had finally given up waiting for Dame's permission.

She hit the red button and dropped her phone on the table with a clatter. No thanks. Whatever bullshit Rachel Suarez was selling, Dame wasn't buying.

When she closed her eyes, though, a series of images weaseled their way into her head. Sometimes, the pictures she deleted off her phone had the bad habit of reappearing in her brain, like algorithm-generated slideshows: *Featured Photos*, or *Memories for You*, or *Nine Years Ago Today*. In her mind's eye, she saw a much younger version of herself, standing next to her new husband. Young Dame looking slightly uncomfortable in her dress and veil. Young Adam addressing an unseen crowd of friends and family. And there was that other picture, too, of Young Dame and Even Younger Rachel Suarez, side by side, blushing bride and maid of honour.

Soon enough, the pictures blurred and faded. But just as Dame edged toward the precipice of sleep, there was an impossibly loud knocking at her front door. Dame scrambled off the couch, awake like someone had doused her with a bucket of ice water.

She looked at her phone again. It couldn't be. Could it?

Dame steeled herself and walked the few steps to her front door. When she opened it a crack, she was relieved to see Meera on the other side. Her hair, as Lewis noted earlier, was decidedly down.

"Did I wake you up?" she said. "You look like you just rolled out of bed."

Dame shrugged. "I think that's just how I look now."

Meera smiled as she walked past Dame and sat down on the couch. Out of her bag, she produced a bottle of El Silencio. "We're going to need a couple glasses."

Dame returned a moment later with tumblers and poured them each a drink. "To the Merc."

"May it never be another condo." Meera touched her glass to Dame's. She took a swig and winced a little. "You know, we worked on that case for months. The least you could've done was stick around and celebrate a little."

"Dodge has Rosie on Thursdays. Plus, he and Fatima just took her for an overnight on Monday, so I didn't want to keep them waiting."

"I get it. You're busy these days." Meera took another, more careful sip of mezcal. "But sometimes it feels like — I don't know — like it's more than just a scheduling issue."

Dame looked up at her. "What do you mean?"

Meera shrugged. "I mean that ever since you came back from mat leave, things have been a little different."

Dame glanced at the door to the nursery. "Life *is* different, now."

"You just don't seem as keen on the job as you used to be. Your heart's not really in it."

"Maybe. Ever since I had Rosie, I'm just a little more interested in the future than ancient Torontonian history."

"Hey, pal" — Meera pointed a finger at Dame — "ancient Torontonian history keeps that little girl of yours in macaroni and yogurt. '*Just because you're done with the past doesn't mean it's done with you.*'"

"Is that Nietzsche?"

Meera shook her head. "I think it's from one of those *Jurassic Park* sequels Lewis made me watch."

"Well, speaking of the past" — Dame picked up her phone from the coffee table — "Rachel called me tonight."

"Like, *Rachel* Rachel?"

Dame nodded.

"What did she want?"

"Don't know. Didn't answer."

"You aren't the least bit curious?"

"Nope."

"Huh. Maybe you really are moving forward." Meera finished the rest of her glass and gave a little shiver. "Speaking of which, I should probably get going. If I leave Lewis alone for too long, the cat starts bullying him."

"How is Elwy Yost these days?"

"Oh, man. I'm telling you, Dame" — Meera yawned — "this whole parenthood business is a *slog*."

Dame smiled. "I've heard that."

MOMENTS AFTER MEERA shut the door, Dame lay back down on the couch. Almost immediately, she could feel the arms of sleep pulling her into a black embrace. At least until the sound of a second knock dragged her back into the real world.

"Oh, for fuck's sake," she croaked from the couch. "Just come in."

Undoubtedly, it was Meera again. No more than ten minutes had passed since she'd left, which — for Meera — was just enough time to realize she'd forgotten either her phone, her wallet, or both somewhere in the apartment.

"You lose something?" Dame asked when she heard the door creak open.

But the woman who stepped inside wasn't Meera.

"Dame?"

The woman standing in her front hall was Rachel.

"I need your help."

Rachel Rachel.

"Adam's missing," she said. "He's been gone for over a week."

CHAPTER THREE

"OKAY. SLOW DOWN. Start again from the start."

Dame put a mug of tea in front of the woman and then sat down across from her at the kitchen table. Less than an hour ago, she was drifting off into a well-deserved unconsciousness, and now, she was making tea ("*Do you have any almond milk?*") for Rachel Suarez. Rachel-*husband-fucking*-Suarez.

"Adam turned forty last month." Rachel dabbed her eyes with a tissue. She was one of those irritating pretty criers. "For his birthday, I booked him some recording time in this studio on Toronto Island."

"Okay," Dame said, "then what happened?"

"Well, he scheduled the Monday off work —"

"He's still with the Parks Department?"

"Yeah" — Rachel sniffed — "he manages a team now. Does mostly office work."

Dame nodded.

"He was supposed to stay on the island for three days. Just three. The guy there — the engineer or whatever — said he could sleep on the couch and that there was a bathroom and shower and stuff. So, he just took a duffle bag, an old hunting jacket, and his acoustic guitar. You know, Suzanne?"

Dame nodded again. She knew Suzanne.

"And he left. Then, three days went by, and then four, and then *six*." Dame could hear the panic blossoming in her voice. "He never came home. He never showed up to work. He wouldn't respond to my texts or calls."

As Rachel twisted the gold band on her third finger, Dame couldn't help but wonder what happened to her own wedding ring. She almost threw it away when she found out about her husband's infidelity, and then managed to lose it when she got her own place. Not that it really mattered to her anymore.

"Is it possible, Rachel" — Dame proceeded with caution — "that Adam just left? I mean, it wouldn't be the first time he stepped out on someone, right?"

There was a momentary quiet in the room. "It'd be the first time he stepped out on me."

Dame adjusted her glasses. "Well, I'm sorry this is happening to you, and obviously, I'm concerned about Adam" — she wasn't really, he was probably off fucking some twenty-five-year-old — "but what exactly do you want me to do about it?"

Rachel frowned at Dame. "I want you to *find him*. Isn't that what you do? Don't you have some sort of — I don't know — side hustle now?"

"My only 'side hustle' is trying to get my daughter to sleep through the night."

Rachel stood up. She crossed the room and leaned against the counter. "We read about you in the *Star*. About how you caught Gus Morrow. What were they calling him? The West End Arsonist?"

"That wasn't really detective work, Rachel. That was just bad taste in men. Something we have in common."

The woman sat down at the kitchen table again and put her face in her hands. "He wouldn't do this to me," she said. "He wouldn't do this to Luka."

The mention of Rachel's son filled Dame's chest with ice. "What did the police say?"

"I filed a missing person report." She shrugged. "They said they'd look into it."

"Well?"

"Come on, Polara. He's a six-foot-tall middle-aged man. Nobody's going to be worried about him."

"Exactly. Because Adam can take care of himself."

"You learned all that private eye stuff from your dad. You're good at this kind of thing. Let me hire you. I'll pay you. Whatever it costs."

"Rachel, I —"

"You *know* Adam. If anyone could find him, Dame, it's you." She was getting louder, now. Her hands gripped the table. "*Please*, just —"

"Rachel."

From the other room, Rosie started mewling. "Ma-maa …"

Dame took a deep breath. "Look, I haven't spoken to Adam in nearly three years. I have no idea who he is anymore — where he goes, what he does — and to be perfectly honest, I'm not all that sure I really knew him when we were married. I certainly didn't know him when he started sleeping with you."

"*Maa-mah* …" Rosie's little voice came again from the nursery.

Rachel stared at the floor for a moment. "Do you think it was easy to come here?" Her voice was quiet. "Do you think I would've come here if I had any other choice? I need your help."

"*Maa-maah!*" Rosie's voice was reaching peak levels of agitation.

"I'm sorry, Rachel." Dame stood up. "I hope you find Adam. I really do. But I have someone else who needs my help now."

"SO?" MEERA LEANED against Dame's desk and lowered her voice. "How's the new guy working out?"

"Who, Terrence?"

They glanced over at the young man sitting at his computer.

"Seems nice," Dame said.

"'Nice'? That's it? Just, 'nice'?"

Dame frowned. "What do you mean?"

"You don't think he's handsome? Or funny? Or" — Meera looked over at Terrence again — "kind of broad-shouldered?"

Dame snuck a peek at her new colleague. He was certainly handsome and broad-shouldered, but he was also a good decade younger than she was.

"Meera —"

"Did you know he has a six-year-old nephew? He's probably really good with kids."

"Meera, you're his *boss*. You shouldn't be talking about him like that."

"Well, there's a reason I hired him, Dame, and it wasn't just because he's 'nice.'" She gave Dame a pointed look. "You're not getting any younger, you know."

"God, Meera. You're an HR nightmare."

She sighed. "Being single is wasted on the unwed."

"So did you just come in here to play matchmaker? Because some people have work to do."

Meera was quiet for a moment. "Okay. Here's the thing. I've got a teensy bit of news."

"What now?"

"The Crown Attorney needs someone from Heritage Planning to testify in the new Marinetti case."

"And?"

"And I may have suggested you."

"Again? Come on, Meera —"

"I'm sorry. I know you spent months in court after everything that happened with the Sainte-Marie Hotel, but this new case has some real teeth. And if the Crown can prove that he's — shit, what did they say? — that he's 'engaged in a pattern of concealment and obfuscation,' then there might be real consequences this time."

"Meera, *none* of the developers that Peggy helped cheat the system faced 'real consequences.' They all got a slap on the wrist and then kept on tearing down whatever piece of history they wanted."

"Well, it didn't help that Peggy basically disappeared from the face of the Earth before the trial started."

"So, what's another trial going to do?"

"You know Marinetti's rap sheet better than anyone. Maybe you could make it stick this time. Think about it. He's the biggest player, the worst offender, and this trial could really hurt him."

"When's it happening?"

"In about a month."

Dame sighed. For years she'd hated Phillip Marinetti — blamed him for the fire that ruined her father's health and killed a little boy — but she'd been wrong. Marinetti hadn't torched the Sainte-Marie Hotel, and he wasn't a murderer. He was just a run-of-the-mill corporate crook.

"Well, I'll do my best, but I've still got a ton of permits to deal with this month."

"Just give them to Terrence." Meera smiled and started heading for the door. "He's got to be good for something around here."

Dame hadn't told Meera about Rachel's visit the night before. She was still actively trying to pretend the whole thing had been a bad dream. But at lunch, she made the mistake of Googling "*Adam Hoffman.*"

When she used to creep her ex online, she'd find his social media posts, his name on the Parks Department website, or even old interviews from when he was still playing in a band: "*When asked why they named themselves Long Walks on the Beach, guitar player Adam Hoffman, 28, just smiles and adjusts his Expos ball cap. 'Well, everybody likes long walks on the beach, don't they?'*"

Now, the first hit was "*Police Searching Toronto Island for Missing Forty-Year-Old Man.*"

Dame wasn't sure whether she should be more or less concerned that he'd made the news. On one hand, it seemed unlikely that she could chalk this up to Adam flaking out. On the other, it meant the police were doing their job, regardless of what Rachel said.

WHEN SHE GOT home from work that afternoon, Dame had a solid hour before she had to pick up Rosie from daycare. It was an hour to tidy, wash a few dishes, and prepare for the long haul single mom weekend.

The apartment really was a disaster, but she was trying to cut herself some slack. Since Rosie was born, she cleaned the place more in a day than she ever had in a month, and somehow it was still filthy. She was amazed, at times, that any of her plants could survive under these conditions. She couldn't remember the last time she watered them, but the snake plant, the devil's ivy, and Peggy's old monstera were all thriving. It was as though all of her maternal instincts had kicked in at once. This past weekend, Dame had even tried her hand at baking.

She fished a blackened chocolate chip cookie out of a very cracked, tiger-shaped ceramic jar. The cookie was rock hard and likely carcinogenic, but still, she nibbled on the burnt sugar as she shuffled through the mail on the kitchen table: credit card statements, bank statements, laughable offers to sell the house she didn't own. When she came across her name in a familiar hand, she stopped.

The return address on the envelope read "*Central North Correctional Centre, Penetanguishene, Ontario.*"

Bad guy in jay-yo.

She didn't open the letter, but instead added it to a stack of seven or eight just like it, in the little cupboard above her fridge.

THAT EVENING, DAME had to cycle through Rosie's bedtime routine four times before the kid finally fell asleep. It was a lot of *night nights* for one night. She managed to catch a few hours of uninterrupted sleep before Rosie started hollering again, but when she got her eyes unstuck and looked at the clock, it was barely five in the morning. Living with a two-year-old was like living with a smoke detector that had a faulty sensor. She could go off at any moment. And often did.

When Dame stumbled into her daughter's bedroom, Rosie was already standing up in her crib, gripping the bars, demanding her release. For a brief, unguarded moment, Dame's brain let her think about Rosie's father. She quickly pushed the thought out of her head.

"Good morning," Dame said.

"Poop," Rosie said.

In the beginning, changing diapers had been high on Dame's list of Scary Things About Motherhood. But with the exception of one very messy and very public incident on the TTC, it hadn't been the ordeal she'd expected. Breastfeeding turned out to be the real horror show. Latching, pumping, leaking — her body seemed to fight the process every step of the way. Not to mention the damage Rosie's baby teeth had done. Dame didn't think her nipples would ever be the same.

At the change table, she strapped the new diaper onto her daughter and dropped the old one in the Diaper Genie. A sour belch escaped the waste container before she could shut it.

"Pee-ew!" Dame said. "That's stinky."

Rosie wrinkled her nose. "Pee-ew!"

Dame coaxed a little food into her daughter and then coaxed her daughter into some clothes. She slathered the little girl's face and arms and chubby thighs in sunscreen.

"What do you think, partner?" she asked. "Should we hit the road?"

For the past couple years, Dame had been driving her father's Buick. But the old sedan needed a new transmission, and neither she nor her father had the four grand needed to fix it. So instead, Dame pack-muled her way down the front steps of her house, Rosie in one arm, umbrella stroller and diaper bag in the other. By then, the sun was just starting to show itself, not in the flashy colours of dawn, but the slow, grey retreat of night.

After she had clipped her daughter into the stroller, they headed south on O'Hara, then east on Queen. They spent most of their morning at Masaryk Park, Rosie trying to climb the play structure, and Dame trying to keep her from falling off of it. Occasionally, the little girl would toddle around in the grass, dragging her stuffed raccoon, and Dame would stare into her phone, hoping her daughter didn't discover a used condom or an uncollected pile of dog shit.

It was following one of these moments of digital distraction that Dame looked up and noticed a white Chevrolet Caprice crawling down Cowan Avenue. A brief chill flashed through her body, but when the car pulled over, Dame was relieved to see two teenage girls climb out and disappear down the sidewalk. She reminded herself that Anton Felski, the man Peggy Beckers hired to kill her, was still behind bars.

By nine o'clock in the morning, Dame felt like she had put in a full day. As they started to head back, she was surprised to receive a text from Meera. *Hey are you home?*

Funny she was already up. Maybe the new cat had meowed her out of bed. *Not yet*, she replied. *Should be in about ten minutes. We're going to stop by.*

Dame was hoping the "we" included Elwy Yost. So far, the only animal Rosie had regular contact with was the cataract-riddled, incontinent poodle that lived in the apartment next to Dodge's. Maybe when life was a little more sane, they could get a dog. Maybe a rescue. Something gentle and steady.

But when she got to her end of O'Hara, Elwy Yost was nowhere to be seen. Instead, Meera and Lewis sat waiting on her front stoop, their eyes both disguised by sunglasses. Meera's hair was up in a bun.

"Hey, guys." Dame crouched down to unclip Rosie from the stroller. "You're here bright and early."

"Dame," Lewis said, "have you heard about Adam?"

She hoisted Rosie up into her arms. "Well, I mean, yeah. Rachel made a surprise appearance at my apartment on Thursday. She had some sob story that he was missing."

Meera and Lewis looked at each other.

"He's not missing anymore," Meera said. "They found him this morning."

CHAPTER FOUR

NOTHING ABOUT ADAM'S service felt real. Maybe it was all the weird ceremony — the bowed heads, the boxy suits, the cloying a cappella performance of "American Pie." None of it seemed to reflect the man she once knew.

The closed casket, in particular, gave her the odd sensation that this was a funeral for somebody else. As she stood there, bits of wet grass sticking to her new, uncomfortable shoes, she could almost convince herself that she was at the wrong cemetery, that her ex-husband wasn't dead at all. She could imagine him off living some life that had absolutely nothing to do with her. And yet here she was, once again pulled back into his stupid orbit.

Only the faces — made unfamiliar by both time and grief — anchored her in lousy reality. Funerals were always a little awkward, but there was something about being the deceased's ex-wife that elevated Dame to a whole new level of social anxiety. Where else could she encounter her ex-mother-in-law, her ex-sister-in-law, her ex-nephews, and a wide assortment of ex-friends, all in the same crowd? Dame didn't want to even think about the fact that, only four days ago, she had booted Adam's widow — her ex–best friend — out of her apartment. As Dame listened to a hired officiant describe Adam's modest accomplishments — family, musicianship, fatherhood — Rachel's hard, guttural sobs punctuated the eulogy. Eventually, her four-year-old son crawled up onto her lap and buried his face in her neck.

Luckily, Meera and Lewis had come with her so she wouldn't have to confront Adam's mourners alone. To her ex-husband's credit, there were a lot of them. Dame had never really thought of Adam as a popular person, but she knew there was often a strange, sad correlation between how young someone dies and how many people show up to the funeral.

In addition to all the people she recognized and wanted to avoid, there was one woman she recognized but couldn't place. Twice they made eye contact, and the second time, she gave Dame a little nod of greeting. Was it a cousin she had met at a Hoffman family reunion? Or one of the chickadees that used to hang around Adam's band?

When the service ended, Dame nudged Meera. "Who's that woman in the black dress?"

"It's a funeral, Dame. We're all wearing black dresses."

"The one with the sheer sleeves. And the chunky bracelet."

Meera craned her neck to see. "I don't know who she is, but I like that bracelet."

Lewis, who had disappeared right after the service, wound his way back through the departing mourners.

"Apparently some people are going to O'Sullivan's," he said.

"That fake Irish pub on the Danforth?" Dame asked.

"Ben invited us." Lewis gestured toward Rachel's brother, a boyish-looking man with floppy hair. "We should put in an appearance at least."

"Where's Ben's wife?" Meera asked. "I haven't seen her around."

"I think he and Fiona are separated," Lewis said.

"Guys" — Dame sighed — "I'm not really feeling this whole *how-long-has-it-been* scene."

"Well, obviously. But aren't you curious?" Meera said.

"About what?"

"Someone here has to know what actually happened to Adam. There's nothing online about how he died."

Dame watched as the woman with the sheer sleeves and chunky bracelet made her way toward the cemetery gates.

"Okay," she said. "But I'm not drinking any of that room-temperature Guinness shit."

O'SULLIVAN'S HAD ATTRACTED a slightly different crowd than the funeral. Dame had never attended a high school reunion, but she imagined that this gathering came pretty close. It was like looking at a pencil sketch of old friends, but all the lines had started to fade.

"Is that Hùng Ngô?" Meera pointed out a man whose prominent belly and receding hairline seemed to be actively moving in opposite directions. "God, he used to be so hot. And — holy shit — is that Tabby Stuart? Guess her face finally caught up to her personality."

As Dame scanned the crowd, she caught the occasional glimpse of Rachel. Adam's widow sat with other middle-aged moms, their collective sadness rendered inert by Botox. Even at her own husband's funeral, Rachel still had the wherewithal to be the best dressed woman in the room. Her hair was tied back, revealing her slender neck, and her black dress was cut just low enough to reveal what the two of them used to jokingly call "first date cleavage." Now, Dame supposed, it was funeral cleavage.

She remembered meeting Rachel and Ben not long after they had lost their parents in a car accident. It was at that lame-ass peer support group their guidance counsellors forced them to join. Rachel called it the "Dead Parents Society." A room full of sad sacks prodded to weep under fluorescent lights. They were like Molly Ringwald and Ally Sheedy in a post-mortem Breakfast Club. But somehow they became friends. Best friends. For *years*. Until Rachel finally did what Dame always assumed girls like her did: fucked her best friend's husband.

On the other side of the room, a number of Adam's musician friends sat haggard and hunched over their pints. Compared to the aging jocks and pageant moms at Rachel's end, they seemed more at home in the dimly lit bar, as though they already lived in the perpetual twilight of some long, sad Rolling Stones song.

Of the two major clans currently dominating O'Sullivan's, Dame figured they were the least likely to bear her any ill will.

"I'm going to use the little leprechaun's room," Dame announced.

On her way to the can, she offered her condolences to the grieving rockers. "Hey," she said, approaching the table. "How are you guys holding up?"

A thick-spectacled vagabond squinted up from his beer glass. "Shitty."

Drummers always had such a way with words.

"I'm sorry, Hobie," Dame said. "When was the last time you saw him?"

The vagabond shrugged. "Lee's Palace. Couple months ago. We talked about doing a Long Walks reunion, but nothing really came of it. I just — I can't believe the guy's really gone."

Hobie's real name was Cobie Howdell, but a graphic designer had misspelled it "*Hobie Cowbell*" on their first EP, and the name stuck.

"Are you playing much these days?"

"Nah," Hobie said. "Kyle's got a new band, though. Don't you, Kyle?"

A sleepy-eyed man raised his balding head. "It's like, mainly post-rock stuff. Dame probably wouldn't like post-rock."

"It's like post-*post*-rock," Hobie said. "It's basically jazz."

"Hey," Dame leaned in a little closer, "do any of you guys know what actually happened? I mean, I know Adam was missing for almost a week, but no one seems to know how — you know — how he died."

The musicians looked at one another.

"I heard he drowned," Hobie said, "but I think the police are still investigating."

Kyle nodded his head. "I just talked to Adam's cousin before the service. Said he washed up on shore by the Port Lands."

"The Port Lands?"

"He was doing some recording on Toronto Island," Kyle said. "I guess somehow he wound up in the water. Drifted for a few days."

"Jesus," Dame said, steadying herself against the table.

She had seen the body of a drowning victim once, by accident, when she was still working cases with Dodge. It was blue, and bloated, and something had scuttled out of its mouth. To think that Adam, that beautiful, stupid boy she once —

"Good to see you guys."

Dame made it to the toilet just in time. She hadn't had much to eat for breakfast, but whatever was in her stomach didn't stay down. The stall filled with the stink of her bile, and for the first time since she'd learned of her ex-husband's death, she cried real tears. Six years she'd been with him. Four years they'd been apart. The entire time she'd been loving or hating him, and the truth was, sometimes those two things weren't all that much different. She carried him with her every day for a decade. And now he was gone.

When she finally pulled herself together, she flushed the toilet and checked the mirror to see if there was puke on her dress. That was when she realized she wasn't alone.

Standing next to her, checking her lipstick, was the woman she'd noticed at the funeral. The woman with the sheer sleeves and chunky bracelet.

"You okay?" the woman asked.

"Yeah, I guess." Dame ran the faucet and scooped a handful of water into her mouth. She spat it out as discreetly as she could.

"Here." The woman yanked a paper towel out of the dispenser and gently dabbed Dame's chin. "You've got a little something there."

"Thanks." She caught the woman's eye. "We — we know each other, don't we?"

"Dame," she said. "I played bass in your ex-husband's rock band for six years."

"Oh my God." She looked at her again. "Oh my God! I'm so sorry."

The last time Long Walks on the Beach had performed live, their bass player had jumped around the stage, scraggly-bearded and bare-chested. Clearly, a couple of things had changed since then.

"It's Grace." The woman held out her hand. "Nice to meet you. Again."

Dame smiled sheepishly and shook her hand. "Are you still playing music?"

"Not as much as I'd like. I've been spending most of my time working at Deacon Blues."

"That place in Kensington?"

Grace nodded.

"Adam loved that store. He'd drag me in there and spend hours making me listen to different guitar tones."

"Best second-hand music store in the city," Grace said. "Basically, I spend all my time selling equipment I wish I could afford."

"Well" — Dame looked at the bathroom door — "guess I should head back out there."

"Hey, before you do, there was something I wanted to ask you."

Dame frowned. "Me?"

"Yeah. It — it's actually about Adam. I was closing up the shop the other day, and —"

The door to the bathroom swung open, and another woman walked in. One of Rachel's friends. Everybody smiled at each other, and the woman disappeared into a stall.

"You know, maybe it would be better if I just show you," Grace said. "Do you think you could stop by Kensington tomorrow? Around five o'clock?"

"I don't know," Dame said. "I have to pick up my daughter, and —"

"I could stick around 'til about six if it makes a difference. I think" — she hesitated — "I think it might be important."

The look in the woman's eyes made Dame believe her.

"Okay. I can do six."

"Good," Grace said. "There's something you should really see."

DESPITE MEERA'S OFFER to drive her home, Dame left early and by herself. She figured a walk would do her some good. Help her clear her head a little. But as she stepped out of O'Sullivan's, she found herself face to face with Rachel, and two other women who looked like slightly less attractive versions of Rachel. They stood on a spotty patch of sidewalk passing around a slender vape.

"Well, look who it is," said one of the less attractive Rachels. "The famous detective. Leaving so soon?"

"She must have better things to do."

Who were these awful women?

"Rachel," Dame said. "God, I'm so sorry. I can't imagine —"

"What are you even doing here, Dame?" the real Rachel interrupted.

"Rachel," Dame tried her best to tread lightly, "of course I'm going to come to Adam's funeral."

"Why? You didn't care about Adam when you were married to him. And you sure as hell didn't care about him when he was married to me."

"Rachel, that's not —"

"When he went missing, you wouldn't even answer my calls."

"I didn't know —"

"And when I begged — *begged* — you to help me, you practically threw me out of your house."

"I'm sorry, but —"

"Yeah, you're sorry now, aren't you? Look, don't come to *my* husband's funeral and start sniffing around for sympathy, okay? You sure as shit don't deserve any."

She took one last haul on the vape and let a dense, strawberry-smelling cloud roll between them. As the three women paraded past Dame and made their way back into the bar, Dame stood there and wondered if Rachel was right.

CHAPTER FIVE

DEACON BLUES WAS a little cubby hole off Nassau Street. Near the door, a glass-fronted counter was stuffed with candy-coloured effects pedals. Behind it, the wall was racked with guitar strings, cables, and patch cords. Synthesizers smiled out from the shelves like rows of perfect teeth, while the shining fruit of vintage guitars hung from the ceiling. Dame eyed a price tag and noted that most of the equipment in the store would cover her rent for at least a month.

She put Rosie down in front of her and crouched to meet the little girl's eye. "Okay, partner," she told her daughter. "Don't. Touch. Anything. Got it?"

"Touch anything," Rosie parroted.

Dame sighed and checked her watch. It was ten to six. Where was Grace?

The empty store smelled vaguely of pot smoke and dude sweat. It was a desperate smell, the smell of expensive gear on layaway. It was also a smell inextricably linked to her ex-husband.

"Hello?" she finally called out.

Immediately, Grace appeared from a backroom. Her hair was tied in a ponytail and she was wearing a Daniel Romano T-shirt.

"Oh, hey," she said. "Sorry I didn't hear you. We used to have a bell on the door but it broke."

"No problem," Dame said.

"And who is *this*?" Grace said, putting her hands on her knees and smiling at Rosie.

Dame's daughter smiled back shyly and hid behind her mother's legs.

"This is Rosie," Dame said. "And Rosie has promised not to break a single thing in the store while we're here. Haven't you, Rosie?"

Grace waved away the implied concern. "Don't worry. We have insurance."

Dame kept a firm grasp on Rosie's hand, nevertheless. "So, what was it you wanted to show me?"

A shadow fell over the woman's face. "Hold on one sec." She disappeared into the backroom again and returned a moment later. In her hand was a battered black guitar case. She hoisted it up on top of the glass counter and snapped open the latches. As Dame watched her lift the lid, she was surprised to see something so familiar inside.

"Is that —?"

"A 1967 Gibson Hummingbird." Grace lifted the acoustic guitar out of its case and weighed it in her hands. "Mahogany body. Spruce top. Rosewood fingerboard and bridge. Adjustable ceramic saddle. All original. There's a little bit of wear and tear below the pickguard, but overall it's in pretty great shape. We'll probably get four grand for it. Maybe five."

"God. It looks just like Suzanne."

"Well, that's why I wanted to show it to you. It reminded me of Adam's guitar when it first came in, but it wasn't until I cleaned out the case that it really twigged."

Carefully, Grace laid the guitar on the glass countertop. She returned to the felt-lined cavity of the guitar's case and opened a small compartment in its neck. Inside was a piece of heavyweight sketchpad paper, off-white, and folded into quarters.

"Have a look."

Dame fished the paper out and unfolded it. "Jesus."

"I found it hidden behind the liner in a little secret pocket," Grace said.

On the paper was a pencil drawing of Adam lying on a bed. His eyes were closed, and he appeared to be asleep. But strangest of all was that he was naked. Completely naked. His hummingbird tattoo — identical to the little bird depicted on the pickguard of the guitar — hovered over his heart. His flaccid cock drooped on his thigh.

"Seemed like a pretty good likeness," Grace said. "I mean, as far as I could tell."

"That's Adam, all right. Do you know who drew it?"

"No idea. There's a signature on the bottom right, but I can't make it out, can you?"

Dame adjusted her glasses and squinted at the squiggle. "Nope."

Rosie pulled on her mother's hand. "Go outside?"

"We'll go outside in a minute, partner." She looked at Grace. "Who brought this in?"

"Some guy. I don't think he knew that much about guitars, but he knew it was worth something."

"Cash or consignment?"

"He wanted cash. Three thousand dollars in paper money. He didn't want a cheque or a money order."

"Weird."

"Yeah. People usually make more when they sell on consignment, but he seemed like he was in a bit of a hurry."

"Have you seen this guy before?"

"Never. Didn't look like a lot of the guys that come through here. Kind of a short and heavy-set. Big, long beard. Little hat. Loud Hawaiian shirt. Didn't really look like a musician, to be honest."

"What did he say about the sketch?"

"Didn't mention it. I don't think he knew it was in there."

"Go *outside*," Rosie tried again.

"Did you get his information?"

"Yeah, I wrote it down." She reached beside the cash register and gave Dame a scrap of paper. An unfamiliar name and number were scrawled across it.

"Have you told the police anything?"

"I wasn't really sure what to say. I mean, I didn't think Adam would've sold his father's guitar, but you never know. People do a lot of weird things for money."

"Have you told Rachel?"

Grace shook her head.

"Why not?"

"Well, I'm not sure who drew that picture, but I'm pretty sure it wasn't Rachel. She was never much of an artist."

"Good point."

"*Go outside!*" Rosie tugged again at Dame's arm.

"You're the only person I've told so far," Grace said. "I read that article about you in *blogTO*, so I figured you might know what to do."

Dame breathed in the smoke and sweat of it all. "Honestly, I think you should just call the cops."

"Yeah?" Grace almost seemed disappointed. "Okay."

"But would you mind if I took a picture of that sketch?"

"Of course not." She smiled down at the artwork as Dame pulled her phone out of her pocket. "He was a good-looking guy, wasn't he? Real lead-singer type."

Dame tried to operate her phone with one hand and keep Rosie from fleeing the store with the other.

"Hard to let go of a guy like that, huh?"

"Yeah," Dame said. "Hard to hold on to him, too."

IT WAS ONLY after Dame had put Rosie to bed that she allowed herself to think about Adam and the guitar he inherited from his father.

Adam's grandparents had left Poland in the late thirties before war broke out. When they immigrated to Montréal, they hoped their youngest son would become a doctor, or a lawyer, but like so many of his generation, he was instead swept away by beat poetry, folk music, and vast quantities of hashish. By the late sixties, Eryk Hoffman had a regular gig at the New Penelope Café, strumming out political observations on the brand new Gibson Hummingbird he named after his favourite song. Dame had seen blurry black-and-white photos of Eryk — horn-rimmed glasses, skyscraper of Dylanesque curls — singing into a microphone with Suzanne on his lap.

Eryk died a few years after Adam moved out to pursue his own musical aspirations, and along with just enough money to buy a second-hand Subaru, he willed his son the Hummingbird. As long as she'd known him, Suzanne had been a feature player in Adam's life. He used to joke that he'd sell his first born before he'd sell Suzanne. Right around Dame's second miscarriage, he stopped making that joke.

Dame sat down at her kitchen table and drummed her fingers on the scrap of paper Grace gave her. Written in blue ink was a name: "*John Rackham.*" The man who sold her Suzanne. A nine-digit number waited beneath the name.

Unbidden, the questions started to push their way to the front of Dame's brain: Who was John Rackham? What was he doing with Adam's Hummingbird? Who drew the picture in the guitar case? And of course, how did Adam — a former Bronze Cross lifeguard at the Alex Duff Memorial Pool — wind up with two lungfuls of Lake Ontario?

She picked up the piece of paper in her hands. The name and number were likely fake, but even if they weren't, where would this information lead her? She already knew what she would say to this man — the lies she might tell him, the lies he might tell her in response. The conversation ran through her head like it had already happened — a little chess game that would lead her to another and another. A series of gambits and counterattacks all in the name of *What really happened? What was the truth?* It was the same, endless, quixotic fact-seeking that left her father scarred and speechless. Dame turned the paper face down on the table and stood up.

On the kitchen counter lay the file folder she'd brought back from Dodge's apartment: the Weatherhead Case. She meant to throw it out as soon as she got home, but it was still sitting there, radiating a melancholy nostalgia. She shimmied the elastic band off the file and opened up the cover. On top of the tidy stack of papers was a yellowing photocopy of a suicide note: "*I'm sorry. It's not your fault. There's no future for me. For us.*"

God. How did Dodge think it was okay to drag his twelve-year-old daughter along to investigate the death of a teenage girl? Dame dropped the folder back down on the counter. She walked over to the threshold of her daughter's bedroom and watched the simple rise and fall of the little girl's breathing.

Here was the truth: Adam was dead. Maybe he drowned and maybe he didn't. Maybe he was murdered and maybe he wasn't. But either way, he was gone. And here was another truth: Dame was alive, and she didn't want to spend her life chasing ghosts.

She didn't want to drag her daughter though the same bullshit her father dragged her through. Let the police ask their questions, if they were so inclined. Let them dig through their crime scenes and solve their stupid riddles. Like Rachel's awful friend said at Adam's funeral, Dame had better things to do.

CHAPTER SIX

"IT'S SO NICE *your daughter takes an interest in your work.*"

Hanh Elliot was showing the detective into the living room. The kid followed close behind, admiring the wide hallways and painted wainscotting of the old Edwardian home. Compared to their little bungalow, the place seemed like a palace.

"Honestly," the woman continued, "I can barely get Spencer to come out of his room most evenings." Hanh directed the detective toward an ornate chaise longue. The kid sat down beside him.

"Well, I can assure you her interest is purely economic." He smiled. "I had to start paying her an hourly wage when she turned twelve this year."

"Maybe I should try that with my son." Hanh's laugh was a nervous, sad sound. "Can I get you anything to drink? Juice? Tea? I just put on a pot of coffee about ten minutes ago."

"Coffee," the kid said. "Tons of sugar."

"I'll have the same, thanks," the detective said. "Minus the sugar."

Hanh left them sitting together on the frilly piece of furniture.

"Okay, partner," the detective turned to the kid. "What do you see?"

"Well, for starters, they're not rich."

"*How do you know?*"

"*The house is nice and all, but*" — *she patted the chaise longue* — "*this furniture is pretty beat up. A lot of the fixtures and light switches are left over from the seventies. After they bought the house, they couldn't really afford any updates.*"

"*Okay. What else?*"

The kid got up and walked around the room. The walls were lined with leaded glass bookshelves. She stopped at an old-fashioned typewriter. "*I think Mrs. Elliot wanted to be some kind of author, but*" — *she tugged at a little brass latch that wouldn't budge* — "*that dream's all locked away now.*"

"*She's a speech pathologist,*" *the detective said.* "*See all those textbooks on the next shelf?*"

"*More Than Words Can Say,*" *the kid read,* "*A No-Nonsense Guide to Living with Aphasia by Edward Hasselblad. Sounds like a thrilling read.*"

"*What does her husband do?*"

"*Well, I can tell you what he doesn't do.*" *The kid crossed the room and stood next to a series of garish family portraits signed* "*Gabe Elliot.*" "*At least, not professionally.*"

"*He's an architect,*" *the detective said.*

"*How do you know?*"

"*Looked him up in the Yellow Pages.*"

"*Well, I hope he's better at architecture than he is at painting.*"

Hanh returned, balancing five cups on a pewter tray. The kid sat back down next to her father.

"*You have a lovely home, Hanh,*" *the detective said.*

"*Oh, thank you. It was actually Cheryl that found it for us.*" *She sat down and turned toward the detective.* "*Cheryl Weatherhead. Jill's mother.*"

The name of the dead girl created a sudden vacuum in all the formalities.

"She was our" — Hanh cleared her throat — "our real estate agent. That's how we met."

The detective and the kid picked up their cups and sipped at their coffees.

"Gabe? Spencer?" The woman's voice rang out with a frail, optimistic melody. "The detective is here."

A man in a paint-splattered smock swung into the room on crutches. A plaster cast was wrapped around the better part of his right leg. He stopped a few feet from the detective and held out his hand. The detective stood to shake it.

"Gabe Elliot," the man said. "We spoke on the phone. Sorry to keep you waiting."

"Looks like you've got a pretty good reason to be late."

The man looked down at his cast. "Got doored on my bike about a month ago. Compound fracture. Three breaks and four pins."

"Sounds painful."

"Doctor's got me on enough pain meds to take down a giraffe." He shifted on his crutches. "Sorry if I'm a bit foggy."

The detective sat beside his daughter and the man eased himself down beside his wife. "Where's Spence?"

Hanh shrugged.

"Spence?" the man bellowed.

The four of them listened to the reluctant trudge of footsteps on the stairs.

Spencer Elliot was already taller than his father, and he had his mother's coal-black eyes. A spray of boyish freckles dotted his face, and his unkempt hair and oversized clothes exuded teenage indifference. He looked nothing like the dark-haired blob in Gabe Elliot's painting.

"Grab a seat, hon," Hanh said. "We're just about to get started."

The boy slunk into an armchair and scanned the new arrivals. "Are you really a private investigator?"

"I am."

"So who's she?" He gestured toward the kid. "Your trainee?"

"Spence," Gabe warned.

"This is my daughter," the detective said. "She helps me out on cases sometimes."

"Aren't you a little young to be a detective?" Spence asked the kid.

"I don't know" — the kid took a sip of her coffee — "aren't you a little young to be a murder suspect?"

CHAPTER SEVEN

"HEY" — MEERA LEANED against Dame's desk — "any chance you finished looking at the permit for that apartment building in Regent Park?"

Dame turned her head. "Uh, just working on it now."

"All good. After that, though, you'll probably want to start reviewing the old Marinetti files. Okay?"

Dame sighed. "I'm pretty up to date on what a craterous asshole Phillip Marinetti is."

Meera grabbed a chair and rolled it over beside Dame. "I'm just saying — the guy illegally demolished, like, a third of Toronto's heritage properties in the last thirty years. If they can get him this time —"

"Don't worry," Dame said. "I know what's at stake."

"Thanks." Meera's hair was up in a bun. Dame hadn't seen her wear it down since Adam's funeral. "I know it's been a crazy few days. Sorry to be so bossy."

"It's okay." Dame smiled. "I mean, you are kind of my boss."

"Oh, shit. I almost forgot" — she reached into her pocket — "someone stopped by the office looking for you at lunch."

Meera handed her a card. It was emblazoned with the Toronto Police Service logo. There was a name and contact information. "A cop?"

"Yeah. Think it has something to do with Adam?"

"Not sure. Maybe."

Meera was quiet for a moment. "Do you think Adam really — you know — drowned?"

"Seems like it. Why?"

Meera shrugged. "I just keep thinking of him. All alone. In the dark. I mean, how long could anyone last down there?"

"Adam was a pretty good swimmer. And he had those lead-singer lungs." Dame smiled and wiped tears away with the heel of her hand. "I bet he held his breath for a long time."

THE COP IN question showed up at her door about an hour after Dame had brought Rosie home from daycare. On Thursdays, Dodge and Fatima looked after the little girl, but every other day of the week, Rosie came home slightly cranky and overstimulated from Sunny Day Childcare.

"Don't *want* abble sauce," she insisted. "Want straw-baby kiwi!"

"I'm sorry, partner," Dame said, "but we don't have strawberry kiwi."

"Yes we *do-o-o*!"

The sudden knock at the door startled Rosie, and the once-ravenous two-year-old slid out of her booster seat and retreated to the living room. When Dame opened the door, the stranger flashed her badge.

"Dame Polara? I'm Detective Connie Radovich. Toronto Police. Can I come in and ask you a few questions?"

"Uh, sure."

The woman walked past Dame. She removed an expensive-looking pair of tortoiseshell sunglasses and took a look around.

"Hi, Sweet Pea!" She waved at Rosie who was peeking out from behind a bucket of Duplo. "I didn't interrupt your dinner, did I?"

"We were pretty much done," Dame said.

"Oh my goodness" — the woman's eyes lingered on the little girl — "would you look at those *cheeks*. How can you *stand* it?"

Connie Radovich was in her late forties but dressed younger. Slim-cut leather coat, Gucci shades, and on her feet, what Meera would call fuck-me boots. She had the barfly energy of an older woman on the prowl. Dame would be surprised if she wasn't someone's favourite aunt.

"And look at these beauties. So *healthy*! Is this a monstera?"

Dame nodded.

Radovich leaned toward the plant and whispered, "*Is she taking good care of you?*" She turned back toward Dame. "I read somewhere you're supposed to talk to your plants. You ever do that?"

"I mostly just try to give them their space."

"Huh. Maybe I should try that." At the kitchen table, the police detective unzipped her coat, sat down, and stretched out her long legs.

"Can I get you something?" Dame asked. "Water? Tea?"

"You know, I could really go for a cup of instant if you've got it. Or even" — she glanced around the kitchen optimistically — "one of those fancy Keurig coffees. *Terrible* for the environment, I know, but *so* convenient."

"Sorry." Dame sat down across from her. "I quit drinking coffee."

"Rats. Well, I shouldn't keep you any longer than I need to, anyway. So" — she reached into the inside pocket of her coat — "let's get down to brass tacks, shall we?"

She produced her phone, swiped through a couple screens, and put it on the table. Out of the corner of her eye, Dame could see Rosie moving stealthily toward the kitchen, her favourite stuffed raccoon under one chubby arm.

"I had a very interesting conversation with your friend Grace Maxwell yesterday." Radovich pointed at the phone. "Could you confirm for me that the guitar in that picture used to belong to your ex-husband?"

Dame looked down at the image. Unmistakably, it was the same Gibson Hummingbird she had seen at Deacon Blues. "Yeah, that's it."

"Now, there was a picture in the guitar case — a risqué little pencil sketch of your ex-husband." She swiped through a couple more photos. "Ah, here it is. *Hubba hubba.* Ms. Maxwell showed this to you, right?"

Dame nodded.

"Any idea who drew this little sketch?"

Dame shook her head.

"There's no way that *you* might have drawn this little sketch, is there?"

Dame smiled. "I'm strictly stick figures and smiley faces."

"Remind me of that if we ever play Pictionary. Now, when did you last spend time with your ex-husband?"

"Uh" — Dame thought — "he gave me a ride home from work a few years back."

"Would you describe the time you spent together as amicable?"

"I guess," Dame said. "I mean, it was a long time ago."

"And you haven't spoken to him since?"

"I saw him once on the street, but we didn't speak."

"Not a word?"

"Nope."

"And his new wife — Ms. Suarez — have you had any contact with her?"

"I have, actually," Dame said. "When Adam went missing, she asked me to look for him."

"That's right." Radovich snapped her fingers. "You're something of a detective yourself, aren't you?"

"Well, I wouldn't say —"

"Oh, come on now, I read all about you in *The Globe and Mail*."

Rosie crossed an ocean of floor and clung to Dame's leg like a life preserver. Dame smiled down at her and tousled her hair.

"Now, I have to ask" — Radovich continued — "you don't have any plans to investigate this particular pickle, do you?"

"No. God no."

"Phew. Probably wise to leave this one to the professionals, right?"

"Panda!" Rosie stepped out from behind Dame's leg and presented her stuffed animal to Radovich.

"Panda?" She looked at Dame. "You know this is a raccoon, right?"

Dame shrugged. "I just work here."

Radovich turned back to Rosie. "Well *hello* Panda. It's *very* nice to meet you!"

Rosie grinned and retreated back to the shelter of Dame's legs.

"Okay" — she stood up and looked at her watch — "I should get going. It's just about wine o'clock, or — as I like to call it — three gin rickeys and a Long Island iced tea o'clock." She punctuated her joke with a short blast of laughter.

Dame walked the police detective to the door. Rosie scrambled over to her mother, and Dame lifted her up into her arms.

"Grace gave me the contact information for the guy who sold her Adam's guitar," Dame said. "Did she pass that along to you?"

"She did," Radovich said. "Mr. *Rackham*. Total dead end. Number's a fake. And turns out 'John Rackham' is a pretty popular alias. There's about thirty-six John Rackhams in the Greater Toronto Area, and over two hundred John Rackhams on Facebook. Apparently, it's the name of some eighteenth-century pirate."

Rosie pulled Dame's glasses off her face and put them in her mouth.

"No, thank you, Rosie." Dame took the glasses away from her daughter. When she put them back on, everything was just a little blurry with slobber. "What about security footage?"

"Camera hasn't worked in years. We just have your friend's description: Big beard. Little hat. Ugly shirt. Not a lot to go on."

"Thought it might be worth a shot."

"Well, thanks. If you think of anything else that might be helpful, don't hesitate to call. Otherwise, I wouldn't concern yourself. You just worry about this troublemaker. Okay?"

She booped Rosie on the nose with her index finger. The little girl giggled.

"Okay. Thank you, Detective Radovich."

"Oh please," she said as she stepped outside, "call me Connie."

Dame closed the door and pressed her forehead against its cool surface.

"*Shit*," she whispered to herself.

CHAPTER EIGHT

"It's probably just standard procedure," Fatima was saying. "A man dies — makes sense the police want a word with his ex-wife."

"What do you think, Dodge?"

"*Always s-suspect*" — Dodge cleared his throat and worked his lips around the next words — "*th-the ex.*"

Dame was hoping for a little insight from her father — something more than one of his pat rules — but it seemed as though he was preoccupied with his macaroni pie. Fatima was right, of course. It made sense for Radovich to give her the once-over. But getting a visit from a cop was like making eye contact with a cologne-soaked bro on the TTC. Once you had their attention, it was hard to shake.

"All done! All done!" Rosie was twisting around in her booster seat.

As Fatima navigated another spoonful of macaroni toward her, the little girl clamped her mouth shut.

"Just a little bit more," Fatima coaxed.

Rosie unlocked her jaws to release an indignant "*No!*" then slammed them shut again.

"Come on now, Rosie," Fatima said. "Don't you want to be big and strong like your mama?"

Rosie considered this for a moment, then, "*No!*"

"Well, you're as stubborn as your mama. That's for certain."

Dame smiled. "We should probably get going. This kid's pretty exhausted." She pointed a thumb at herself. "This one is, too."

MR. KIRBY WAS sitting in the bus shelter outside the LCBO like he was every Thursday — spine straight, hands folded on his lap, eyes obscured by enormous wraparound sunglasses — as though he was waiting for a bus that would never arrive.

"Well, good evening, ladies," he said.

"Hi, Mr. Kirby."

"How is Ms. Rosie doing this evening?"

"She's okay. A little fussy."

"Well, that's understandable." He looked down at his watchless wrist. "You're a bit off schedule today."

Dame made the walk from Dodge and Fatima's apartment to her place every Thursday evening. The route took them up Jameson and east on Queen Street, past the jewellery repair store, the Western Union, and no less than six Tibetan restaurants. A former internet café stood wrapped in signage that read: "*Coming Soon! Houdini's Escape Room Palace!*" All told, the journey took less than twenty minutes, which — for the last couple months — included this brief transaction outside the liquor store.

"Could I petition you two lovelies for a little spare change?"

Dame had started keeping five-dollar bills in the zippered compartment under Rosie's stroller for this very purpose. She fished one out and stuffed it into the man's front pocket.

His face lit into a grin. "Thank you kindly."

Mr. Kirby was a dignified drunk. Every time Dame saw him,

he was wearing the same crumpled linen suit, yellowing shirt, and dark glasses. She suspected he was at least partially blind, but he never failed to recognize her and Rosie as they walked by. At his feet stood a bottle wrapped as always in a brown and green LCBO bag. He couldn't have been much older than Dodge, but he seemed like a caricature of age, like a bronze statue tourists took their picture sitting beside.

"Mama, home. Go *home*," Rosie complained from under her stroller straps.

"Uh-oh. You better get going." The old man smiled. "Don't want to make the boss angry."

"*Ho-o-ome*," Rosie insisted.

"Okay, Rosie. We're going," Dame said. "Have a good night, Mr. Kirby."

"Same to you, my lovelies."

Mr. Kirby seemed only to exist in the liminal space of Thursday evenings. Other days, when Dame walked by the liquor store, he was nowhere to be found. She wondered what he did with his time. Where did he go? Did he have a home? Did he have someone to help him stumble into bed?

Dame knew she would never learn the answers to her questions. Just as she knew that one Thursday evening she would walk past the LCBO and the bus shelter would be empty.

AS EXPECTED, ROSIE fell fast asleep once they started moving again, and Dame decided to risk taking the scenic route back to O'Hara. She headed north and cut through the parking lot of the West Lodge Apartments. A back lane lined with garage doors led her up to Seaforth Avenue, and a few moments later, she arrived at a little bungalow, wrapped in once-white vinyl siding, now yellow with age. Her childhood home.

"Well, this is where it all began, partner," she told her daughter.

A snore whistled through the little girl's nose.

"Appropriate response."

She hadn't walked past the old place in a while, but little had changed. Same rickety railing on the front steps. Same chain-link fence she used to hop as a kid. Same rusty mailbox with the words "*No Flyers*" stencilled across the front. The only real difference was the sign hammered into the yard out front. On it, a cheerful, goateed man smiled out below the word "*Sold.*"

"Huh."

Dame hadn't even known the place was for sale — not that she could've afforded it. Still, she had dreamed of one day tearing off the ugly siding and seeing what was underneath. Restoring the old house to whatever former glory it once possessed. She was a little sad to learn that she'd missed her chance.

LEWIS PUT A few sweet potato fries into his mouth. "So, wait. Does this mean you're a suspect, now?"

On Friday, Meera insisted Dame accompany her and Lewis to the new vegan place on Queen. Over a guava mezcal mule, Dame told them about her visit from Connie Radovich.

"Haven't you ever watched a crime drama?" Meera gave her husband the stinkiest of stink eyes. "They always interview the ex-wife."

"Oh," Lewis said. "I guess that makes sense."

"Motive and opportunity make a suspect," Dame said. "A little evidence never hurt, either. But right now, I think the cops are just covering their bases."

Meera waved down a server and pointed to their mules. "We'll get three more of these, please."

"Two," Dame corrected her. "I have to pick up Rosie in exactly seventeen minutes."

"Aww," Meera groaned. "Call and tell your daycare provider you're at a work meeting."

"Can't."

"Tell them your team leader *insists* you stay for another drink."

"Sorry."

"Did I mention I invited Terrence? He should be here any minute."

Dame shook her head. "Meera, I think you're the worst boss I've ever had."

"What do you mean? Your last boss tried to burn down a hotel with you inside it."

"And yet somehow, you're still the worst."

Lewis put another small bundle of fries into his mouth. He chewed thoughtfully and swallowed. "Do you think anyone is capable of murder?"

"Probably." Dame started to stand up. "I'm pretty sure my daycare provider is going to murder me if I'm late again this week."

"Hold on," Meera said. "We haven't even talked about how that guy wound up with Adam's guitar. I mean, Adam loved that thing more than you — no offence — and what about that Rose-on-the-*Titanic* pencil sketch? Exactly *who* is drawing him like one of their French girls?"

Dame dug around in her pockets for her share of the bill. "I don't know, Meera. Maybe Adam made some bad investments and had to pawn the Hummingbird. Maybe one of his old groupies sent him some extra creepy fan art and he forgot it in the case. It doesn't matter. The police will sort it out."

"So, you're not the least bit interested in what happened to Adam?"

"Of *course* I'm interested. We were together for six years. But it's not my job to investigate his death. That detective made it pretty clear that I shouldn't get involved."

"I hate to break it to you, Dame," Meera said, "but you're already involved."

CHAPTER NINE

ROSIE'S FAVOURITE TOY that week had been Crocodile Crunch, a game where she tested each of the plastic teeth of an open-mouthed croc, until pressing the one dull fang that made the jaws snap shut on her hand. It was a relatively painless chomp, but Rosie was consistently thrilled by the reptile's unpredictable act of violence.

The week before, it had been Duplo — the little girl built great Rosie-sized towers that clattered to the floor in climactic disasters. Before that, a toy cash register on which she rang up inexplicable transactions, pulling the bright lever and dropping fat plastic coins into the hollow of the bottom drawer.

Dentist, architect, accountant — it was foolish to impose a real-world future on the imaginary present, but sometimes Dame couldn't help herself. She wanted her daughter to have a life free from the dangers and obligations of the past.

"You be careful now." Dame pried open the crocodile's spring-loaded maw. "This guy's gonna getcha!"

"Gonna *get* me!"

She left her daughter on the carpet in front of the little green beast. With any luck, she'd have a couple minutes to herself before Rosie pushed down on the wrong tooth. She took advantage of the opportunity to fill the kettle with water and put it on the stove's element. While she was at it, she also filled a pint glass with water and tipped a little into the nearby snake plant.

Snap!

The little girl cackled and called out. "Mama!"

She walked over and pried open the jaws again. As Rosie considered the options, Dame poured a little water into her monstera. Detective Radovich was right. These plants were healthy. Vibrant, even. But she couldn't remember the last time she'd even watered them.

"Hello?" she addressed the philodendron experimentally. "You're looking very ... alive?"

Steam drifted up out of the kettle and she could hear the water beginning to bubble inside. While she waited, she sorted through the wad of paper she'd freed from her mailbox. Credit card bill, credit card offer, and *ooh* — half-off coupon for Bogey's Perogies.

As the kettle worked itself into a whistle, the letter she'd been dreading appeared in her hands. The same thin envelope. The same Penetanguishene return address. It was the second one this month, which meant he was writing more often, and not giving up as she thought he eventually would. It was almost enough to make her open the envelope, but not quite. She filed it away with the rest of the collection in the cabinet above her fridge.

After she took the noisy kettle off the burner and poured boiling water on top of a tea bag, she stopped and was surprised by the silence of the house. She realized this whole time she'd been waiting for the next *Snap!* The next *Mama!* But there was nothing.

She poked her head into the living room to find that Rosie had abandoned Crocodile Crunch for a new toy. A large plastic fire engine with a movable ladder and lights that would flash on and off when she rolled it back and forth on the carpet.

"What you got there, partner?"

"Fuck!"

Dame raised an eyebrow.

"Fire fuck!"

In the cabin of the vehicle, behind the little steering wheel, Dame couldn't help but notice a little plastic seat designed for a little plastic person, but the engine was apparently operating on autopilot. The firefighter was nowhere to be seen.

"YOU'RE ON SPEAKERPHONE," Dame said, lifting the legs of her two-year-old with one hand and wiping the little girl's bum with the other.

"Why?" Meera's voice sounded small and far away.

"Because I've taken up juggling. Why do you think?"

"Isn't that kid potty-trained yet?"

Dame sighed. Rosie had managed to smear a thick frosting of shit up her backside. "Can we cut to the chase, Meera? I'm a little busy."

The line was silent for a moment. Finally, "Rachel called me last night."

Dame contained the disaster in the diaper and dropped it into the Genie. "And?"

"She was pretty upset. I think all the not-knowing is really starting to get to her."

She wrapped Rosie in a fresh diaper and pulled her T-shirt down over her tummy. "Yeah, I mean, she's not exactly my favourite person, but I can't imagine how hard this must be for her."

"I think she feels pretty alone right now."

"Why? She's got plenty of friends."

"I'm not so sure she does."

"What about all those people she was hanging out with at the funeral?" She plopped Rosie on the ground and the little girl wobbled toward her toys.

"Yeah, but did you meet those people? They're the worst."

Dame smiled. She washed her hands and dried them on a towel.

"Listen," Meera said, "I'm going to stop by tomorrow and bring her some food."

"Some food?"

"Yeah, Dame. Food. That's what you do when someone's in mourning. You bring them food."

"If you say so."

"Anyway, I think you should come with."

"Uh, I'm not so sure about that. I don't think Rachel really wants to see me."

"Honestly, Dame? I think she needs all the help she can get."

CHAPTER TEN

WHEN MEERA TURNED left at an enormous dog park, navigated past an adorable coffee shop, and pulled to a stop in front of a cheerful-looking duplex in North Riverdale, Dame turned to her friend in wide-mouthed astonishment.

"How the *hell*?"

Besides the shiny black Range Rover parked outside it, there was nothing particularly ostentatious about the house. But still, owning a home in Riverdale was owning a home in Riverdale.

"Beats me," Meera said. "Last time I talked to Rachel, it wasn't about finances."

"Isn't she a yoga instructor?"

"She runs a twenty-four-hour personal fitness studio. There's a difference."

"Still" — Dame looked back at the house again — "it must take a lot of downward dogs to pay the mortgage on this place."

Meera frowned at her friend. "You don't get to be jealous of a recent widow, okay?"

They got out of the Jeep and walked up the front steps. Meera knocked on the door, while Dame steeled herself for more of Rachel's wrath. She was starting to wish she hadn't left Rosie with

Dodge and Fatima. Sometimes, it was nice to have a little person to hide behind. But when the door opened, it wasn't Rachel that greeted them. It was Adam's mother.

"Meera?" she said. "And is that" — she peered over a pair of bifocals — "Dame? Oh, girls, it's so good to see you."

She embraced them one at a time. When it was Dame's turn, the smell of her ex-mother-in-law's Chanel No. 5 brought back a strange cocktail of residual feelings: guilt, gratitude, indignation, disappointment.

Meera held out a large Tupperware container. "I brought Rachel some chicken *karahi*. It's my mom's recipe."

"I'm sure she'll love it."

Dame stood there and felt useless while Meera said all the right things.

"We're so sorry, Mrs. Hoffman. We both really cared about Adam."

"Thank you, girls. Do you have time to come in for a drink? I've been overstaying my welcome, and I'm sure Rachel could stand to see some new faces."

"Actually," Dame started, "we should probably get —"

"Of *course* we have time," Meera interrupted.

When they walked into the house, they found Rachel and her brother Ben sitting on a sectional, polishing off a bottle of Zinfandel. Dame's ex–best friend looked years older than she had the day of the funeral. Her chestnut curls were tied up in a greasy topknot (a hairstyle that has only ever looked good on *Destroyer*-era Gene Simmons), there were dark circles under her eyes, and an angry-looking pimple announced itself on her chin.

"It's nice to see you, Meera," Rachel said. "Dame, I'm surprised you could find the time."

As the new arrivals sat down, there was a brief, uncomfortable silence, and Ben hurried to fill it. "We were just talking about Dave Bachinsky's wedding."

"I barely remember that wedding," Meera said.

"Yeah," Dame said, "because you single-handedly made them regret having an open bar."

As if on cue, Mrs. Hoffman put two glasses of wine down on the coffee table.

"So, Dave had hired this videographer for the night," Ben continued, "and the guy was going around interviewing guests about, you know — 'What's your favourite memory of Dave and Cynthia?' or 'What advice do you have for the happy couple?' — that kind of thing. Eventually, Dave and Cynthia watch the video, and the first guest starts talking, but all you can hear is Adam in the background describing the time he met Spookey Ruben at the Greyhound Station."

"Oh my God" — Dame took a sip from her glass — "he would not shut up about that."

"Apparently, you can hear Adam in the background of almost every single interview talking about Spookey Ruben. How nice Spookey Ruben was. How Spookey Ruben signed his T-shirt."

"Oh, Jesus," Dame said.

"Poor Dave says, 'I don't even know who Spookey Ruben is, and he's the star of my whole goddamn wedding video.'"

Everyone laughed.

"Adam was so loud," Meera said.

"Even his text messages were loud," Dame said. "He always wrote everything in capital letters. I'd text him to pick up milk while he was out, and he'd be like, DO WE NEED BREAD?"

Everyone laughed again. Everyone except Rachel.

"You know" — the widow stood up — "I'm going to look for another bottle. I don't really care for this vintage."

Rachel squeezed past her brother and made her way toward the kitchen.

"I'm sorry," Dame said. "Maybe I shouldn't be here."

"We're *glad* you're here," Mrs. Hoffman said, reaching out to pat Dame's hand.

"She's just exhausted," Ben said, standing up. "I'll go check on her."

They watched him follow his sister into the kitchen.

"It's good to see Ben again," Meera said. "Has he been spending a lot of time here?"

"Ben actually lives here, now," Mrs. Hoffman said. "He moved in about six months ago when he split up with Fiona."

"That's too bad," Dame said. "I liked Fiona. Does she still run the little stationery shop on Queen?"

"I'm not sure," Mrs. Hoffman said. "But the silver lining is that Ben has been chief cook and bottle washer around here since everything happened."

"And he's still working at that clinic in Leslieville, right?" Meera asked.

"He decided to go down to part-time," Mrs. Hoffman said. "It's been a challenging year."

There was a sudden rattle at the doorknob, and a teenage girl with long braids came through the door carrying a familiar four-year-old in her arms.

"Luka!" Mrs. Hoffman exclaimed. "Come give your grandma a hug. She needs one."

The babysitter put the child down and he ran over to his grandmother.

"Did you have fun with Zoe?" Mrs. Hoffman asked mid-squeeze.

The child squirmed out of his grandmother's arms and crawled up beside her on the couch. "We went to the park!"

He had a big voice for a four-year-old. Big like his father's.

"Did you go on the curly slide?"

"No," the boy said, pushing his big toe through a hole in his sock. "Too scary."

"Did he eat all of his snack?" Mrs. Hoffman asked.

"No." Zoe put a piece of gum in her mouth. "He said he had a stomach ache."

"Did he eat the apple slices?"

"Just the yogurt, I think."

"You've got to eat your fruits and vegetables, mister" — Mrs. Hoffman poked at the boy's belly — "so you can grow up big and strong like your —"

She stopped herself. The room was suddenly silent.

"Can I go watch *Backyardigans*?" the boy asked.

"Sure." Mrs. Hoffman wiped a rogue tear from the corner of her eye. "You go watch TV."

"I'm going to take off now, Mrs. Hoffman."

"Sure thing, hon. We'll see you tomorrow."

The babysitter closed the door behind her and Mrs. Hoffman pushed a sad smile across her face. "She's been such a help. Everyone's so helpful and all I can do is sit around and feel useless." She sighed, long and deep. "The police won't tell us anything. Nobody seems to have any answers. It's too bad your father got sick, Dame. We could use a good detective right about now."

Meera gave Dame a look and Dame ignored it.

"I'm sure Dodge would help if he could, Mrs. Hoffman." She shifted in her seat. "Would you mind if I used the bathroom?"

"Of course, hon. Up the stairs, down the hall, and to the left."

DAME SCRUTINIZED THE face looking back at her in the mirror. Why did she agree to come today? Was she only making things worse?

She dried her hands on decorative towels. They were the good towels, with little birds on them, the towels people put out for company. Now they were soiled and damp with overuse.

When Dame started making her way back down the hall, she stopped at an open door. It was a bedroom, but not the primary bedroom. If anything, the place looked like it had belonged to Adam and Adam alone. Next to a well-worn futon, a small Orange amplifier sat unused. Above, the walls were decorated with old Long Walks on the Beach posters and a series of guitars hanging from plastic mounts. Some of the guitars Dame recognized: the Fender Jaguar Adam bought in high school and the oddly shaped Domino Californian that aped Ian Curtis's Vox Phantom. There were a few new additions as well: a butterscotch Telecaster and a Deering Goodtime banjo. Only one wall mount was unburdened by an instrument, its plastic fingers reaching out for a 1967 Gibson Hummingbird.

"He was starting to use this room as a studio. But then I moved in and messed everything up."

Dame hadn't even heard Ben come up the stairs.

"Sorry. I was just —"

"No, it's okay." Rachel's brother pushed his floppy hair off his forehead. "Take a look around. I haven't really changed anything."

Dame stepped inside the room. The futon was pulled out into a bed. It was neatly made with pillows and a comforter.

"I'm guessing you cleaned the place, at least. Adam was never *this* tidy."

"Yeah. I'm a bit of a neat freak. The crazier life gets, the cleaner my room gets."

"That might be the defining quality of adulthood."

"You think so?"

Dame had always thought of Ben as Rachel's kid brother,

but even as a grown-up, he still had a kind of boyish enthusiasm about him, as though at any moment he might pull a new baseball card or action figure out of his pocket and show it to her.

"So, you're like a real deal psychologist now, huh?" Dame said.

"Yeah. Other people's problems. That's my business."

"I was sorry to hear about you and Fiona."

"Oh, don't be. It's honestly for the best. I think we'll both be happier in the long run."

There was a cautious optimism in his voice, and she admired him for it. He seemed to be handling his separation better than she had handled her divorce.

"So" — Dame surveyed the room — "I see Adam's posters, and Adam's guitars, but I don't see Old Neil."

Ben raised his eyebrows. "Old who?"

"Old Neil," Dame repeated. "Don't you remember? That hideous terracotta bust of Neil Young he made in high school?"

"That was Neil Young? I always thought it was a slightly deformed Pat Benatar."

Dame laughed. "Luckily, he was better at guitar than sculpture. But still, he loved that thing. Refused to get rid of it."

"Beauty's in the eye of the beholder, I guess."

"Well, I had to *behold* that thing in my living room for the better part of six years. I wonder if Rachel finally convinced him to throw it out."

"Probably. You know what Rachel's like. She once had her living room repainted because it was the wrong shade of white."

Dame smiled and looked again at the guitars on the wall. "Do you know if Adam was writing new music?"

"A little bit. I mean, I think that's why Rachel organized the recording time on the island."

"Who was he recording with?"

"Some guy from up north. They used to play his song on Q107 all the time. Something about a cold heart."

"Rings a bell."

"At least he got to document some of his songs before —" Ben let the conclusion of his sentence fade away like a bad smell.

"Was he happy?" Dame asked. "You know, in your professional opinion."

"Well, Adam always seemed pretty happy to me. But, if there's one thing I've learned as a psychologist" — Ben smiled — "it's that we tend to show people the face we want them to see."

CHAPTER ELEVEN

THE DETECTIVE LEANED forward on the Elliots' chaise longue. "Spencer, why don't you start by telling me what happened on the night of Tuesday, July 16?"

"God" — the tall boy slumped further down into his seat — "do I have to go through all this again?"

The detective took another sip of his coffee. "Police report said you were at home in your room playing video games, and then sometime after midnight, you entered the Weatherheads' house. Is that right?"

Spencer nodded.

"Pretty late to borrow a cup of sugar, wasn't it?"

"Jill was supposed to call me, but she never did. I knew she was home — at least, I saw her light on — and her folks were out of town."

The detective turned another page in his notebook. "Cheryl and Bruce Weatherhead had gone to their cottage in Southampton for the week."

"Yeah. So when she didn't answer the door, I let myself in."

"The door was open?"

The boy shrugged. "I have a key."

"Spencer and Jill have been close since they were little," Hanh offered.

"Well see now, that's interesting, because your other neighbour" — the detective turned back a few pages in his notes — "Mrs. Schulz told the police that the Monday before, she heard Jill and Spencer arguing. Quite loudly, she said. Lots of profanity. Any truth to that?"

"No," Spencer said.

"Any idea why she would say that?"

"Because Mrs. Schulz is a senile old Nazi who has nothing better to do than spread rumours about people."

The detective looked at Hanh and Gabe.

"We didn't hear anything," Gabe said.

"So, you walked inside the house. Then what happened?"

"I called out but nobody answered. I went upstairs to her bedroom, but Jill wasn't there. And then, down the hall, the bathroom door was shut but there was light coming from under the crack. So I knocked, and when no one answered, I turned the knob and —"

Spencer stared out the window, his dark eyes fiercely resisting tears.

"You found her," the detective said. "In the bathtub."

"She wasn't — she wasn't the right colour."

"Did you notice anything else unusual? Shampoo bottles knocked over? Signs of a struggle?"

He shook his head.

"The coroner's report says you dialled 911 from the Weatherheads' house at 12:27 a.m. Paramedics brought her to the hospital, but Jill was dead on arrival."

"Look, if you've got the coroner's report, why do you need to drag me through all this shit again?"

"Spencer," Gabe warned.

"I understand this is difficult," the detective said. "I'm just trying to figure out what happened to your friend."

"My friend?" The boy stood up. "Jesus, you don't understand a goddamn thing, do you?"

"Spencer," Hanh said.

"Forget it. I'm not going to waste anymore of my time with Inspector Gadget, here."

"Come on, Spence." Gabe pushed himself up on his good foot.

"I've talked to the cops, the lawyers, the therapists, and now I've got to talk to this guy? This private dick?"

Gabe put his hand on the boy's shoulder. "He's trying to help."

"Don't touch me." The boy jerked away from his father and stormed out of the room. They listened to his feet punish the stairs and the door to his bedroom slam shut.

Hanh let out a long sigh. "I'm sorry. This has been very difficult."

"On all of us." Gabe sat back down and took his wife's hand.

The detective sipped at his coffee. "Do you mind if I ask — when did Spencer's relationship with Jill become romantic?"

Gabe frowned and shifted in his seat. "It's hard to say, really."

"Growing up they were always such good friends," Hanh said. "I guess things changed just after they started high school."

"There were traces of semen on Jill's bedsheets. Were they having intercourse?"

A red glow crept into Hanh's cheeks. She glanced at the detective's daughter.

"It's okay," the kid said. "I've been briefed."

"We — we don't really know," Gabe said.

"Yes, but they were a couple of teenagers in love" — Hanh looked at her husband — "so it stands to reason."

The detective took another sip of his coffee. "I thought it was a bit strange that Spencer refused to give consent for a DNA test."

"Our lawyer didn't think it would help our case," Gabe said. "Spencer was always next door. His DNA's probably all over that house."

"Gross," the kid said under her breath.

"Tell me about the last time you saw Jill," the detective said.

"She came by the house Tuesday evening," Hanh said. "She was looking for Spence, but he was still out with his friends."

"Can you remember what you talked about?"

"Nothing important, really."

"Any details at all might be helpful."

"She had a killer headache," Gabe said. "She got migraines sometimes."

"I offered to make her some tea," Hanh said, "but she just wanted to go home and take a hot bath. She was three-quarters of the way through one of those Anne Rice vampire novels and she was hoping to finish it if she felt better."

"Well, it doesn't really sound like she was in crisis. And according to the Weatherheads, she didn't have any reason to kill herself."

"I'm not so sure about that," Hanh said.

"What do you mean?"

"Jill was a wonderful young woman." Hanh seemed to choose her words carefully. "She was thoughtful and smart — she used to show me her poetry — but she was also very troubled. I think she may have been experimenting with drugs."

The detective looked again at his notes. "There were traces of opioids in her system. And there's no record of any prescription."

Gabe shook his head. "I think that poor kid got high, ran a bath, fell asleep, and drowned. We'll probably never know if she did it on purpose."

"Well, at first glance, it sure looks like something between a suicide and an accident. But it's a little funny there's no note. Kids usually leave a note. And, the coroner said Jill had fresh bruises on her sternum. Any idea where those came from?"

Both Hanh and Gabe shook their heads.

The detective drained the rest of his coffee. "Well, so far, Spencer hasn't been formally charged with anything. But he's a person of interest because of his proximity, the suspicious nature of Jill's death, and because of what Mrs. Schulz told the police. Do I have all that right?"

"Spencer is a 'person of interest'" — Gabe bunny-eared his fingers — "because Bruce Weatherhead is a sanctimonious asshole."

"That would be Staff Inspector Bruce Weatherhead — Jill's father. You think he may be using his position to influence the police investigation."

Gabe imploded with hollow laughter. "We know he is. He can't bear the thought that his little girl was unhappy. He needs someone to blame, and he's got Spencer in his crosshairs."

"So you can see," Hanh said, "why we need your help."

CHAPTER TWELVE

"HEY THERE, SWEET Pea. Remember me?"

Detective Radovich poked at Rosie's tummy and the little girl smiled and turned away into her mother's arms. "Aw," Radovich said. "Somebody's shy."

"Hi, Connie." The detective's first name felt strange in Dame's mouth. Possibly because it was competing for real estate with a toothbrush.

"Thought I'd try and catch you before you head off to work."

"Can you give me one sec?"

"Of course." Connie took off her Gucci sunglasses and put them on her head. "I know mornings can be *cuh-razy*."

Dame hurried back into the bathroom and spat toothpaste foam into the sink. She looked at her watch. What was Radovich doing here, anyway?

When she came out of the bathroom, the police detective was in her front hall staring up at the ceiling. "Is that all original crown moulding?"

Dame nodded.

"And that stained glass in the transom window — is that original, too?"

"No. The original was cracked. My landlord actually just had it replaced."

"Sounds like your landlord's okay."

Dame shrugged. "Yeah. She's pretty cool."

Rosie toddled away from them and picked Panda up off the ground.

"Listen," Dame said, "I really only have a few minutes before I have to go."

"Well, I'll just have to speed things up, won't I?" She took a notepad out of her back pocket and flipped it open. "I've done a little more digging since our last chat. Your father's name is David Polara, isn't it?"

"Yes."

"And you worked as his assistant for a while, is that right?"

"Yeah."

"So, as someone who knows all about professional detective work, you probably know it's illegal to operate as an unlicensed private investigator, right?"

Dame shrugged. "I went through all this with the police when the Sainte-Marie Hotel burned down. I was just acting as a concerned citizen back then."

"*Concerned citizen.*" Radovich scrawled something in her notepad. "Right. Well, Dame, I also have a statement from your former landlord — a Mr. Ray Hobart. He said he *paid* you to investigate his now *ex*-wife Aki Miyamoto. Is that right?"

"Well, technically, he —"

"You weren't acting as a 'concerned citizen' then, were you?"

"No, but —"

"And isn't Aki Miyamoto your landlord now? The one who replaced your stained glass transom window? The one who's 'pretty cool'? If you don't mind me asking, how much are you paying for rent these days?"

Dame figured it was time she stopped talking.

"Honestly, I get it." Radovich put her hands on her hips. "We're all working our own angles. And we all have to bend the rules to make ends meet. Especially in this city. But you and your father — you have a long history of operating just a *smidge* outside the law. Don't you?"

"I think my father and I worked pretty hard to operate within the confines of the law."

"How about you just confirm a couple details then, okay? From what I understand, Mr. Hoffman left you for Ms. Suarez. Is that correct?"

Dame was starting to get that prickly feeling under her collar. "That was over four years ago."

"Sure, but Ms. Suarez was your maid of honour, and — one might safely assume — your friend. And she had *his baby* before you were even officially divorced. That must've cut pretty deep, right?"

"Look, Connie" — the name still felt strange, even without the toothbrush — "either I take my daughter to daycare, or I call a lawyer. Which is it going to be?"

"Almost done. Promise." Radovich smiled. "So, on Monday, July 30, Mr. Hoffman's last night on Toronto Island, your father's girlfriend — Fatima Cooper — picked Rosie up from daycare. According to your daycare provider, Ms. Cooper also brought her back the next day. Seems like you had the whole night to yourself. Mind telling me what you got up to?"

"I *slept*," Dame said. "For the first time in months, I slept for more than six hours straight."

"Is there anybody who could corroborate that story? Any friends at the slumber party?"

Dame shook her head.

"That's a shame."

Radovich wrote something else down in her notepad. Dame didn't have to see it to know what it said. The police detective had just sourced out two key ingredients for a murder suspect cocktail: motive and opportunity. But Dame also knew that, without hard evidence to spike the punch, nobody was going to drink it.

"So unfortunately, that brings us to the matter of Mr. Hoffman's phone records."

"Phone records?"

"According to the good people at Bell Canada, the last number that Mr. Hoffman ever dialled" — Radovich trained her eyes on Dame — "was yours."

"What?" Dame was reaching into her pocket, fumbling for her phone. "I haven't spoken to Adam in years."

Radovich shrugged. "Phone records show he called you Monday, July 30, at 9:44 p.m."

Dame scrolled to the date. There it was. A missed call from an unfamiliar number.

"I didn't answer it." Dame showed Radovich her screen. "See? I didn't even talk to him."

"Maybe not. But why was Mr. Hoffman calling you in the first place?"

"How should I know?"

"Well, as a detective — even an unlicensed one — you're probably aware that all of this is just circumstantial at best," Radovich said. "But you have to admit, it's something."

It was something. *Motive, opportunity,* and now, *evidence.*

"Am I under arrest?" Dame asked.

"Not yet. But if I were you" — she gave her a sympathetic smile — "I'd consider contacting that lawyer now."

DAME DIDN'T NEED to be told twice. When she finally got to work, she put in a call to an old friend. By lunchtime, she was opening the door to his Moss Park law office.

"Well, shit" — Bernie Hargrove stood up to greet Dame — "it's been a minute."

He shook her hand and invited her to sit down. He was about the same age as her father, dressed in a checked grey coat and bright yellow shirt. His hair was cropped short, and he sported a manicured salt-and-pepper beard. The watch on his wrist looked expensive, and he took a moment to glance at it as they settled into their respective chairs.

"Hope you don't mind if I eat," he said. "I'm slammed all afternoon. Got about twenty minutes before my next client."

"No problem. Thanks for squeezing me in on such short notice."

Hargrove's office was small and tidy. The smell of fast food radiated from a brown paper bag on his desk. Beside it, a framed CFL trading card featured a much younger Hargrove, decked out in the black and gold of the Hamilton Tiger-Cats. Number Sixty-Seven. Defensive Tackle.

"How's your old man doing these days?"

"He's okay. He had a stroke a few years back, but he's doing better."

"I got shingles last year. Hurt like a son of a bitch. Tell your dad to get the shot — the shingles shot — whatever they call it." The big man leaned back in his chair. "How the mighty have fallen, huh?"

Dame smiled.

"When your pops and I used to play ball together, Coach called us 'Dodge and Bern.'" He laughed a little at that. "We were citywide champs three years in a row. Pounded the hell out of Humberside."

"Dodge never talks about football."

"Your old man was the best. Fast as hell. Shame he didn't keep at it."

"He'll be happy to hear you said that."

"Heck of a private eye, too. I miss working with him."

"I miss working with him, too." Dame smiled. "I just don't miss the work."

Hargrove reached into the paper sack. He unwrapped a burger and took a bite. "So," he said, his voice muffled by two all-beef patties, "what do they have on you?"

"Well, my ex-husband Adam is dead. Probably murder."

"Cops are looking at you?"

Dame nodded. "He cheated on me, I've got no alibi, and I'm the last person he called before he died."

Hargrove let out a low whistle. "Special sauce, lettuce, *and* the cheese. You sure you didn't do it?"

Dame raised an eyebrow. "Yeah, I'm sure."

"Are you the only suspect?"

Dame shook her head. "Some guy with a big beard and a little hat sold Adam's guitar to a consignment shop in Kensington a couple days after he died."

"Are they sure it was Adam's guitar?"

"There was a nude sketch of Adam stuffed inside the case, so yeah. Pretty sure."

"Have they found the big-beard-little-hat guy?"

"Nah. Police couldn't get a positive ID on him."

"Who's the lead detective on the case?"

"Radovich. Connie Radovich."

"Radovich, huh?" Hargrove nodded. "She's good. Really tough, really honest."

"I'm not sure if that's supposed to make me feel better."

"Hey, at least she gave you a chance to lawyer up, right? Could be worse. Some of these downtown cops like to railroad you. They knock you off balance and don't let you back up."

"So, what do we do?"

"Well, I'm going to need the whole story from start to finish, but if the cops are building a case against you, we need to build a case against someone else. Throw a little reasonable doubt in their eyes."

"How do we do that?"

"Normally, I work with a couple guys — guys sort of like your dad — unfortunately, one of them's golfing in Hilton Head and the other's in jail." He pushed the final bite of his burger into his mouth, dusted his hands, and chewed thoughtfully. "You wouldn't happen to know a half-decent private investigator, would you?"

"Yeah," she sighed. "There's one that comes to mind."

CHAPTER THIRTEEN

DAME HAD ASKED the cabbie to wait for her. She wasn't sure if she was staying, and she might need a ride home. But when Rachel didn't slam the door in her face, she waved him away.

"What do you want, now?"

"I want to know who killed Adam," Dame said.

"You didn't give a shit before. Why the sudden enthusiasm?"

Dame sighed. She realized she was going to have to tell Rachel Suarez something she hadn't told her family or friends. "Because the police think I did it."

Rachel frowned. "Why do the police think *you* did it?"

"Well, besides the whole *fucking-my-best-friend* motive, I don't have an alibi for that night, and for some reason I was the last person Adam called before he disappeared."

"Adam *called* you? Why? What did he say?"

"I don't know. I didn't answer."

Rachel shook her head. "Of course you didn't."

"I didn't even *know* he called me. Dodge took Rosie for the night and I was out cold by eight thirty."

Rachel held Dame's gaze for another moment, and then turned on a heel and walked away. Unsure what to do, Dame walked inside and closed the door behind her. She took off her shoes. Eventually, she found Rachel in the kitchen, staring at her phone.

"He messaged me just after eleven thirty that night. He said he was coming home the next day. He said he loved me and he'd see me Tuesday."

"Rachel, no one's doubting that Adam loved you." She took a step toward her. "We all know he chose you over me, okay?"

"How do I know you *didn't* kill him? If the cops think you did it, maybe you did."

Dame sighed. "Honestly? Four years ago I *wanted* to kill him. But if Adam hadn't left me, I would've never had Rosie, and she's the best thing that's ever happened to me. Besides" — Dame pulled a chair out from the kitchen table and sat down — "if I was going to murder him, I wouldn't have done such a piss-poor job of it."

Rachel eyed her warily. "Do you want a coffee?"

"Don't drink it anymore."

"Tea?"

"No thanks."

"Tequila?"

"Bingo."

Rachel found a bottle in the cupboard and poured two glasses. She sat down across the table from Dame.

"So, what's your plan? Are you going to go down to the Port Lands and look for clues?"

Dame took a long pull and looked at the woman across from her. Her eyes were swollen. Her hair was greasy. The pimple she had sported earlier was fading, but like some kind of dermal Hydra, two more had taken its place.

"It's been over a week since they found him. The police would've searched that scene pretty carefully, and if they missed anything, it would be long gone now."

"So, then what?"

Dame cleared her throat. "You paid for studio time on the island for Adam's fortieth birthday. Is that right?"

Rachel nodded.

"And — remind me — how many days did you arrange?"

She thought for a moment. "Friday was just a set-up day. And he took the Monday off work. So, three and a half."

"Why wasn't he going to come home Monday night?"

"Well, I teach a private class Monday night —"

"Late-night Pilates?"

"Something like that. So Adam figured he'd stay as late as he could and then go straight from the island to work Tuesday morning."

"Did Adam call you or text you while he was on the island?"

Rachel shook her head. "Only that message on Monday night. I wanted to give him some space. Let him get some work done."

"And Monday night was the last you heard from him?"

Rachel nodded. She grabbed a Kleenex and blew her nose.

"Toronto Island might be the best place to start, then."

Dame worked her way through a few more questions: Did Adam have any separate bank accounts? Separate credit cards? Did he have any recent conflicts? Did he leave his phone lying around or did he hide it away?

As a child, she initially watched Dodge conduct these interviews with a quiet admiration. She wondered how he decided which questions to ask first. Ask last. How did he know which questions would get him the answers he needed? Now she understood. He was making it up as he went along, just like she was.

"Hey, did Adam ever talk about selling or trading his acoustic guitar?"

"Suzanne?" Rachel stared at Dame like she was stupid. "Of course not. He loved that thing. Why?"

"Somebody — no one seems to know exactly who — sold it to Grace Maxwell at Deacon Blues."

"What? That doesn't make any sense."

"I know. That's why it's a clue."

"Right."

"Look, there's something I'm going to need you to do for me. Something you're not going to like."

"What?"

"I'm going to need you to call the coroner and get the autopsy report."

Rachel stood up, folded her arms, and crossed to the kitchen counter.

"I know it's upsetting, but I can't do it because I'm not family, and —"

Rachel dropped a file folder on the surface of the table.

Dame looked up at her. "You've read it already?"

"Started to. Couldn't finish. That ... *thing* they're describing — that's not Adam."

Dame flipped open the file and read the first page. The report identified the body as Adam Robert Hoffman. It got his age right. His eyes and hair colour checked out. He may have gained a little weight in the past few years, but to be fair, Rachel was a pretty good cook.

The story seemed to lose the plot when it noted how tall her ex-husband was. His one hundred and eighty-three centimetres was described as "length" rather than "height" because — it occurred to Dame — Adam would never stand up again. He would be forever horizontal.

There was a brief description of his clothes. His jacket, shirt, and jeans. Pre- and post-mortem tears in the fabric. One of his boots was missing.

"Did they find his Expos hat?" Dame couldn't remember a day when Adam hadn't worn that ball cap.

"They did eventually. It was about thirty feet down the shore. One of the cops recognized it from the 'Missing' photos."

"Anything else?"

"They gave me this vinyl bag full of his personal effects. I haven't been able to look through it, yet. There's a list that itemizes everything somewhere in the report."

Dame turned a couple pages. "Okay, I see it."

She read through the list. Wallet, watch, wedding ring — all accounted for. It didn't seem like he'd been mugged. "What about his phone?"

Rachel shook her head. "Probably at the bottom of Lake Ontario."

Dame nodded and kept reading. It wasn't long before she understood why Rachel had stopped. Besides a few familiar details, there was very little of the man she knew on the pages that followed. All that was left was the history of a body's final violence. Adam had only been in the water for a few days, but the lake had done a number on him: vascular marbling of soft tissue, pink discolouration of the teeth, fluid accumulation in pleural cavities, lacerations on the face and neck, sloughing of the skin on the hands and feet. The report read more like a Cronenberg screenplay than a description of someone she once loved.

"Says there was a hematoma on the back of his head," Dame said. "x-rays showed comminuted fractures of the occipital bone."

"What does that even mean?"

"It means someone hit him in the back of the head. Really hard."

"So the police are right. This wasn't an accident."

"Doesn't seem like it." Dame read for another moment. "It also says they found traces of algae in his lungs and liver and kidneys."

"What does that mean?"

"It means he was still alive when he went into the water." She sighed and closed the file. "It means he drowned."

Rachel excused herself and disappeared into the bathroom. When she sat back down, Dame whiffed the parmesan tang of vomit under the lilac air freshener.

"Look, it might not get any better," Dame said.

"What do you mean?"

"I mean, what if I find something you don't want to know?"

"I just want the truth."

"People say that" — Dame thought of the naked Adam sketch — "but sometimes they don't like the truth they get."

"I already know this isn't a happy story," Rachel said, "but I still need to know how it ends."

A door slammed, and the two women looked toward the sound it made.

Luka came airplaning into the room and crawled up onto his mother's lap. Once again, Dame was gut-punched by how much the boy looked like Adam.

"Hi, Lukie," Rachel said. "You're back early."

"Sorry," the babysitter said, entering the room and heaving a pale pink backpack off one shoulder. "I know I wasn't supposed to bring him back until five thirty."

"No sweat, Zoe. I know how it goes."

The girl unzipped her backpack and pulled out a small fluorescent green baseball bat and child-sized glove. "Oh, and I finished that Rupi Kaur book you loaned me."

She pulled a copy of *The Sun and Her Flowers* out of the bag and put it down on the kitchen table.

"Wasn't it *amazing*? My book club was in *love* with it."

Zoe took a piece of gum out of its wrapper and put it in her mouth. "It was okay."

"Mom," Luka said, "can we have chicken nuggies tonight?"

Rachel sighed. "I was going to make a broccoli stir-fry —"

"*Pleeeease?*"

"Okay. Chicken nuggies. For my little athlete."

Luka hopped down and zoomed figure eights around the kitchen. "Chicken nuggies!" he cried triumphantly.

"Careful baby, you're going to —"

The boy knocked over Zoe's unzipped backpack. Books, granola bars, and a coil of white earbuds scattered across the floor. A bottle of pills went rattling across the kitchen tile.

"Luka!" Rachel scolded.

The boy's flight plan conveniently took him into the next room.

Rachel sighed. She and Zoe hunched over the scattered items and started stuffing them back into the bag.

Dame looked beneath her chair where the bottle of pills had rolled to a stop. When she picked it up, she couldn't help but notice the label read "*Folic Acid.*"

"Thanks." Zoe was beside her, arm outstretched, palm facing up.

Dame smiled and put the bottle in her hand.

"That kid" — Rachel was saying — "he's a walking disaster just like his father."

The babysitter hoisted her backpack onto her shoulders. "I'm going to head home."

"Okay, Zoe. Thanks."

The door clicked shut, and Dame turned to Rachel. "Seems like a nice kid. Kind of quiet."

"Yeah, she's a little shy. But honestly, I don't know what I would've done without her the past few weeks."

"Has she been working for you for a long time?"

"About six months. Adam loved her. She actually used to be one of Ben's clients. He vouched for her."

"And that didn't break any professional boundaries?"

"Nah." Rachel shrugged. "She's not his client anymore. And just between you and me, he said she wasn't seeing him for anything too serious. Just a little social anxiety. Why? Do you need someone to look after Rosie?"

"I've already got daycare. And I don't think a babysitter's in my budget right now, but" — Dame looked toward the door — "I'll be sure to keep her in mind."

CHAPTER FOURTEEN

IT DIDN'T SMELL like death inside the Weatherheads' house. If anything, it smelled a little like cedar and citrus. Like money.

"Six minutes and thirty-four seconds," the detective said, checking the glow of his Casio. "Not bad."

The kid handed him back a tension wrench and a half-diamond rake, and the detective zipped them safely into a small leather case. "Should've went with the camel back," she said. "Probably could've shaved off another minute or so."

"There's no sign of forced entry," the detective said, running a gloved hand over the door jamb. "If someone actually did kill her, they didn't break in."

The kid aimed her flashlight's beam at the keyhole. "Maybe they didn't lock their door."

"In this neighbourhood?"

The detective had a point. During the day, the Beaches had a breezy affluence to it, all sunshine and boardwalks and homey, patchwork shops. But at night, the neighbourhood drew a cool exoskeleton over itself. Front doors looked grim and impassive, like well-dressed nightclub bouncers. Audis and Volvos shrugged moonlight from their black windscreens.

"Should we start in the girl's room?" the kid asked.

The detective shook his head. "Bathroom."

The Weatherheads, the kid learned, were no longer living in their Kenilworth Avenue home. In fact, it seemed unlikely they would ever return. Cheryl and Bruce were temporarily residing at the Four Seasons, while Jill Weatherhead enjoyed a more permanent stay in Park Lawn Cemetery.

This knowledge did little to untie the knot of anxiety that was twisting up her insides as she followed her father through the midnight shadows of the massive house and up the stairs to what might very well be a murder scene.

The bathroom was the last door on the right. "You can wait out here if you want," the detective said.

"No. I'm okay."

By street light, it looked like any other bathroom — like their bathroom — except bigger and swankier. There was no ratty bath mat, no torn linoleum floors, no bleach-resistant mildew in the grout. Instead, there were two ceramic pedestal sinks, a glass block shower stall, fluffy towels still hanging from brass rings. The jacuzzi tub was a corner unit that looked out over two windows. The detective lowered the venetian blinds and switched on his flashlight. The kid followed suit.

"The forensic guys would have been all over this room," she said. "What's the point of looking at it now?"

"Well, what do you see?"

"I don't know. For a fancy bathtub, it's not all that deep."

"So?"

"So, it would be hard to drown in it by accident."

"They say children can drown in an inch of water."

"Yeah, but she wasn't really a child, was she? I mean, even if she was on drugs, you'd think she'd start to choke and wake up when she went under the surface."

"Maybe." The detective opened the medicine cabinet and shone his light inside. He closed it. "Maybe we should take a look at her bedroom."

They moved down the hall. Outside Jill's door, there was a little plastic sign with her name written in bubbly cartoon characters. The kind of memento parents buy for their children at amusement parks. By the time the detective pushed the door open, the kid was starting to realize that trading a murder bathroom for a dead girl's bedroom might not be the upgrade she anticipated. As the kid played her light over a vanity mirror, a stuffed unicorn, and a Mitsou poster, she couldn't help but feel the sad echo of a girl who was once very much alive.

"This is kind of cool." She pointed her light at a seafoam green typewriter.

"Looks like an old Hermes Rocket."

"Mrs. Elliot said Jill was into poetry." The kid ran her fingers over the keys and they surprised her with a loud clacking.

"Try to keep it down," the detective said. "And you can turn that flashlight off. We're getting enough light in here from the street."

She did as her father asked. "So, what exactly are we looking for?"

The detective cast his eyes around the room. "Well, the Elliots are pretty convinced that Jill killed herself. And the Weatherheads are pretty sure Spencer did it. I'd like a little evidence to support one of those two theories."

Taking care not to disrupt the scene, they began to search the dead girl's room. As the kid poked through the strappy, sparkly, complicated clothing in her closet, a picture of Jill Weatherhead began to take shape in her mind. She was only four years older than the kid, but already, Jill was on some unfamiliar precipice of adulthood.

In her nightstand, the kid found more evidence of the girl's maturity: lipstick tubes, mascara, a box of tampons, and four or five pill bottles.

"Was Jill on any meds?"

"Nope. No prescriptions, anyway."

She took a closer look at the bottles. There was nothing unusual. Advil. Vitamins. Except —"What's 'folic acid'?"

The detective, who had been sorting through a rack of CDs, stopped. He turned around. "Can I see that?"

The kid passed the bottle up to her father, who leaned against the window frame and tried to read the tiny print in the dim light.

"What is it?"

"Well, people take folic acid for different reasons," he said. "They take it for anemia, and heart disease, but most people" — he tossed the bottle back to his daughter — "take it to prevent birth defects."

The kid gave the pills a little rattle. "This bottle's half empty."

Just as the lightbulb went off in her brain, another light went on in the house next door.

"Shit!" The kid flattened herself against the wall and snuck a peek out the window. "Is that Spencer's room?"

"No. Spencer's room is upstairs."

"Then who —?"

Before she could ask her question, it was answered for her. Gabe Elliot stood at the window, leaning on his crutches and looking up toward the kid and the detective. From thirty feet away, his eyes seemed to penetrate the darkness of Jill's bedroom.

"Think he sees us?" the kid whispered.

The detective shook his head.

"Then what's he staring at?"

But as the kid looked back at Gabe Elliot, she started to recognize what she saw in his eyes. It was the same thing she saw in her father's eyes when he stared at an old photograph of her mother.

It was longing.

CHAPTER FIFTEEN

THE NEXT DAY, Dame knocked on the door to Meera's office. "I need a day off."

"God." Meera leaned back in her chair and stretched her arms behind her head. "Don't we all."

"No, I mean, I need to take tomorrow off."

"Oh. Right. Let me just check the schedule ..."

As Meera clicked her mouse and squinted at her computer screen, Dame sat down and wondered how many times she had come into this office to ask her old boss for something — a day off, a favour, a little advice. Peggy Beckers had managed to squeeze a jungle of greenery into this little room, and after her disappearance, Dame wanted to steal her bonsai tree, but someone beat her to the punch. Instead, she wound up snagging the healthy-looking monstera. What happened to the rest of the plants was unclear, but Dame assumed they died a slow death in some TPS evidence locker. Or Dumpster. In a way, it was a shame. The ficus, the philodendron, the English ivy — Peggy had always taken such good care of them. Now, the only thing decorating the office was a picture of Lewis holding an adorable kitten and looking mildly terrified.

"Oh, crap." Meera looked up from the computer. "We're supposed to fill out the online form *and* submit a paper copy to

Human Resources, now." She opened her desk drawer. "*Shit*. Where did I put the paper copy ...?"

For the first time, Dame registered just how tired Meera looked. "You doing all right, boss?"

"Yeah, I'm fine. Just a little busy. What do you need the day off for?"

"Errands."

Meera smiled. "Since you're being intentionally vague, I'll just assume you're doing a little *investigative* work."

"Now who's the detective?"

There was a quick, professional knock on the office door. "Ms. Banerjee?"

"Hi, Terrence."

Meera's handsome new hire stood holding a cardboard box. "I brought those old insurance agreements over from Archives."

"Oh great. You can just leave them on that chair by the door."

Terrence put the box down. A little wisp of dust escaped from under its lid.

"Ever notice that Archives smells kind of funny?" Terrence said. "It's kind of like —"

"*Vegetable soup.*"

Dame and Meera said it simultaneously. They looked at each other and laughed.

"Yeah." Terrence shook his head, slightly mystified. "Vegetable soup."

"No one really likes going to Archives," Dame explained, "but after a while you won't notice the smell so much."

"Good to know." He turned and headed in the direction of the Heritage Planning office.

Meera looked at Dame. "Okay. Be straight with me. What are you doing tomorrow?"

"I told you. Errands."

"Errands my ass." Meera looked past Dame and into the fluorescent lights of the hallway beyond. "How long have you worked here?"

Dame shrugged. "I don't know. I started here just a few months before you, right? So, eight? Maybe nine years?"

"Nine years." Meera shook her head. "And a hundred more to go."

"I figure it's more like twenty."

Meera frowned at Dame. "You think you'll still be working here in twenty years?"

"Sure. It's decent money. Guaranteed pension. We can grab drinks every Friday and watch each other go grey. What's wrong with that?"

"Twenty years is a long time when your heart's not in it anymore."

"It's a paycheque, Meera. My heart doesn't need to be in it."

"See, that's the thing. For me, it's not just a paycheque. It's a career. I'm here for the long haul and I'm okay with that. But you" — she looked at Dame — "you can do something the rest of us can't. Hanging around here is a waste of your talent."

"In this economy, talent's overrated."

"Look, you're my best friend, so don't take this the wrong way."

Dame frowned. "Meera, don't."

"Every morning I roll into City Hall pretty early. Eventually, you show up and we get down to work. We have a few laughs, and it's great."

"Don't do it, Meera."

"But you know what the best part of my day is?"

"I'm serious, Meera. Don't you dare *Good Will Hunting* me."

"It's that half hour before you come into the office. Because I think maybe that day, I'll walk over to your desk, and you won't be there. No goodbye, no see you later, no nothing. You've just left."

Dame sighed and started heading for the door. "So that's a yes on the day off then, right?"

THERE WOULD BE weeks, months maybe, when Dame forgot that she lived on a lake. Toronto often seemed, in and of itself, like a twisting system of asphalt rivers that emptied out into an ocean of concrete. But on that bright Wednesday morning, Dame was not only confronted with the Great Lake itself, but the understanding that this vast body of water swallowed up and spat out the body of Adam Hoffman.

Dame hadn't gone back to visit her ex-husband's grave since the funeral. She wasn't sure that she would. Looking out at all the blue of Lake Ontario, she wondered if Adam's headstone would make her feel any different than she did at that moment — small and temporary, a misstep away from the abyss. Only Rosie, the warm weight on her hip, the ache in her bicep, kept her tied to the present.

"Look at the seagulls" — she pointed out at the demon birds — "look at the sailboats."

Birds, boats, buoys. The journey between the Jack Layton Ferry Terminal and Hanlan's Point Ferry Dock was a series of white flags. Beside her and then behind her, the city rose up like grey, uneven teeth.

The *Ongiara* was a squat diesel ferry that chugged through the water like a bulldog learning to swim. It had none of the venerable grandeur of the *Trillium* or the *Sam McBride*, and none of the amenities either. No polished wood railings, no observation deck, no seats. It was a car ferry, a floating parking lot crowded with human traffic because private vehicles were not allowed on the island. Tourists with their backpacks and coolers and Blue Jays T-shirts. Commuters carrying bags of groceries to get through the week. Dame was surprised how many people had herded themselves onto the boat that Wednesday morning. She wondered if one of these people knew something about her ex-husband's murder, if one of these people was responsible for Adam's death.

After the initial excitement of the *Ongiara*'s departure turned into tedium, Rosie was lulled to sleep by the static churn of the engine and the distant horizon. Dame eased her into her stroller and spent a good part of the twenty-minute journey watching the sun through closed eyes: a bright red darkness. The sun and wind felt unexpectedly good on her face, and she thought that maybe there was something to all of Meera's Afflecking. Maybe a life spent working from a cubicle wasn't what she was meant for. Or maybe — more likely — the cheerful menace of Connie Radovich's handcuffs made these small freedoms all the more precious. Dame would have to remember she was here on business, not pleasure.

With a certain anticlimactic inevitability, the journey whittled itself down to precious inches. One of the ferry operators, dressed in a weathered ball cap and a fluorescent safety vest, stepped out of the cabin to eyeball the remaining open water. The rumble of engines reversing startled Rosie and she woke up angry and frightened as the gate crashed down and the crowd moved forward in a slow surge.

"It's okay, partner." She unwrapped a fruit bar and put it in the little girl's hands. "We're going to go see about a rock star."

After a few more minutes of tearful protest, Rosie fell back to sleep in the stroller. Dame didn't blame her. In the 1940s, Centre Island Village was Toronto's West Egg. Wealthy urbanites went there to lawn bowl and booze and yuck it up until the sixties, when the city told them all to amscray and reduced the village to democratic parkland. The island still had a lot going for it: amusement rides, nude beach, disc golf course, haunted lighthouse. Unfortunately, according to Google Maps, none of these attractions were en route to Dame's destination. The tree-lined asphalt lanes and manicured boulevards were nice enough, but nothing to write home about. Still, it was the path Adam must have taken.

Dame could remember spending one ambling, beautiful, Lou Reed–perfect day with her husband on the eastern side of the island. Sometime after the wedding and before their soul-crushing, marriage-destroying efforts to start a family, they took the ferry to Ward's Island. There, they raced their rented bikes and tried each other's ice cream. They found a little restaurant that served burgers and cold beer. In the heat of the afternoon, they followed the shore to the concrete ruins of an old dock. Adam walked out as far as he could, stripped down to his underwear, and dove into the E. colied waters of the most polluted Great Lake. That time, he survived.

I've never understood how you can do that.

He smiled. *It's not so bad. I didn't swallow any used Band-Aids this time.*

No, not that. I mean, you were down there forever.

They walked along the shore, water squelching in Adam's shoes.

My lifeguarding instructor gave me three tips for holding your breath. He searched his memory in the middle distance. *Slow your heart rate, keep your movements to a minimum, and don't think about the time.*

Dame laughed. *Sounds like business as usual for you.*

It may have been that very night when the idea of recording on Toronto Island had occurred to Adam. They had stretched out on the cooling, emptying beach and watched as some private party yacht from the mainland cruised by, playing Top 40 dance music and blasting fireworks into the sky.

I've heard there's a little studio around here, he said between shimmering blooms. *It's called the Outhouse. Not a lot of people know about it.* The band had been on hiatus for ages. A seemingly permanent pause in his music career.

Maybe you should come back on your own sometime. Record some of the solo stuff you've been working on.

Had she said that? Had she put the idea in his head to come here? Maybe Radovich was right. Maybe she had killed him, after all.

CHAPTER SIXTEEN

THE OUTHOUSE DIDN'T have a website, and it wasn't listed in any formal directories. It had no real online presence at all. The place was more rumour than recording studio, but Dame had a feeling she was getting close when she heard the sound of David Byrnesque vocals accompanied by an acoustic guitar. One of the two was out of tune. Possibly both.

As she followed the path around a corner, the guitar player came into view. He sat cross-legged on a picnic table in shorts and a T-shirt. The sleeve of tattoos down his right arm — not to mention the overgrown topiary of his asymmetrical hairdo — clearly marked him as an ambassador for hipster musicians everywhere.

"Hey, there," Dame said over the music. "Would you happen to know where I can find the Outhouse?"

He stopped playing. "The Outhouse?"

Dame was a little surprised to hear the German in his question (*"Ze Outhaus?"*).

"Yeah," Dame said. "The recording studio?"

"Ah, yes. The studio." He climbed down from the picnic table and leaned over Rosie's sleeping form.

"Uh, she's actually just — maybe don't —"

"Hello, little one!" he said. "Are you having a nap in there? Yes?"

Rosie's eyes fluttered open and registered the musician's unshaven mug. Her sudden reply was shockingly loud.

"*Heiliger Strohsack!*" He took a step back. "What lungs!"

"Could you tell me where the studio is?" Dame asked over the sound of her daughter.

"On the other side of the school." He pointed in the general direction. "Beside the bicycle repair shop."

"Okay, thanks!"

"But, you know," he shouted over Rosie, "I don't think you should bring such a loud baby to the school, yes? Some of the artists, they sleep late and you might wake them up."

Dame mimed deafness and continued on her way.

THE BEACON POINT Art Centre was, in fact, an old elementary school — the original elementary school for children who lived on the island — and while it still featured a swing set and the faded remains of a hopscotch court, its current incarnation wouldn't be particularly appealing to kids. It was a squat clapboard structure, guarded by unruly bushes and slathered in a sage-coloured paint that peeled away from the previous colours underneath. Separated from the beach by a patch of scrubby Jack pines, Beacon Point couldn't even boast a decent view of Lake Ontario.

The city had wanted to tear down the school not long after they turned the island into a public park, but the structure was saved, not by Dame's predecessors at Heritage Planning, but by a small group of activists and former school employees who petitioned to turn the place into a residence for artists.

And while it hadn't looked like much from what she could glean from Google Maps, as Dame walked through the school grounds, she had to admit there was some heartening quality to the place she couldn't put her finger on. Maybe it was the August sunlight, the cages of fat tomatoes in the vegetable garden, or the lazy drone of bumblebees, but Dame felt oddly comforted that this was where Adam had spent his last days. Even Rosie seemed to be awed by her surroundings, or at the very least, found them interesting enough to stop crying.

Beside the school's main building were a few structures, inconveniently undesignated by any signage. She didn't see anything that was obviously a studio or a bicycle repair shop. Luckily, Dame noticed a young woman wearing a wide-brimmed hat and working in one of the gardens. Once again, she attempted to secure directions.

"That's the one you want," the gardener said, pointing out an aluminum-sided double-wide trailer. "I think he's got a band in there right now, so maybe wait until the music stops."

As if to prove her theory, a muffled cacophony of live music filled the air.

"Thanks. Will do."

She pushed Rosie's stroller over a cracked and weedy asphalt path. The rickety wooden steps that led up to the door were overgrown with goldenrod and thistle, and nailed to the door itself was a faded plastic moon. Abbey Road, it was not.

As advised, Dame waited for the music to stop, and when all the clamour finally stumbled to its uncertain end, a man came out onto the steps and lit a cigarette.

Jesse Maracle looked different than Dame had imagined him. About fifteen years different. His hair was longer and greyer, and it was tied back behind his head. He still had his rock-star good looks and swimmer's build, but Dame could see how the years had softened both his jawline and his belly.

Adam had owned a couple of Jesse Maracle records. Not the one with the big hit — "Common Cold Heart" had made heavy rotation on MuchMusic — but the later albums, the ones that were quieter, more introspective. The last records, as far as she knew.

"Yeah?" he was asking.

"Uh, hi. Do you have a few minutes to talk?"

"About what?"

"Adam Hoffman."

Maracle took a long drag on his cigarette and then stubbed it out on the door jamb. "Well, come in if you're coming in."

He turned back into the darkness of his studio. Dame unstrapped Rosie from her stroller and followed him inside. The sound booth smelled of sandalwood and body odour. Maracle was seated at a massive console of knobs and sliders and switches, and through a large picture window, Dame could make out four shaggy-haired twentysomethings — boys, really — standing or sitting at their respective instruments.

"You a cop?" Maracle asked, not looking up from the sound-board.

"No."

"You're going to have to wait a bit, then. I'm on the clock."

"I don't mind. Except" — Dame gestured her head toward Rosie — "will it be loud?"

"Should be okay in the booth. Grab a seat."

Against one wall, a cracked vinyl couch was covered with notes and what looked like lyrics scrawled on binder paper.

"Just shove all that shit over," he said. "I wasn't exactly expecting company."

Dame did as she was told and Maracle pressed the talkback button. "Okay, folks," he said. "How did we feel about that last one?"

Through the glass, she could see one of the boys shaking his head.

"Sean went into the chorus too late." The voice came through the speaker.

"That's because Paul started singing too early."

"I always sing it that way."

Maracle released his finger from the button and they watched as the boys continued to bicker.

"I've got these guys in here until Monday."

"What are they called?"

"Laces Undone. Ever heard of them?"

Dame shook her head.

"Yeah, you probably won't."

Just then, the door to the studio opened and the four boys filed into the sound booth.

"Hey, Jesse, we're going to take five and head over to Centre Island for a slice. You want anything?"

Maracle shook his head. The boys left the studio, and the former rock star turned in his chair to cast his dark eyes down on Dame.

"So?"

She had thought about pretending to be Rachel. It might've opened some doors, but people tend to clam up around widows. That said, she also wasn't sure how people would react to a woman investigating her ex-husband's death. Did people still consider her some kind of widow? What did you call someone whose ex-husband dies? The only word that came to mind was *suspect*.

"Adam was an old friend of mine." Dame played it safe. "I guess I'm just trying to understand what happened to him."

Maracle was quiet for a moment. "Popular topic of conversation these days."

"Oh yeah?"

"This one detective interviewed me three separate times. Figured I should start charging her my hourly rate."

"Sorry. I know you're busy."

Maracle sighed. "He was your friend. Makes things a little different. What did you want to know?"

"What was Adam recording before he died?"

"He finished a handful of songs. Not exactly sure what he planned on doing with them. They were good, though. Guy had some talent."

"Could I listen to something he was working on?"

Maracle squinted at the soundboard. "Guess there's no harm in that. Give me a minute to pull up a file."

Dame kept a tight grip on her squirmy child. The sound booth's electronic equipment was a dessert cart of blinking lights and candy-coloured buttons that likely looked as attractive to Rosie as they did expensive to Dame.

"Here's one that turned out pretty well, I thought." He pushed the faders up on the board and Adam's voice leapt out of the speakers. The sound of it caught her off guard. Dame had heard him sing a thousand times — with his band, in the car, in the shower — but there was something so unadorned about the recording, so *Adam*, that for a moment, it felt like he suddenly was in the room with them. And when she realized he would never be in any room with her ever again, unexpected tears filled her eyes.

"Mama sad?" Rosie put her hand against the side of Dame's face.

"I'm okay, partner." She kissed the top of her daughter's head and turned to Maracle. "Has Rachel heard this?"

"His wife?"

Dame nodded.

"Not yet. I haven't finished mixing it."

"You should send it to her. I think she'd appreciate it."

They listened a little longer. When the song reached the chorus, she was surprised to hear a second voice, a cool current running through Adam's ragged baritone. A woman's voice.

"Who's the other singer?"

"That's Greta."

"They sound nice together. Was she a friend of Adam's?"

"Uh, kind of. She's one of the artists doing a residency here."

Dame adjusted her glasses. "What kind of art does she make?"

"I'm not really sure. A lot of artists come through Beacon Point. It's hard to keep track."

"Any chance I could meet her?"

"Well, I haven't seen her for a couple days, but —"

Maracle was interrupted by the sound of boots on the steps outside. In the doorway, a man stood silhouetted against the daylight.

"Hey, Jesse, could I borrow some coffee?" the man asked. "I don't want to go all the way to the mainland today. I just need enough to get me to the weekend."

"Sure, Yosef," Jesse said. "On one condition."

"What's that?"

"My new friend here wants to meet Greta. Think you could arrange it?"

Yosef stepped into the studio. He was tall and thin, with curly dark hair and fine features. He made a sound like he was measuring his love of coffee against Maracle's request.

"You still have that Grizzly Bear blond roast?"

"It's in my bin."

He sighed. "Okay. Deal."

"SO, THIS IS the common area." Yosef was digging through a clear plastic tote marked "JESSE." "We usually get a little more cupboard space, but Jesse's new clients dragged in two giant cartons of Mr. Noodles."

"How long have you been staying here for?"

"A few weeks." He scooped coffee grounds into the coffee maker. "Different people stay for different periods of time. All depends on their funding. You want a cup?"

She absolutely did. "No, thanks."

Dame followed Rosie as she toddled around, exploring the large room. She imagined it had once been some sort of teacher's lounge, with wide windows that looked out into a grove of birch trees. There was a full kitchen, a large maple harvest table, and a little nook with a couch and a TV. The walls were decorated haphazardly, in a way that suggested public space more so than private residence: a diagram indicating what to do in case of fire, a hastily — perhaps angrily — scrawled message that reminded residents to wash their own dishes and put food scraps in the compost.

By the door, a cork bulletin board had become a hectic collage: news clippings about the emerald ash borer, a speckled seagull feather, and — hiding under a printout of a BuzzFeed listicle ("*25 Mattresses That Look Like Celebrities*") — Dame spotted a piece of off-white, heavyweight paper that featured a pencil sketch of a lopsided Jack pine.

"Do you know who drew this picture?"

Yosef crossed the room to get a better look. "Uh, nope."

"That signature" — she pointed at the illegible squiggle — "you don't recognize it?"

He shook his head. "Sorry. There's a lot of people around here working on different projects."

Dame pulled her phone out of her pocket and flipped through her photos. Moments later, her suspicions were confirmed. The illegible squiggle below the Jack pine sketch was identical to the one below the sketch of a naked, sleeping Adam.

CHAPTER SEVENTEEN

IN SPIRIT, BEACON Point reminded Dame of the Ossington art studio Meera had recently saved from the wrecking ball. But whereas the Merc was a tightly wound beehive of coffee breath and elbows, Beacon Point had a breezy calm about it. The echoes of school children were long silent, and the long, academic hallways were cool and empty. Residents lived and worked in private, classroom-sized studios. Every day they could choose: solitude or community.

"Greta's room's on the other side," Yosef was saying, "so it's a bit of a hike."

"You and Jesse seem" — Dame chose her words carefully — "a little *hesitant* about her."

"Greta's a doll. She can just be" — it was his turn to choose his words — "a lot."

As they made their way down the hall, the gardener Dame had seen earlier came in through a side door cradling a thatched basket of something green and leafy.

"Hey, Maudie," Yosef said.

"Oh hey." She was small and slender, but her arms were strong and smudged with dirt.

"You coming back for the campfire on Saturday?"

"Probably. I'll stop by your room later, okay? I just want to get all this kale into the kitchen before I completely run out of gas." She smiled and walked past them.

"Is she one of the artists?"

"Groundskeeper. Comes in a couple times a week to look after the garden and mow the lawn."

"Do you guys have a lot of campfires around here?"

"Every Saturday, pretty much. That's how I met Adam. He actually caused a little bit of campfire controversy."

"What do you mean?"

"Well, there's this one guy here — Christoph — he sort of fancies himself the Official Island Troubadour."

"German guy? Bad haircut?"

"That's the one. I think when Adam busted out his acoustic guitar, Christoph got a little jealous."

"Adam was a pretty good musician."

"Yeah, but it was more than that. When Adam started singing that Jeff Buckley song — you know, 'Hallelujah'?"

It was a Leonard Cohen song, but Dame let it slide.

"Anyway, Greta started singing along with him — it must have made Christoph *nuts*. She *never* sang with him. And then later, when a few of us met up with Maudie — she grows this really good weed — Greta brought Adam along."

"Christoph wasn't invited to the after-party?"

Yosef shook his head.

"And I'm guessing he has a bit of a thing for Greta?"

"Oh, honey," Yosef smiled at her, "what straight man on this island doesn't? Ever since I got here, I've been watching Christoph and the other dudes fight over her like seagulls fighting over a french fry."

Yosef stopped at the end of the hall. "This is Greta."

He knocked on the door, and after a few moments a voice

replied, "*Entrez s'il vous plaît.*"

Inside the little room, a single bed was pushed up against one wall and a small student desk against the other. A hand-knotted Persian rug dominated the floor, and on top of the rug, sitting cross-legged, was Greta. Despite the heat of the day, she wore blue cotton coveralls decorated with paint splatters. She was gouging at a block of linoleum with some kind of tool while a Cartier watch slid up and down her delicate wrist. Beside her on the floor were a number of similar tools — small wooden doorknob handles that ended in cruel-looking metal.

"Greta, this is —"

"Dame. And this is my daughter, Rosie."

The young woman got to her feet and stared at the two-year-old. "Hello, little Rose," she said. "Do you have any thorns?"

Dame realized, with an objective, almost clinical assessment, that she was staring at one of the most strikingly beautiful people she had ever met. Wide, bright eyes, full lips, and tousled Brigitte Bardot updo. It was an audacious, intimidating beauty, unaided by makeup or fashion, and for a brief, demoralizing moment, Dame felt like everyone else in the room were simply figments of the woman's imagination.

"Dame was hoping she could ask you some questions," Yosef explained, "about Adam Hoffman."

"Poor Adam," Greta said. "I'll always treasure the part of himself he shared with me."

Dame looked at the chaos of the woman's unmade bed and wondered which "part of himself" Adam had shared with Greta.

"Okay then" — Yosef was already halfway out the door — "I'm sure you two have lots to talk about."

Dame and her daughter found themselves alone with Greta, her pale blue eyes locked on them, like a snake hypnotizing its victim. She put Rosie down but kept a firm grip on her hand.

"So, you were Adam's lover?" Greta said.

"Uh, not exactly."

"But you were intimate with him, weren't you? I can see it in your colours. There's a place where your aura overlapped with his."

"Yeah, I guess you could say that. Did your aura ever" — Dame cleared her throat — "*overlap* with Adam?"

Greta sat down on her unmade bed and smiled an effortless, nose-wrinkling smile. "When I first heard Adam sing, I knew we would be a part of each other's lives, however briefly. I'm so glad Jesse was able to document our ... *entanglement*."

Dame caught Rosie reaching for one of the sharp tools littering the floor. She picked the little girl up into her already-aching arms. "So, what is it you're working on?"

"Oh this? This is part of a series of linocut prints."

"Those blades look pretty sharp."

"Our life is so temporary, so ethereal — I wanted to capture transient moments with something more permanent."

"And that's linoleum you're carving into?"

She nodded. "I used to work with a different medium" — she turned over her forearms to reveal an intricate pattern of scars — "but some people found it upsetting. I don't like upsetting people."

A detail from Adam's autopsy report surfaced in Dame's brain: *lacerations on the face and neck*. Behind Greta, the student desk was scattered with an assortment of chisels and razors. And then Dame noticed something else: a spiral-bound sketchpad, the cover of which advertised its cream-coloured, ninety-pound drawing paper.

"Do you use any other mediums? Do you ever paint? Or ... sketch?"

Greta nodded. "I like to sketch my subjects before I carve them. The pencil lets me feel their truth. The blade lets me reveal it."

Dame held her daughter a little closer. "Could I see the work in your sketchpad?"

"Oh, no. Those are my first drafts. It's a very private part of my process."

Dame shifted Rosie to her other hip — the little girl was starting to feel like a sack of bowling balls. "Could I show you something?" She dug her phone out of her pocket and thumbed to the pencil sketch of Adam.

As Greta took her time admiring every detail of the image, Rosie got progressively squirmier.

"He was such a beautiful man," Greta said, "wasn't he?"

"Could you tell me who drew this picture?"

"I could" — she smiled again — "but like I said, I don't like upsetting people."

CHAPTER EIGHTEEN

BY THE TIME she left Greta's room, Dame was plenty upset. Upset, frustrated, hot, and responsible for a two-year-old who was making it very clear that she felt exactly the same way. What had started out as such a beautiful, hopeful day was quickly starting to feel like a bust. The only person who had any answers about Adam seemed incapable of giving her a straight one.

Had Adam been fucking Greta? Or just "documenting" their "entanglement"? And, if they were fucking, who knew about it? In any case, Dame was out a day's pay and had nothing to show for it. Not only that, she'd missed the twelve-thirty ferry, and the next one didn't run until two o'clock. She and Rosie were going to be stuck on this island for at least another hour.

She let Rosie toddle ahead of her. The little girl squatted and poked at a fallen leaf, floppy hat shading her eyes, skin glowing with a fresh coat of sunscreen. As they slowly made their way back to locate the stroller she'd abandoned beside Jesse Maracle's studio, Dame discovered the ex–rock star himself smoking a cigarette and talking to a bearded, big-bellied man wearing a small straw fedora. She noticed a camera hanging from the man's neck. As she got closer, she could tell they were arguing. When the bearded man stormed away, Maracle put out his cigarette and went back inside the Outhouse. Dame heaved Rosie up on her hip and followed him through the door.

"So Laces Undone aren't back yet?"

Maracle shook his head. "Still on break."

"Dang. I was hoping for an autograph."

The aging rocker smiled.

"Your friend sure left in a hurry," Dame said.

"Who? Houseboat Harry?" Maracle turned his head toward the window. "Wouldn't exactly call him a 'friend.'"

"Oh, no?"

"Harry's this amateur photographer who lives on a boat in the marina. Likes to hang around the artists. Thinks he's some kind of modern-day buccaneer."

"A pirate, huh?" Something pinged in the back of Dame's brain.

"Pain in the ass is what he is. Guy just loves drama. Last few weeks, he and that German guy have been scrapping over Greta. As far as I can tell, Greta doesn't want anything to do with either of them." Maracle sat down in front of the massive mixing board and made a few adjustments. "Speaking of which, how did your visit with her go?"

"A little strange," she said.

"Yeah, that sounds like Greta."

"Do you think there was something going on between her and Adam?"

"You're starting to sound a little more like an ex-wife than an old friend." He seemed to consider her for a moment. A broad smile crept across his face. "You're the detective, aren't you? The one with the funny name."

"I don't really —"

"Babe? Dolly? Dollface?"

She sighed. "Dame."

Maracle snapped his fingers. "Right. Dame. Adam spoke very highly of you."

The detective fought back a blush. "So, any thoughts on Adam and Greta?"

"Well, I can tell you this much: Sometimes I can arrange for musicians to stay in a vacant studio, but Beacon Point's running at capacity right now, so Adam had to crash here — on the couch."

Dame looked at the cracked vinyl, still busy with papers — lyrics, lists, forgotten notes. She supposed it was a little better than the floor.

"Saturday and Sunday morning I woke him up around ten o'clock. But on Monday, he wasn't here. Eventually, he rolled in wearing the same clothes he'd worn the day before."

"You think he spent Sunday night with someone?"

Maracle shrugged. "I didn't ask."

"Did you tell the police about it?"

"They didn't ask."

Dame adjusted her glasses. "Around when did you last see him?"

"Originally, he planned to leave Tuesday morning, but we finished up early on Monday afternoon, and I think he was looking forward to sleeping in his own bed."

"So, Monday night?"

Maracle nodded. "Last ferry goes out at ten o'clock. Adam grabbed his guitar, threw on his jacket, and left here on foot a little after nine."

Dame frowned. If Adam had gone home Monday evening, why had he texted Rachel to say he was leaving Tuesday morning?

Just then, the dull musk of the recording studio was interrupted by a new, unmistakable reek.

"Poop!" Rosie said.

Maracle raised an eyebrow.

"Sorry," Dame said. "Do you mind if I change her in here?"

"Wouldn't be the first turd ever produced in this studio." Outside the window, Laces Undone were playing hacky sack. "Probably won't be the last."

Dame laughed.

"Here," Maracle said, "let me get this stuff off the couch."

As he gathered up the pieces of paper, one fell to the ground. It wasn't cheap loose-leaf, and there were no lyrics or notes on it. Instead, it was a piece of off-white, heavyweight paper that featured a pencil sketch of the engineer himself, bent toward the mixing board. Beneath the drawing was a very familiar-looking squiggle.

Dame held out the paper to Jesse. "Did Greta draw this picture?"

"Nope. That there's a Maudie Beresford original."

"Maudie? As in, the gardener?"

"One and the same."

The lightning strike of realization sizzled through Dame's body.

"You wouldn't happen to know if she's still on the island, would you?"

Maracle looked at his watch. "Not sure. Sometimes she hangs around. You might want to check the common room. Someone there might know."

Dame had her daughter changed and dressed in record time. "Thank you," she said to Maracle. "I know making music with you meant a lot to Adam."

"He was a good songwriter. I was sorry to hear what happened to him."

Dame slung the diaper bag over her shoulder, hoisted her daughter into her arms, and as quickly as she could, hustled back to Beacon Point's main building. When she got to the common room, Yosef was sitting at the harvest table drinking Maracle's coffee and reading a book.

"Hey again," Dame said. "Any chance you've seen Maudie around?"

"Uh" — Yosef furrowed his brow — "she took off on her bike about half an hour ago."

Rosie squirmed and pushed against her captivity. "Go *home, Mama.*"

"Was she heading to the ferry?"

Yosef shook his head. "She's buddies with a guy who runs a water taxi. He usually takes her to the mainland after work."

Rosie kicked her legs. "Wanna go *home, Mama.*"

"There's no way I could catch her, is there?"

Yosef shook his head. "Not on foot. Best bet might be to come back on Saturday."

"*Go home no-o-o-ow!*" The little girl's animal shriek echoed through the school.

A raw-looking, grey-haired woman stomped into the common room. "This is an artist's residency. Not a *lunatic asylum.* And some people are trying to work!" The woman turned and stomped away.

Dame sighed. She knew when she was beat.

CHAPTER NINETEEN

DR. KANNAN SETH *was not a creep. He did not wear a white, gore-stained labcoat. He did not wolf down sloppy joes sitting beside partially vivisected cadavers. He wasn't even meeting the detective in the chill menace of some institutional basement.*

"Is that him?"

As they walked into the Bloor Street deli, the kid pointed out a man sitting alone in a booth next to the window.

"You sound disappointed."

Dr. Seth stood up to greet them. He shook the detective's hand and invited them to sit down. He was about the same age as the kid's father, dressed in a pink paisley shirt and a grey overcoat. He looked up at the clock as the detective and the kid settled themselves into the booth.

"I've got about forty-five minutes before I have to get back. Mind if we order first?"

When the waitress materialized, he ordered a corned beef on rye and a pickle on a stick. The detective got a hamburger and the kid asked for a grilled cheese sandwich. Three cups of coffee arrived before the food.

"So," the forensic pathologist said, "you wanted to talk about Jill Weatherhead."

The detective nodded.

"Well, I didn't examine the body. But I did manage to glance over the autopsy reports. Ms. Weatherhead's a bit of a celebrity on Grosvenor Street. Anything in particular you wanted to know?"

"Was there anything unusual?"

Dr. Seth took a sip from the ceramic mug. "Death is always a little unusual. We've both been in business long enough to understand that."

"Was there anything to suggest that she didn't commit suicide?"

"We-ell, from what I understand Ms. Weatherhead had a lot of reasons to live. Daddy is rich. Mummy is good-looking. Handsome boyfriend, too." He took another sip of his coffee. "I'd say the living was very easy for Ms. Weatherhead."

The food arrived and everyone was quiet for a moment as they tucked into their sandwiches.

"Was there something in the autopsy to suggest that Jill's life had changed in some way?" the detective said. "Maybe something that didn't show up in the official police report."

"Something to suggest her life had changed in some way." The pathologist repeated the detective's words.

"Maybe in a family way?"

For a moment, the kid thought Dr. Seth was going to choke on his corned beef.

"My friend, why do you always have to ask me the difficult questions?" he said when he regained his composure. "Ask me nice questions, okay? Questions that won't get me fired."

The detective smiled.

Dr. Seth took a bite out of his pickle on a stick. "Okay, fine. From what I heard, Jill Weatherhead was three months pregnant when she died. But mummy and daddy didn't want the media to get hold of that particular detail. They were — you know — one of those good, Christian families. And Jill was only sixteen.

From what I understand, daddy had it scrubbed from the official report."

"Wouldn't that impede the investigation?"

"Staff Inspector Weatherhead doesn't want an investigation. He only wants justice. Or at least, his version of justice. He made up his mind that the neighbour boy did it. He's just angry they haven't found any hard evidence."

"Why does he think Spencer did it?"

"He got his little girl pregnant. That alone makes him guilty."

"A neighbour heard them arguing." The detective carved out an angry face in his puddle of ketchup. "Maybe Jill wanted to keep it and Spencer didn't."

"Sure, sure," the pathologist said. "A crime of passion."

The kid adjusted her glasses. "I don't buy it."

Both men paused and looked at her.

"They were old friends," she continued. "Isn't that what Mrs. Elliot said? Close since they were little?"

"She's got a point," the detective said. "They weren't exactly Sid and Nancy. And their parents had the resources to support them if Jill decided to keep the baby. Seems like a bit of a stretch as far as motive goes."

Dr. Seth finished his pickle and washed it down with the rest of his coffee. "Well, these are all interesting theories" — he put a purple bill down on the table — "but I've got to get back to work."

"I wish you'd let me buy you lunch."

"Lunch, my friend, I can afford." He stood up and brushed crumbs off his pants. "The company I keep" — he smiled — "now that might cost me one day."

"See you around, doctor."

"See you around, detective."

CHAPTER TWENTY

"SO?" MEERA RESTED her arms on top of Dame's cubicle. "How was your day off?"

Dame shrugged. "Wasn't much of a day off. I ran around Toronto Island all day and then I was up half the night with Rosie."

"Well," Meera said, "I know you've got a lot on your plate right now, so Lewis is going to take over the designation of the old town hall in Dufferin Grove, and I've got Terrence" — she waved at the handsome recruit — "looking after all your incoming permits for the next two weeks."

Dame frowned into her computer screen. "So, what am I supposed to be working on?"

"You" — Meera crouched down beside her — "are just going to focus on the Marinetti trial. Okay? I want you to go over those development violations with a fine-tooth comb."

"Meera —"

"Shareholders, investors, accountants, mortgage firms, architects, insurance providers, contractors, subcontractors, landscapers, the guy who does his laundry, the guy who cleans his eavestroughs — I want you to run it all under the Dame Polara microscope, okay? Work every angle. Be ready for any question."

Not all that long ago, catching a crooked developer like Marinetti would've consumed Dame. She would've spent every spare minute making sure she had the evidence necessary to bring him down. But these days, Marinetti seemed like the least of her worries.

"Okay." She forced a smile to her face. "You got it, boss."

ON HER LUNCH break, Dame put in a call to Bernie Hargrove.

"So, I might have a bit of a lead on the woman who drew that picture of Adam."

"Great! What are we talking about? Temperamental painter? Capricious poet?"

"Uh, no. Groundskeeper."

"Groundskeeper. Okay" — the lawyer sounded a little disappointed — "I think we can work with that."

"Her name's Maudie Beresford. I did a little digging online. She's twenty-six and lives with her parents."

"Just a kid, huh?"

On the other end, Dame could hear Bernie biting into his lunch.

"Yeah. But a kid with a master's degree in microbiology and a part-time job with an environmental consulting firm. I think groundskeeping is what she does for fun."

"Sure. Groundskeeping and sketching the occasional nude. You going to talk to her?"

"I could swing by her work, or her house, but she's probably going to be on the island this Saturday."

"And you might get more naked sketch talk out of her when she's not around her parents or colleagues."

"Yeah, that's what I was thinking."

"So, does that mean you're going back on Saturday?"

"I think I have to."

"Wish my other investigators worked as hard as you."

"Try hiring more murder suspects. We're a very motivated demographic."

THAT EVENING, WHEN Dame arrived at Dodge's apartment, Fatima opened the door before she could even knock.

"I made sweet potato and black bean curry," Fatima said. "And I won't take no for an answer."

Dame smiled. The poor woman had been translating Rosie's id and Dodge's ego all day, and she wasn't about to begrudge her some adult conversation. But when they all sat down for dinner, Dame found she didn't have much to say. Luckily, Rosie had plenty.

"Grampa stinky," she informed the table from her high chair. "Grampa make stinky smell."

Dame raised an eyebrow.

"Grampa toot! Pee-ew!"

The old man frowned.

"It was the burrito you had for lunch," Fatima said. "You know those beans don't agree with you."

Dodge grumbled and changed the subject. "*M-Mari-Marinetti.*"

"Oh," Fatima remembered, "they mentioned that Marinetti man on the news today."

"Phillip Marinetti?" Dame said.

"I hope they put all of those real estate thugs in prison," Fatima said. "I hope they catch that Beckers woman, too."

Dame also hoped 'those real estate thugs' would go to prison, but she knew it was unlikely. When Anton Felski botched Dame's murder and got himself a sixteen-year sentence, he rolled over and named a lot of names. Suddenly, all these reputable developers — bigwigs like Chuck Moffat at Okusha Corporation, Sandra Grant at Titun, Jimmy Tanaka at Neos — were linked to the biggest arson conspiracy in the city's history. Still, they were careful. They had expensive lawyers and enough junior staffers to throw under the legal bus. They made sure they were never in the wrong place at the wrong time. None of them spent a minute behind bars.

And more important than all the names Felski could name was the one he couldn't. The one he didn't know. The name of the man who, on Peggy Beckers' orders, had murdered Dame's mother when Dame was just eleven years old. *Kind of strange looking*, Felski had told her. *Has two different-coloured eyes*. It was hard to care about a bunch of white-collar real estate criminals when the man who killed her mother was still at large.

AS USUAL, MR. Kirby sat waiting in the bus shelter outside the LCBO, a bottle wrapped in brown paper by his feet.

"Hello, lovelies," he said as they approached. "How are we this fine Thursday?"

"We're good, Mr. Kirby," Dame said. "How are you?"

The old drunk raised his face toward the setting sun. "You know, Dylan Thomas told us to rage against the dying of the light." His dark glasses flashed. "Frankly, I don't see what there is to be so angry about."

Dame laughed.

"Miss Rosie" — he directed his attention to the little girl in the stroller — "are you being good for your mama today?"

"Yes," she said soberly.

"You're not raging against anything?"

She shook her head. "No."

"Well, that's good to hear. Now" — he looked up at Dame — "is there any possibility that I could trouble you for whatever excess change is weighing you down?"

Dame reached into the zippered pocket under Rosie's stroller and produced her usual blue bill. When she leaned in closer to put it in the man's front pocket, she noticed a series of red scratches across his cheek.

"You pick a fight with a thorn bush, Mr. Kirby?"

He put a trembling hand to his face. "Ah," he said, smiling, "one of the many hazards of being flesh and blood in a world of sharp edges."

Dame adjusted her glasses. "You take better care of yourself, okay?"

"Of course," he said. "I have my modelling career to consider, don't I?"

Dame smiled. "Have a good night, Mr. Kirby."

"You too, my lovelies."

"KUH-BEE STINKY," ROSIE said as Dame freed her from the confines of her stroller. "Stinky like Grampa."

Rosie wasn't wrong. The old man had a bit of an odour to him. Some combination of mothballs, sweat, and a brand of aftershave that Dame was pretty sure they didn't make anymore. She wondered if this was one of the inevitable symptoms of old age. She'd noticed that Dodge was getting a bit smelly as he got on in years. Even when he wasn't eating bean burritos.

Dame plunked Rosie down on the sidewalk, and the little girl wobbled and held on to her pant leg for balance. It was quiet outside their house on O'Hara, and the sun was starting to sink below the horizon. As Dame struggled to collapse the plastic stroller, she smiled at a young couple pushing a tiny newborn in a massive, armoured pram — an Escalade compared to her little Chrysler Neon. She watched as they continued on, dominating the sidewalk, a little army and their own private tank. There were days, certainly nights, when she wondered what it would be like to have a partner again. Someone else to hold the door open while she fumbled through it. Someone else to put Rosie to bed, or get up with her in the middle of the night. Someone else to help carry the weight. For Dame, the concept of romance had curdled like three-day-old breast milk, but division of labour still made her swoon.

"Come on," she told her daughter. "Let's get you inside."

Backpack on her shoulders, diaper bag around her neck, stroller under one arm, she used her one free hand to help Rosie navigate her way up the stairs. When they got to the top, she let go of her daughter to fish around in her pocket for the key.

It was Rosie who made the discovery.

"Door open, Mama."

She was right. It was open. Not hanging wide open in the way her previous landlord would leave it — inviting rats and raccoons and the whole neighbourhood to room with her. It was just open a crack. Nothing you could see from the street. No sign of forced entry. Just open. Unlocked and open. A sudden cold crept through her body. She grabbed her daughter's hand, just a little tighter than before.

CHAPTER TWENTY-ONE

"AKI?" DAME CALLED out. "Is that you?"

It wouldn't be the first time her landlord entered her apartment without permission. But in the last couple years, Aki had been pretty good about giving her a heads-up beforehand. What worried her more was the memory of finding Lewis in her front hall, beaten unconscious by Anton Felski. She picked Rosie up into her arms and held her close.

"Hello?" Dame stepped inside.

Her daughter looked up at her, confused. "Nobody home, Mama."

The little girl seemed to be right, but to make sure, Dame made a cursory scan of each room. The bedroom, the bathroom, the nursery — everything seemed to be in order, until she found her way into the kitchen.

"What the hell?"

On the counter, her plastic watering can stood half full. Dame couldn't remember the last time she'd used the thing, but she was sure it hadn't been that morning. She walked over and pressed her finger against the monstera's soil. It was still damp.

Someone had been in her house. And not that long ago.

Dame checked the door to the back porch. It was also open. So was the exterior door.

She shifted Rosie's weight to her other arm. "You keep holding on tight, okay partner?"

"Okay, Mama."

Dame stepped out into her tiny backyard. Aside from a recent dandelion infestation, nothing seemed particularly out of order. She pushed open the back gate and followed the narrow laneway that ran parallel to her street. Still, nothing out of the ordinary. Just the usual detritus of fast food wrappers, cigarette butts, and — *hold on*. Lying not far from an empty Capital Espresso cup was a pair of relatively new and relatively expensive-looking sunglasses. Dame crouched down, her knees very aware of the extra thirty pounds of toddler they were bearing. The shades were in good shape — not scratched or covered in laneway grime — which meant whoever lost them lost them recently. What's more, they looked familiar. Who did she know that owned tortoiseshell Gucci sunglasses? An image of a woman wearing a slim-cut leather coat and fuck-me boots came to mind. *Radovich.*

Dame stood up. Hargrove had called Connie Radovich "really tough" and "really honest," so why was she breaking into her apartment without a warrant? She hung the sunglasses from her collar and immediately Rosie tried to snatch them.

"Sorry, partner. I might need those for later."

Dame went inside, put Rosie in her booster seat, and put the shades on the coffee table. She went back and collected the letters and fliers from her mailbox. There was yet another envelope with a Penetanguishene return address. She sighed and filed it away with the others above the fridge.

Dame fixed herself a glass of El Silencio, and after she felt the reassuring burn of it in her belly, she made a phone call.

"Hey!" Rachel said when she answered. "How'd it go on the island yesterday? You figure anything out?"

"Uh, maybe."

For the past few years, Rachel had brought her nothing but bad news. Dame thought there might be some small, cruel pleasure in returning the favour. She was wrong.

"I think it would be better if we talked about it in person."

"That bad, huh?"

Dame avoided the question. "Can I stop by after work tomorrow?"

Rachel was quiet for a moment. "Okay," she said finally. "Zoe will drop off Luka around five thirty, so if you could come before then, that might be best."

THE NEXT DAY, Dame left work a little early and took transit to the east end of the city. Rachel let her in and guided her to the kitchen. With a quiet formality, she poured them both a short glass of cheap tequila. "Okay, Polara," she said as they sat down, "what's up?"

Dame sighed and took out her phone. "It didn't make sense to tell you this before," she said, "but Grace Maxwell found this pencil drawing stuffed in the liner of Adam's guitar case." She slid the phone across the table. Rachel picked it up, and Dame watched as understanding fell across her face.

"Who drew this?"

"A woman named Maudie Beresford. She's the groundskeeper at Beacon Point Arts Centre."

"This woman, she" — Rachel zoomed in on some part of Adam's anatomy — "she slept with Adam?"

"I — I think so," Dame said gently.

"And you think she had something to do with Adam's death."

"I'm not sure. But I'm going to find out."

Rachel kept staring at the image. "She did a good job, at least. Looks just like him."

"Guess we're kind of in the same boat, now."

"What boat?"

"The I-Got-Cheated-On-By-Adam-Hoffman Boat."

"Is that what you think?" Rachel handed the phone back.

Dame took another look at her ex-husband in all his nude glory. "Uh, kind of?"

"Polara, Adam and I had an open marriage. He was free to see people as long as he was safe and told me about it. I don't care if he was with someone before he died, but if that someone *killed* Adam, then that's a different story."

"An open marriage?"

"We had a few rules. No friends or mutual acquaintances. And no one who lived in our neighbourhood."

"Jesus. I thought —" She wasn't sure how to finish her sentence.

Rachel smirked and seemed to enjoy Dame's confusion. "Well, maybe that's why Adam chose me. I wanted to be with him; I didn't want to own him."

Dame felt the heat of the day crawl up her collar. "I didn't want to *own* him, Rachel. Monogamy's a pretty standard arrangement in most marriages."

"Yeah, and as you well know, most marriages end in divorce."

Dame was trying her best to stay calm. "At least I didn't turn him into something he wasn't."

"What's that supposed to mean?"

"I mean the desk job, the Range Rover — that wasn't Adam."

"I thought you said you didn't know who he was anymore."

"I know you shoved all his music equipment into the spare bedroom."

"Oh, grow up, Polara. We're almost forty. Do you think I was going to spend the rest of my life tripping over guitars and staring at some hideous sculpture of Neil Young? That stuff *belongs* in a spare room."

"You always hated Adam's music."

"What are you talking about? I *paid* for his studio time."

"Well, maybe if you let him play music at home, he wouldn't have died on Toronto Island."

Rachel stood up so fast her chair tipped over. "Oh, so now it's *my* fault?"

It was at that moment that Ben Suarez walked into the kitchen. "Whoa. Easy. What's going on?"

"My old friend here is blaming me for my husband's death."

"I'm not blaming you for his death" — Dame stood up — "I just think you ruined his life."

"What the fuck do you know about —"

Ben quickly stepped between the two women. "Okay. Everybody take a breath. Why don't we all just sit down for a sec."

The two women eyed each other warily and did as Ben suggested.

"Now, it sounds like maybe you're wrestling with each other instead of wrestling with the actual problem."

"Leave the psychobabble at work, Ben."

"Hey, you can get mad at me all you want if it makes you feel better — but what's this really about?"

Rachel sighed. "Dame's looking into what happened to Adam."

"That's right." Ben snapped his fingers. "I forgot about your whole *Veronica Mars* thing."

"And even though it's a day late and a dollar short," Rachel continued, "she figures she has a lead."

"Which is?"

Dame cleared her throat. "Adam was getting cozy with some Toronto Island gardener before he disappeared."

Ben nodded. "Well, I can see how that might open some old wounds."

Rachel poured herself another drink.

"All this bullshit aside," Dame said, "there's something that's been bothering me."

"What?" Rachel asked.

"The guy who runs the recording studio — Jesse Maracle — he told me that Adam packed up and left around nine o'clock on Monday night. Said he wanted to get home early and sleep in his own bed."

Rachel frowned. "He texted me Monday night, remember? He was going to spend the night on the island."

"Can I see the message?"

Rachel sighed. She flicked through a few screens and gave Dame her phone.

Can't wait to see you tomorrow, the message read. *Love you!*

It had been sent at exactly 11:32 p.m.

"So" — Ben crossed his arms — "what happened between nine o'clock and eleven thirty-two that made Adam want to stay on the island?"

"I don't know," Dame said.

"Maybe Adam wanted one last visit with his gardener friend," Ben suggested.

"But then why would he call his ex-wife at" — Rachel looked at Dame. "When was it?"

"About quarter to ten."

"He called Dame?" Ben raised an eyebrow. "Why would he do that?"

"I'm not sure we're asking the right questions," Dame said.

"What do you mean?"

"Look." Dame held the phone out to Rachel and Ben. "When was the last time Adam used lower case letters in a text? That guy used all caps all the time. Remember?"

Rachel squinted at the screen. "Jesus. You're right."

"So, maybe the question isn't *why* he sent this message. Maybe the question is *who* sent this message."

CHAPTER TWENTY-TWO

DAME CHECKED HER watch as she made her way down the front steps of Rachel's house. It was getting late, and she didn't want to keep her daycare provider waiting. But when she looked up, she saw Rachel's son and his babysitter walking toward her.

"Oh, hey," she said. "I don't know if we were ever properly introduced. I'm Dame."

"Zoe."

"I'm sure you're both in a bit of a hurry — but could I ask you a couple quick questions? I have a two-year-old daughter, and I was thinking about hiring someone to help out."

Zoe bent down and smiled at Luka. "Hey buddy. Show me how you can go into the house all by yourself, okay?"

The little boy did as he was told, slamming the door shut behind him.

"He reminds me so much of his father," Dame said. "Did you know Adam pretty well?"

"Kind of." Zoe took a package of gum out of her pocket, unwrapped a stick, and popped it in her mouth.

"Mind if I bum a piece?"

The girl held out the pack, and Dame took it in her hands.

"So, how long have you been working for Rachel?"

"About six months."

"Just after school?"

"And some weekends."

Dame unwrapped the gum. "Rachel said you usually charge twenty-five dollars an hour."

"Yeah. Works out to about four hundred dollars a week."

"Wow. That's what I used to pay in rent." Dame put the gum in her mouth and chewed. "Hey, listen — were you babysitting on the Monday night that Adam didn't come home?"

"No. I would've dropped Luka off around five thirty. Ben's usually home by then."

"And what did you do after that?"

Zoe frowned. "Went home, maybe? I don't really remember."

Dame nodded. "You're fifteen? Sixteen?"

"Fourteen."

"God, I remember being fourteen. I hated being at home. Always wanted to be out with my boyfriend. Do you have a boyfriend, Zoe?"

She hesitated. "No."

"Sorry. None of my business." Dame took a step back. "Well, I should probably let you go. Nice talking with you."

Zoe turned toward the house.

"Oh, hey. Don't forget your gum." Dame held out the package. "Been a while since I've had the ginger kind. I used to chew this stuff when I had morning sickness."

The girl took the gum. "I just like the taste."

"Yeah, it's great." Dame smiled. "Spicy."

The babysitter jogged up the steps and went inside the house.

SUNNY DAY CHILDCARE was an early childhood daycare service that operated out of a large Victorian on Dunn Avenue. Beatrice, the woman who ran the place, and who everyone — even the adults — called "Aunty Bea," was a grandmother of two and an old friend of Meera's mother. She only took on four children a year, and Dame had been lucky enough to snag a spot for Rosie early on.

"There she is," Aunty Bea said when she opened the door. "Rosie was just starting to get a little restless."

"*Mama!*" Rosie said, running to her mother. "Mama up!"

Dame swung the little girl up into her arms. The warm weight of her daughter felt good and comforting. In the next room, two little boys vroomed cars around a Fisher-Price garage.

"We had a bit of trouble with Rosie's listening today," Aunty Bea said. "And she didn't eat very much of the macaroni and peas that I made for lunch."

The usual sliver of guilt worked its way under Dame's skin. It was so strange to feel responsible for the choices made by a two-year-old.

"Overall, though," Aunty Bea continued, "we had a lot of fun. Didn't we, Rosebud?"

"*Cookies!*"

"We did make cookies, didn't we? Gluten-free walnut and raisin cookies."

"Sounds delicious," Dame lied.

"And what did we do with the cookies, Rosie?"

"Ate them up!"

"That's right. We ate them up."

"Well, that's not very nice." Dame tousled the little girl's gossamer hair. "You didn't save any for me?"

"Don't worry, Mama." Aunty Bea held out a Ziploc full of misshapen blobs. "We didn't forget about you."

They said their goodbyes to Aunty Bea and — after a brief conflict during which Rosie made it abundantly clear that she would *not* ride in the stroller — began their long and excruciatingly slow walk home.

With the wide-brimmed hat, miniature sunglasses, and drunken gait of a toddler, Rosie might have looked more at home at an all-inclusive Floridian resort than she did on a Toronto sidewalk. Suddenly, the little girl stopped and crouched down, her big diapered bum hovering inches over the concrete.

"What do you see, partner?"

"Fuzzy cata-pilla."

Dame stood over the bug and feigned interest. "Cute."

It was during this insect inspection that Dame's phone rang. When she looked at the call display, she saw that it was Bernie Hargrove.

"Hey," she said when she answered. "What's up?"

"Just confirming you're going to the island on Saturday to pin down that Maudie Beresford kid."

"Yeah, I am. Is that the only reason you called?"

"Well, there is one other thing." Dame heard the last of Bernie's milkshake go up his straw. "You haven't had any more run-ins with Connie Radovich, have you?"

Dame thought of the tortoiseshell Guccis on her coffee table at home. "Not exactly. Why?"

"I was just talking to my guy in Homicide, and apparently no one's seen her at work for a couple days. No sign of her at home when they checked her apartment, either."

"Maybe she just found someone who shares her interest in Long Island iced teas."

"Maybe. On the bright side, this could potentially buy us a little more time."

"And on the not-so-bright side?"

"Just — be careful. Something feels a little off about this."

"That's how murder investigations are supposed to feel, right?"

Bernie laughed. "You sound just like your old man."

Dame ended the call just in time to watch Rosie bring her foot down hard onto the sidewalk. "*Smoosh!*" When she stepped away, Dame saw the orange and brown remains of the *fuzzy cata-pilla*.

"Rosie!" Dame said, grabbing her arm and pulling her away from the tiny corpse. "Why would you do that?"

The little girl cackled gleefully. "*Smoosh!*"

Dame thought of Lewis's question again. Was anyone capable of murder?

SEEMINGLY EXHAUSTED BY her insecticide, Rosie finally conceded to ride in her stroller. Dame took advantage of the opportunity and once again cruised by her old place on Seaforth Avenue. It had been over a week since she'd discovered the real estate sign outside her former residence, and she was more than just a little curious to see if the new owners had moved in.

But when she turned onto the street, Dame's heart sank. Even a block away, she could make out a tall metal fence surrounding not only her old house, but Mr. Balanchuk's little brick bungalow next door. She hurried over to examine the sign strapped to the austere barricade. "*Coming Soon*," it read, "*Seaforth Estates*." Below, an artist's rendering of an unimaginative low-rise apartment building looked like the world's saddest Lego set. The name of the developer was one Dame had never heard of before: ZTT Limited. She Googled the name, and soon, her worst fears were confirmed. ZTT was a subsidiary of a far more familiar company; a company that, despite being incredibly successful, had been getting a lot of bad press lately. Optics-wise, it was a smart move, but it still didn't change the fact that fucking Phillip Marinetti was tearing down her childhood home.

CHAPTER TWENTY-THREE

HANH ELLIOT STOOD *at the door to her house, wearing a smile like a question mark.* "Back again so soon?"

"Sorry to just drop by like this," the detective said. "I was hoping we could come in and ask some follow-up questions."

"Of course," Hanh said, stepping to one side. "Please, come in."

They followed her into the living room where they had sat with the rest of the woman's family only two days prior.

"It's just me, I'm afraid. Gabe's at work and Spencer's out with friends."

"Glad to hear your son's leaving his room."

She shook her head. "You know, he used to talk to me. Used to tell me everything. But now —"

The detective walked around a little, his eyes appraising the collection of objects in the leaded glass cabinets. "This old typewriter" — he gestured toward the antique — "it's a Smith-Corona Sterling, right?"

Hanh nodded.

"Could I take a closer look?"

"Sure. Give me just a minute. I keep the key stashed away upstairs."

She returned a few moments later and unlocked the door.

"Wow." The detective crouched down to get a closer look. "This is what? 1942?"

"Yeah. You know your stuff."

"It's in such great shape. I can see why you keep it locked up."

Hanh smiled. "When Spencer was little he had the unfortunate habit of shoving Pop-Tarts where they didn't belong. Cassette decks. VCRs. I've kept it in here ever since."

"Love those glass top keys. So much nicer than the 1950s model." He stood back. "You must be something of a writer."

"I was —" She paused. "I mean — I haven't been particularly inspired these days."

The detective turned his attention to one of the crude family portraits. "So I guess your husband is the painter, then."

"He's an architect — but yes. Painting is his first love. He still manages to find time. Evenings and weekends."

"Does he rent a studio, or —?"

"He converted the spare bedroom into a studio," Hanh said. "Just on the main floor."

"Any chance I could see it?"

"Of course. Gabe's always showing it off to people. I'm sure if he were here, he'd drag you inside and offer to paint your portrait."

"Well, in that case," the detective winked at the kid, "let's take a look."

It was an impressive bit of chaos. Stacks of canvases, used and unused, leaned against the walls. On a long metal table, tubes of paint spilled out of an old cigar box. Bouquets of paintbrushes burst from old coffee cans, while aluminum pie plates lay dappled with every colour.

An unfinished painting sat on the easel. From the file photos, the kid recognized the strawberry blonde hair of Jill Weatherhead.

Despite the crude lines and gaudy tones, there was something almost sweet about the likeness. Of all the portraits, it was certainly his least terrible.

"He loved her," Hanh said. "We all did."

"The evening Jill died — Gabe mentioned she had a headache. Do you remember if you or your husband gave her anything for the pain?"

Hanh shrugged. "Tylenol, maybe? I don't really remember. Why?"

"Just a thought." The detective took another look at the painting. "How did your husband feel about your son dating the girl next door?"

Through the window, the kid could make out the pink curtains of Jill's second-floor bedroom. She realized they were standing just where Gabe Elliot must have been standing when they saw him the night before.

"He was against it, to be honest. He wanted to stop them from seeing each other, but how do you stop kids from falling in love?" Hanh sighed. "Should we head back to the living room?"

They began to follow her when the detective stopped beside a blocky oak dresser. "Is this a Cavalry Campaign Chest?"

Hanh smiled. "Good eye. Gabe bought this years ago. Before we met. I remember it used to have pride of place in his old apartment. Now I think he just uses it to store acrylics and paint thinner."

"I love this old military furniture. It's so" — he gave the kid a strange look — "utilitarian."

As they made their way back toward the living room, Hanh paused at the kitchen door. "We ran out of coffee this morning, but would you like a cup of tea?"

The detective looked at his daughter. "You were just saying how you could go for some orange pekoe, weren't you?"

The kid frowned. "I didn't —"

"Remember?" He held her with his gaze. "After your tap dancing lesson?"

The kid narrowed her eyes. "Sure," she said, disguising a sigh. "I'd love a cup."

"And I'm so sorry," the detective turned to Hanh, "but would you mind if I used your washroom?"

"Not at all. It's just down the hall. Can't miss it." She turned to the kid. "How about I get the kettle going, and you tell me all about your dance class?"

Twenty minutes later, they were sitting outside the Elliots' house in the detective's Buick. "God," the kid said, "why do people drink boiled leaf juice?"

He handed her a red and white peppermint. "Thank you for your service."

She unwrapped the candy and popped it into her mouth. "What were you doing, anyway?"

"I wanted to get a closer look at that Cavalry Chest."

"How come?"

"Army and Navy Store used to make them. They all have a secret compartment that isn't all that secret, and every slick jimmy who has one likes to stuff his skeletons in there."

"Well, did you find anything good?"

He reached into the inside pocket of his coat. "See for yourself."

The detective handed the kid a fat stack of envelopes tied with a piece of twine. She opened one and started to read it.

"Love letters?"

The detective cleared his throat. "Look who they're from."

She turned the paper over and searched for the signature. "Cheryl Weatherhead. Wait" — she turned to the detective — "Jill's mother was having an affair with Spencer's father?"

"Seems like it."

The kid scanned the letter. The paper was already yellowing and the ink fading. *"When did she write these?"*

"Check the postmark."

The kid looked at the envelope. The letters were addressed to Gabe Elliot, care of what she could only assume was his architecture firm. Next to the portrait of Queen Elizabeth was a smudged date.

"1974?" The kid stared in disbelief. *"That's like, a million years ago."*

"Seventeen years," the detective said, *"to be a little more precise."*

"Seventeen years."

The detective turned the key in the ignition. *"Maybe it's time we have a chat with Cheryl Weatherhead."*

CHAPTER TWENTY-FOUR

DODGE AND FATIMA had agreed to look after Rosie for the evening, which gave Dame a few precious hours to travel back to the island and track down Maudie Beresford.

When she disembarked the ferry and got her feet on solid ground, the sun was already well on its trajectory toward the horizon, and she had to get moving. Earlier in the week, it took her the better part of an hour to get to Beacon Point. But this time, Dame was travelling light. No stroller, no diaper bag, and no Rosie. Just a backpack and sensible shoes. She made it there in almost half the time.

The grounds of the old school were quiet when she arrived, but it didn't take long for her to see grey slivers of smoke wending their way up into the sky. She walked toward them until she could smell the burning wood and hear the welcome crackle of a bonfire. From twenty feet away, she could see an orange blaze flickering on Beacon Point Beach and the grey-blue of Lake Ontario stretching out beyond.

"So, you want a beer? Or are you here on business?"

Yosef was standing next to the fire, poking at it with a stick, his dark curls twisting away from his head.

"Strictly business, I'm afraid."

"This isn't really a place for business." Christoph sat on a piece of driftwood, tuning his acoustic guitar. "Maybe you should take your business elsewhere, yes?"

Dame surveyed the group. A small collection of people Dame didn't recognize sat in plastic chairs around the fire. A few feet away, the bearded man Dame had seen arguing with Jesse — Houseboat Harry — leaned against a tree, drinking a can of Boneshaker IPA. No one was looking particularly friendly.

"I was actually hoping I could have another chat with Maudie. Or" — she raised her voice strategically — "maybe Greta?"

At the sound of the second name, Christoph and Houseboat Harry exchanged glances.

"You gentlemen wouldn't happen to know where I could find them, would you?"

Houseboat Harry shook his head. "Hard to find people who don't want to be found."

"Maybe," Christoph offered, "Greta and Maudie do not want to have this chat, yes?"

"No, I can't imagine they do." Dame turned to Yosef. "What about you? Any ideas where Greta and Maudie are?"

"Look, I know you just want to find out what happened to your boyfriend," Yosef said, "but everyone's getting pretty tired of all the outside interference."

"He wasn't my boyfriend," Dame said, taking a few steps back. "He was my ex-husband. And seeing as though all three of you are trying really hard not to look at the Arts Centre behind me, I'm going to do us all a favour and take my outside interference inside."

AS DAME BREEZED through the corridors of the artist's residency, she noticed the grey-haired woman who had yelled at her during her last visit. She was sitting at the harvest table alone, drinking a cup of coffee.

"You're not going down to the campfire?" Dame asked.

The old woman shook her head.

"How come?"

A wry smile crossed her face. "You know, this place used to be a sanctuary for people to make art. But now these goddamn kids — with their stupid haircuts and grant money — they're always drinking or fighting or fucking, and this is the only time I get the place to myself. Only time I can hear myself think."

"You haven't seen Greta around tonight, have you?"

"That sociopath in Room Twelve? No. Not tonight."

"How about the gardener? Maudie Beresford?"

"Saw her mowing the lawn earlier today." The woman took a sip of her coffee. "Nice kid. Works hard. She's actually talented, too. Not sure why she hangs out with these hacks."

"Okay, thanks. I'll leave you to it."

Dame made her way down the hall to Greta's room. When she got there, she put her ear to the door. Nothing. She knocked. Still nothing.

"Hello?" she said. No answer.

She gave the doorknob a rattle. It was locked.

"You know, this knob looks like a Corbin," Dame said. "Probably late fifties. Kind of a tough one to pick, but" — she knelt down and took a closer look — "there's a lot of wear in the keyway. Probably a few thousand cycles or so. I'm guessing it'll take me about fifteen, twenty minutes to break. You could sit tight until then. Or, you could just save me the trouble and open the door yourself."

Dame put her ear to the door again. There was nothing. Another whole minute of nothing.

"Okay," she sighed. "Suit yourself."

But just as she started to dig around in her backpack for Dodge's old lockpick kit, the knob turned and the door swung open. On the other side of it stood a very sheepish-looking Maudie Beresford.

"Just the gardener I was looking for. Mind if I come in?" Dame didn't wait for an answer but pushed past Maudie, crossed the room, and sat down on the unmade bed.

"No Greta tonight?"

Maudie shook her head. "She has a boyfriend on the mainland. Some crypto-investor guy who pays for her studio time. She lets me crash in her room when she stays with him."

"I kind of thought she might have a sugar daddy," Dame said. "You don't get to be that footloose without someone else footing the bill."

Maudie allowed herself a little smile. She sat down on the Persian rug across from the bed. "So, you're his wife, right?"

"Is that why you've been playing hide-and-seek with me?"

Maudie looked at her shoes and nodded.

"Well," Dame said, "I'm not the wife you're worried about."

"What do you mean?"

"I'm Adam's ex-wife. His current wife — his widow, I guess I should say — asked me to find out what happened to him."

"That sounds ... complicated."

"You don't know the half of it."

"So, you're not angry with me."

"Nope."

"Is his ... other ... wife angry with me?"

"Nope. Open marriage. You're in the clear."

"Okay. Then why were you looking for me?"

"I thought you might know something about Adam's last day on the island."

"Oh." Her brows furrowed a little. "That was the Monday,

right? I didn't really see him that day."

"So when did you last see him?"

"Well, Greta had left Sunday afternoon, so Adam and I spent Sunday night here."

Dame patted the mattress. "Here?"

Maudie nodded.

"Did you tell the cops about any of this?"

Maudie shook her head.

"And then what happened?"

"Well, on Monday he was working in the studio and I was working in the garden, so we didn't cross paths. I decided to spend another night here because Greta was still on the mainland. Adam and I had talked about meeting up again, but when I stopped by Jesse's studio, he'd already left."

"When was that?"

"Sometime after nine. Nine thirty maybe?"

"So, you really didn't see him all day? What about in the morning — you know — before he left?"

"He left before I got up. I told him to let me sleep in. I probably would've slept until noon if Harry hadn't woken me up."

"Harry?"

"Yeah. You know Houseboat Harry? There was a huge crash outside my door, and when I poked my head out there was this whole tray of breakfast stuff — eggs and bacon and coffee and strawberries — all over the floor, and I could see Harry hurrying down the hall. I guess he was going to get a mop or something."

"He was bringing you breakfast in bed?"

Maudie sighed. "He probably thought he was going to surprise Greta."

"He's done that before?"

"Yeah. Greta told him to knock it off, but the guy's pretty relentless."

"Did Harry see you when you poked your head out?"

"I don't think so. He was moving pretty fast in the opposite direction."

"And he thought Greta was in here?"

"I mean, I guess. If he was bringing her breakfast."

"Okay. This next question's kind of important. Do you think Harry saw Adam coming out of Greta's room?"

"I don't know for sure" — Maudie looked up at Dame, and Dame watched something in her eyes come into focus — "but, yeah. Maybe."

CHAPTER TWENTY-FIVE

ON THE ISLAND, August evenings took a long time to die. It was way past Rosie's bedtime — a time Dame would herself be trying to get some shut-eye — but across the water, the city's skyline was framed by a pretty pink light.

Dame would've preferred the cover of darkness.

She sat at a picnic table, just on the edge of the Toronto Island Marina, waiting. The docks were at capacity, stuffed with tall-masted sailboats, fancy yachts, and slick cigarette boats, but there was also the occasional boxy vessel that suggested semi-permanent residence.

As the light started to fade and the crowds started to thin, Dame wondered which boat was Harry's. She stood up and walked along the docks, noting the names stencilled on every stern. They ranged from the whimsical to the lewd, and Dame started to develop a pretty clear sense of just who captained these ships. Seafaring moms and dads came up with cutie-pie names like *Splish Splash* or *Beach Bum*. The rich asshole contingent called their enormous floaters *Liquid Asset* or *Naut on Call*. And then, of course, there was the Jimmy Buffett crowd — retired, drunk, horny — who used names like *Breakin' Wind*, *Wet Dream*, and *Cougar Catcher*.

So, what, then, would a photographer and wannabe pirate name his houseboat?

Dame slowed when she passed *Viewfinder*, but decided it was a little too clever. And *Siren Chaser* was a little too on the nose. But then she saw the *Ranger*. It was a small, late model Adventure Craft, white with turquoise accents (which were, in turn, accented by streaks of rust). Its spartan deck featured two weather-beaten camping chairs and was littered with crushed cans of Boneshaker IPA.

Well, shiver me timbers.

Taking a quick look around, Dame boarded the vessel. The door to the interior was locked, and for the second time that night, Dame thought she might have to pick her way in. Luckily, after a very brief search, she found the key under a welcome mat that read "*Go Away.*"

Inside, the cabin was tiny but made ingenious use of space. There was a closet-sized combination toilet and shower, a kitchen counter with sink and hot plate, and a mini-fridge stocked with beer. Everything seemed too small for a grown man, but the smell was right: stale sweat, Old Spice, and farts. A large flag, emblazoned with a skull and crossbones, hung across a bungee cord and served as a bedroom curtain. When Dame slipped past it, she was reassured that she'd come to the right place.

"Jesus *Christ*," she said, looking around.

Beside the bed was a family-sized bottle of Lubriderm Unscented Lotion. And fixed to the walls, the ceiling — every possible surface — were hundreds of pictures of Greta. Greta singing. Greta walking along the shore. Greta riding a bike in tiny jean shorts. Greta in a bikini and sunglasses.

Dame suddenly wished she had brought hand sanitizer and a pair of rubber gloves. Maybe a black light. As she searched the room, she tried her best to touch as little of it as she could.

Eventually, she found a little storage cabinet built into the side of the bed. Inside it she found a can of beard balm, an unopened box of condoms, and a paperback copy of Jordan Peterson's *12 Rules for Life*. Tucked in the book, there was something else: an envelope containing twenty-six one-hundred-dollar bills. A stamp on the outside of the envelope read *"Deacon Blues."*

"Holy fucking shit," Dame said to no one in particular.

In the fading light, she used her phone to take pictures of the money, the envelope, the Greta shrine, and the Lubriderm. Just as she finished the documentation process, Dame heard a man's voice, and the floor of the boat shifted to one side, as though someone had added two hundred pounds of ballast. An instant later, a swollen hand ripped the Jolly Roger curtain aside, and Houseboat Harry stood between Dame and her way out.

"What the hell are you doing in here?"

"This isn't Captain John's Harbour Restaurant?" Dame said. "My bad. I'll be on my way."

Through an interface of five or six beers, Harry's eyes went first to the photographs of Greta, and then to the open cabinet where he stashed his cash.

"I'm calling the cops."

"Probably not a bad idea," Dame said. "But you should know that I've got pictures of everything: the Greta photos and the three thousand dollars from Deacon Blues."

Harry took out his phone. "Yeah? So what?"

"So, I just happen to know another guy who got three grand for selling a dead man's guitar. The name John Rackham ring a bell?"

Harry stopped dialling and gave her a hard look.

"You know, I searched up that name — John Rackham. He was a pirate, wasn't he?"

"Wouldn't know."

"Sure he was. More commonly known as 'Calico Jack.' Operated in the Bahamas during the early eighteenth century?"

"If you say so."

"You fancy yourself a bit of a pirate, don't you, Harry? A bit of a John Rackham type? I mean even the name of your boat — the *Ranger* — was the name of Calico Jack's ship."

"Like I said, I don't know what you're talking about."

"So, what happened to Adam Hoffman, Harry? You make him walk the plank?"

Harry's hands were slowly turning into fists, and Dame had a sneaking suspicion that he was about to use them on her. "You break into *my* boat, start *accusing* me of —"

"Hold that thought." Dame took out her phone and quickly realized there was no service. She thumbed the keyboard anyway, and made one performative stab at the screen for emphasis. "A-a-and *sent*!"

"What's sent?"

"The cash. The Lubriderm. The Greta jerk-off gallery. All to my colleague on the mainland. And if she doesn't hear back from me in the next ten minutes or so, she'll be contacting the police herself. Which could be pretty bad for you, all things considered."

Houseboat Harry glared at her in silence and Dame waited for him to call her bluff. Instead, he slammed his fist into the wall so hard that two of the photos unstuck and fell down. "God*dammit*!"

"Why don't you start from the beginning?" Dame controlled her voice. Kept it gentle. "You saw Adam coming out of Greta's room Monday morning. And then what? You waited for him to finish up in the studio? You followed him home?"

"I didn't need to follow him," Harry said quietly.

He pushed past Dame and sat down on his filthy bed. He picked up one of the pictures that had fallen off the wall and looked at it.

"You know," Harry said, "it's amazing what people will post about themselves online. I found pictures of his family, pictures of him outside his house, even posts about his running route." He smiled. "Took me less than an hour to figure out where that prick lived. And when I heard Maracle say he was leaving Monday night, I rode the ferry to the mainland, got my car out of storage, and waited outside his place in Riverdale."

Dame's heart started keeping some pretty serious time in her chest.

"The guy had a wife and a kid. A nice house. Why'd he have to go after my girl?"

"She's not 'your girl,' Harry."

"I was just going to scare him, you know? Rough him up a bit."

"But things got out of hand, right? Maybe you hit him a little too hard."

"Fuck, no." Harry stood up suddenly and almost cracked his skull on the roof. "I didn't lay a finger on the guy."

Dame adjusted her glasses. "What do you mean?"

Harry took a long, shaky breath. "It was almost eleven o'clock when he finally showed up. He popped out of an Uber with his duffle bag and his guitar and was inside before I could do anything."

"Eleven o'clock?"

"Yeah. Around then."

Dame frowned. If Adam was alive and kicking around eleven o'clock, then maybe he *did* send that last text to Rachel. Lower case letters and all.

"Why didn't you go knock on his door?"

"I — I didn't want to freak out his family. I waited for a while to see if he was in for the night, and about a half hour later he comes out the side door and starts loading some gear into the Range Rover parked in the driveway."

"You're sure it was him?"

"Yeah — he was wearing that stupid Expos hat he always wore on the island. Fucking Expos aren't even a team anymore."

"So why didn't you confront him, then?"

"I was going to, but then his wife stepped outside."

Rachel was there? "What did she look like?"

"I don't know. Young. Pretty. Wearing a yellow hoodie."

"What were they loading into the SUV?"

"I couldn't see. A few things, though. Looked heavy."

"Was there anyone else around?"

"On a Monday night in Riverdale? Streets were pretty quiet."

"And then what happened?"

"Well, he takes off in the Range Rover and his wife stays at home. I follow him down to this automotive place in Leslieville — Christine's Auto Repair. He pulls in behind the shop and throws a few things into a Dumpster they have out back. After that, he started heading south, but I lost him in traffic."

"He was heading toward the lake. Toward the Port Lands."

"Seemed like it."

But why was he going there? "So, how'd you wind up with his guitar?"

"I got curious and wanted to know what he chucked in the trash, so I went back to Leslieville and took a look in the Dumpster. That's when I found the guitar."

"Was there anything else in there?"

"Yeah. A family of pissed-off raccoons. I'm lucky I got away with the guitar. And then, when I got it home and looked up what it was worth, I realized just how lucky."

"So you sold it."

Harry shrugged. "At first I thought I might teach myself how to play. Thought maybe Greta would think it was cool. I mean, if a couple of morons like Christoph and Maracle can do it, how hard could it be? But when your pal turned up dead, I figured I should get rid of it."

Dame leaned against the wall. Had Rachel lied to her? Had she seen Adam after he left the island? It didn't make any sense.

"So, you're not going to tell anyone about" — he gestured toward the many, many pictures of Greta — "all this, are you? I mean, I helped you, right? You kind of owe me one."

"Sure, Harry," Dame lied. "I'm forever in your debt."

CHAPTER TWENTY-SIX

IT WAS ALMOST eleven o'clock by the time she made it to Dodge and Fatima's apartment. Rosie was conked out on the couch, bathed in the blue light of the television, her arms still wrapped around her stuffed raccoon.

"Sorry I'm so late," Dame whispered.

She expected Dodge and Fatima to be pissed, but instead, they seemed more than a little pleased with themselves. Fatima listed all the food Rosie ate — yogurt, sweet potato, strawberries, carrots, Baby Mum-Mums — while Dodge showed Dame paper after paper covered in incomprehensible Crayola.

"Hey, did you see they sold our old house?" Dame said. "Marinetti Developments bought it. They're going to knock it down and turn it into a fucking apartment building."

Dodge sighed and shook his head.

"He was on the news again," Fatima said. "That awful Marinetti character. Will you be testifying at his trial?"

Dame nodded. "Meera talked to the Crown Attorney. They want me to represent Heritage Planning and answer a few questions about Marinetti's impact on the city, which, obviously, wasn't all that great."

"Well, good," Fatima said. "I hope they put those crooks in prison."

"Yeah," Dame said. "Me too."

Gingerly, she scooped her sleeping child off the couch. The little girl murmured a few incomprehensible syllables before she rested her head on her mother's shoulder. Dame said goodbye to her father and his girlfriend and made her way out of the building. In the elevator, she eased Rosie into the stroller, put her stuffed raccoon next to her, and covered them both with the little blanket Fatima had knitted. Rosie stirred briefly, but sleep kept a firm grip on the kid, and Dame was able to get out onto the sidewalk and cover ground.

She was a dead woman walking. The thought of her bed was the only thing that kept her moving. Luckily, the next day was Sunday, and while she was confident Rosie wouldn't let her sleep past five thirty, she could at least put her daughter in front of some brain-rotting children's TV for a couple hours while she snuck a guilty doze on the couch.

Dame made her way down Queen Street, fantasizing about how many hours she could spend horizontally. She had just passed the sushi place when she noticed something strange: the unmistakable rumpled suit and dark glasses of her favourite blind alcoholic. Mr. Kirby was walking down the street about a block ahead of her and moving at a pretty decent clip. They were both heading in the same direction, and Dame was surprised to see how well Mr. Kirby navigated the sidewalk and his fellow pedestrians. Maybe he wasn't as blind as she'd assumed. Maybe it was all strategy. A blind beggar might rake in a little more spare change than one with 20/20 vision.

Still, Dame couldn't help but be a little curious about the man cutting loose from his usual perch. Where was he going? Why was he moving so fast? As they approached Dame's street, something even stranger happened. Mr. Kirby stopped at the corner of O'Hara and Queen and pulled out a phone. He held it to his ear, seemed to respond to something someone was saying, took a long look up the avenue, and then kept walking. A couple other questions came to mind, like who was Mr. Kirby talking to? And why was he so interested in her street?

Not long after, Dame lost him in the crowd. She considered trying to catch up with him, maybe even fishing for a few answers (*"Fancy meeting you here!"*), but in the end, the promise of sleep won out over her curiosity, and she hung her usual left down O'Hara.

"OKAY, SO WHICH two designated buildings did Marinetti illegally demo in 2007?"

"Uh, the Tanner House in the Junction," Dame's voice reverberated off the metal walls of the Dumpster, "and the King's Crown in Moss Park."

"What about 2008?"

"In 2008, he bought the old National Bank building on Church Street. He had permission to gut it, but claimed the foundation was damaged and tore the whole thing down before anyone could inspect it. The city fined him, but there's no evidence he ever paid the fine."

"2009?"

"We *think* Marinetti's guys burnt down the old hardware store on Queen West in 2009, but no one could ever prove it."

"Not bad," Meera said. "You passed."

"Well, I'm a little more motivated now that Marinetti's tearing down my goddamn childhood home."

"The trial's less than two weeks away. Might be hard for him to demolish houses from prison."

Dame hoisted herself up on the edge of the trash bin. "I wouldn't count on it."

She dropped down onto the asphalt that surrounded Christine's Auto Repair. Meera sat watching her from a moulded plastic chair that someone had dragged out to the edge of the parking lot for smoke breaks. Behind her, the neon "*Open*" sign in the window was a dull grey — the primary reason she could root around in the business's trash on a Sunday afternoon.

"How's it smell in there?" Meera asked.

"Not good."

"You find anything?"

Dame shook her head. "A few burger wrappers and pop cans. Some car parts I didn't recognize. The garbage truck must've been by recently."

"What are you looking for, anyway?"

Dame sighed. "Well, if I'm to believe Toronto Island's favourite stalker and pirate enthusiast, this is where Adam tossed his Hummingbird and some other, as yet unidentified miscellanea."

She kicked at the asphalt where it ended abruptly and crumbled into a strip of brown, brittle grass. "It was nice of Lewis to look after Rosie for a few hours. Think he can handle it?"

"Probably. He's had a lot of practice with Elwy Yost lately."

"Elwy Yost doesn't need diaper changes."

"Yeah, but he'll figure it out."

Dame made a slow circle around the Dumpster. The ground was littered with gravel, cigarette butts, coffee cups. "I left Rosie with Dodge and Fatima yesterday, and now Lewis today. I'm starting to feel like a bad mom."

"Feeling like a bad mom is a sure sign you're a good mom."

"Maybe," Dame said, "but then how do bad moms know they're bad moms?"

"They don't. That's one of the reasons they're bad moms."

Dame smiled and started another lap around the rusty trash bin. "I guess this was a waste of time."

"You told me yourself — all investigations waste time."

"Yeah, but these days, time feels a little less disposable."

Dame stopped. Among the gravel and rock and bits of broken asphalt, she noticed something smooth and flesh-coloured.

"Huh."

Dame reached down and picked it up. It was small, about the size and weight of a genetically modified strawberry. A piece of something that had broken off something else. Debris that had bounced out of the bin by force of impact.

"What is it?" Meera asked.

"Not sure yet."

Dame adjusted her glasses in the fading light and realized that she was holding a nose. A disembodied terracotta nose. She squinted at it again and felt the unexpected thrill of recognition. This wasn't just any nose. This was Old Neil's nose.

CHAPTER TWENTY-SEVEN

WHOEVER WAS KNOCKING at the door sounded like they were trying to knock it down.

"*Dammit*," Dame whispered.

Rosie's eyes fluttered open and then shut again. Dame breathed a sigh of relief. She left the little girl sleeping and hurried to the door before whoever it was knocked again.

Whoever it was turned out to be the cops.

"Good evening, Ms. Polara." The man pulled his sunglasses off his face, folded them, and put them in the pocket of his well-tailored jacket. "This is Detective Carl Oates" — he gestured to the man behind him — "and I'm Detective Andrew Hall."

As if choreographed, they simultaneously produced their identification.

"Hall and Oates?"

"Yes, ma'am."

"You've got to be shitting me."

"No, ma'am. Would you mind if we came inside and asked you a few questions?"

"I would, actually. I just put my daughter to bed."

The detectives looked at one another, working out their next move through cop telepathy. Hall was small and wiry, with sad eyes and an aggressive-looking crewcut. Oates lumbered over him in a sloppy brown suit that did nothing to hide the belly hanging over his belt. She didn't trust either of them one bit.

"My partner," Hall said, "is wondering if he could use your bathroom. He said he didn't have to go when we stopped at Tim Hortons" — he glared at Oates — "but now he seems to think it's an emergency."

Dame sighed and stepped out of his way. "Hang a left when you hit the kitchen."

The detective hurried past her.

"He has an enlarged prostate," Detective Hall explained. "They've got him on some alpha blockers but they don't seem to be helping."

"You might as well come in, too," Dame said, "but if either of you wake up Rosie, I'm going to be incredibly uncooperative."

She led him into the living room. Dame took the chair and Detective Hall took the couch.

"So," Dame said, "how long has the band been together?"

"The band?" Hall was momentarily confused. "Oh — right. We've been partners for about three years. But we're not" — he cleared his throat — "a band."

They hunkered down into an uncomfortable silence for a few moments, until it was truncated by the sound of a flushing toilet. Oates walked into the living room and sat down next to his partner.

"All right, gentlemen. To what do I owe this pleasure?"

"Well, Ms. Polara" — Hall brushed invisible lint off his pants — "we're looking into the murder of Adam Hoffman, and —"

"What happened to Connie?"

"Detective Radovich is currently unavailable. We'll be handling the investigation from here on out."

Currently unavailable? Dame was expecting *on sabbatical* or *assigned to another case* but *currently unavailable* had the sinister ring of truth. She looked down at the Gucci sunglasses on the coffee table.

"And what do you need from me?"

"We've been reviewing Detective Radovich's reports," Hall explained, "and there are a few details that could use a little clarification."

"Such as?"

"Such as" — Hall took a notebook out of his pocket and flipped through it — "you worked for a private investigator — your father, David Polara — for quite a while."

"That's right."

"And then briefly as an unlicensed investigator, correct?"

"Pass." Dame crossed her arms. "I'm not going to answer any questions like that without a lawyer present."

"Questions like what?"

"The incriminating kind."

Hall wrote something in his notebook. "We'd like a little help, Ms. Polara." He produced an unconvincing smile. "And we'd appreciate your expertise."

"Well, if you guys want to hire me" — Dame smiled — "my rates are very reasonable."

"From what we can tell, Detective Radovich had concerns that you might work the case yourself."

"And?"

"Did you?"

"Yeah, that's another pass."

"So, you don't have any more insight into Mr. Hoffman's death?"

Dame adjusted her glasses. "Are you guys just here to crib my notes, or what?"

The detectives looked at one another again, passing some silent message through the air between them.

"Look" — Hall sighed — "we know you spent some time on Toronto Island this weekend, and we know you spoke to a number of Mr. Hoffman's acquaintances. If you have any pertinent information about this case, it's in your best interests to tell us."

Dame thought for a moment. "Actually, there is one thing."

"What's that?"

"There was this guy on the island — Harry something or other. They call him 'Houseboat Harry.' Thinks he's some kind of Great Lakes pirate."

"Harry Buchanan? We're familiar with him."

"He was harassing one of the artists in residence at Beacon Point. A friend of Adam's named Greta. Following her around. Taking pictures of her. That kind of thing."

"We spoke to Mr. Buchanan this morning," Hall said. "He was quite forthcoming. I think he initially thought that you sent us to see him. He's agreed to dock his houseboat somewhere else from now on."

"Well, that's good news."

Hall nodded. "Mr. Buchanan had some other interesting details regarding the night your ex-husband died."

"Oh yeah?"

Oates cleared his throat and, for a moment, stared at Dame through steely-grey eyes. Finally, he asked his question: "You wouldn't happen to own a yellow hooded sweatshirt, would you, Ms. Polara?"

Huh. She hadn't been expecting Oates to be the smart one.

CHAPTER TWENTY-EIGHT

DAME CARRIED OLD Neil's nose around in her pocket all day Monday. As she responded to emails, reviewed files on Marinetti, and made herself tea in the break room, it sniffed against her hip. Every once in a while, she took it out and felt the weight of it in her hand. It was a good nose, a solid triangle with a small bump on the bridge. The nostrils were sculpted, not just painted. Dame could get an inch of pencil inside both of them and, for better or worse, didn't find anything up there. Of all the aspects of Adam's hideous original, Dame was willing to believe that this was the most representative of Neil Young. It was entirely possible that — like so many other aspects of his life — Adam had laboured over the individual details but couldn't bring the component parts together.

After work, Dame took the Queen car east. She got off on Jones and used GPS to find Riverbend Psychology. The clinic operated out of a Second Empire row house, slotted neatly between a shawarma joint and a nail salon. Inside, the place was pretty impressive. Someone had clearly put a few bucks into it. Exposed brick, glass doors, smallish paintings with big white mats. The place screamed "up-and-coming," but of course, in this city, up-and-coming meant you'd already arrived.

"Do you have an appointment?"

The receptionist behind the counter was busy working away at a computer. She was what Dame used to think of as old: tired, middle-aged, somebody's mom. Dame realized that, as she quickly approached forty, she was all of those things, too.

"I was hoping I could catch Ben for a few minutes," Dame said. "Ben Suarez."

The woman didn't look up from the screen. "Dr. Suarez is on a leave of absence."

"Leave of absence?" Dame repeated. "I thought he just went down to part-time."

"No. At present Dr. Suarez doesn't work here."

"Any idea where I might find him? It's not business. I'm an old friend of the family."

She stopped typing and sighed. "Well, this time of day, you might want to try your luck at McLaren's."

"What's McLaren's?" Dame asked.

The woman started typing again. "It's just a couple blocks away."

"BORDERLINES, MAN." THE psychologist was pushing his fingers through his hair. "They can take all the good out of your day."

Ben had already had a few by the time Dame found him. He seemed happy to see her ("*Hey! Veronica Mars!*") and not at all surprised. Maybe just drunk enough to believe that anything and everything was possible — even the sudden, unexplained appearance of your sister's ex–best friend.

"I mean, they don't even *need* your help. But then the hour's up, and they're suddenly a mess and you're the worst doctor they've ever had." He sighed and sat back in his chair. "Sorry. Long day. A lot of sob stories. A lot of noise."

Dame played along. "Between work and Rosie, I get an earful every day. I could use a little peace and quiet."

"*Yes,*" Ben said. "Isn't that what everyone wants? A little peace and quiet?"

"Everyone over thirty, anyway."

Ben laughed and looked around for their server. The sports bar wasn't one Dame would've walked into by choice — too many flat screens broadcasting too many men running across too much Astroturf — but it seemed like this was Ben's regular.

"You know, Fiona and I used to argue about having kids." Ben shook his head. "I think that's when I knew things were over. I mean, I like kids, and I *love* Luka, but I just couldn't invite that kind of noise and chaos into my life on a permanent basis."

"And that's when you moved in with Rachel and Adam?"

"Seemed like the easiest solution. I'd rather give Rach a few bucks for rent than piss it away on some landlord. Besides, she could use the extra cash."

"I thought she was doing okay. Financially speaking, I mean."

"Well, between you and me" — Ben leaned forward — "that fitness studio is *hemorrhaging* money. It's a complete disaster."

"How come?"

Ben shrugged. "Cost of living. Rent's gone through the roof. It's Toronto. Everything's expensive."

A ponytailed server arrived and put a Paloma down in front of Dame and a double shot of bourbon down in front of Ben. "Enjoy!" she said, before vanishing back into the bustle.

Dame took the lime garnish off the edge of her glass and squeezed it into the cocktail.

Ben held up his drink. "To peace and quiet."

They clinked glasses and Dame tried the Paloma. Not bad.

"So?" Ben finally arrived at the obvious question. "Why did you come all the way to Leslieville to track me down?"

"I guess I'm still trying to piece together what happened the night Adam died."

"Veronica Mars is on the case."

"Something like that." Dame took another sip of her drink. "Hey, could you run me through what you were doing on July 30?"

"Okay, let's see. That was a Monday?"

Dame nodded.

"Probably ran a few errands and then came by here for a libation or two. Got home around five. Babysitter dropped Luka off around five thirty. Rachel left around eight to teach her evening class —"

"Did she take the Range Rover?"

"Uh, no. I've been using it. She usually takes the 506 along Gerrard."

"Okay. After that?"

"After that I put Luka to bed, watched an episode of *Storage Wars*, and then hit the hay. Probably around ten — ten thirty?"

"Do you usually go to bed that early?"

"Early to bed, early to rise."

"And you didn't hear anyone come home that night?"

"You mean, like, Rachel?"

"Maybe. Or maybe Adam?"

"You think Adam came home? From Toronto Island?"

"That's what I'm trying to figure out."

Ben frowned and sipped at his bourbon. "I guess that makes sense. I mean, the theory that Adam's body drifted two and a half miles from Toronto Island to the Port Lands in just a few days always kind of bugged me." He took another drink. "But if he came home, what happened to all his stuff? He must've had a duffle bag or a backpack or something. And what about his guitar? How'd it wind up in a consignment shop?"

Dame smiled. "I've been asking the same questions."

They finished their drinks and a few moments later a server swooped in with menus under her arm. "You guys thinking about something to eat?"

"I don't know." Ben ran a hand through his floppy hair. "What do you think, Veronica Mars?"

"Can't. Sorry. I have to go pick up Rosie."

"Duty calls." Ben shrugged. "Guess we'll just take the bill."

Dame waited for the server to head back to the bar before she asked her next question. "So there was one other thing I wanted to ask you."

"Shoot."

"Remember when we were talking the other day? You said you figured Rachel threw away Adam's bust of Neil Young."

"Right, right. Old Neil."

"Do you have any sense of how long ago she might have done that?"

"Not really. I mean, to be honest, I don't know for a fact that she did."

In her pocket, the tip of Neil Young's nose rubbed against the side of her leg. "When was the last time you remember seeing it in the spare room?"

Ben crossed his arms and squinted one eye. "Couple weeks ago, maybe?"

"Was it before or after Adam disappeared?"

"Probably after," Ben said. "How come?"

"Not sure." Dame smiled. "Not yet, anyway."

CHAPTER TWENTY-NINE

THE DECOUPAGED PHONE booth outside the library was Dame's go-to pay phone. She wasn't sure what she'd do when they inevitably yanked it and all the other phone booths in the city. Blocking your own number seemed like an obvious red flag, and there was something wasteful about using a burner phone.

When the sugary voice on the other end of the line said, "Uplift Fitness! How may I direct your call?" Dame tried to summon a comparable cheer and failed. It was too early to be that chipper.

"A friend of mine recommended one of your instructors to me a couple weeks ago, and I've forgotten her name."

"Well, I bet if we put on our thinking caps, we can figure it out!" The receptionist punctuated her wager with a little giggle. "Do you remember what kind of class it was?"

"Uh, Pilates class?"

"All right. Do you remember *when* your friend took the class?"

"Monday night. Sometime after eight o'clock, I think."

Dame could hear the woman clacking away at a keyboard. "Hmm. We don't have any Pilates classes on Monday nights. Jacqueline teaches Pilates on Wednesday night. Does that ring a bell?"

"No, I'm pretty sure it was a Monday night."

"Okay, well on Monday evenings we have spin classes and hot yoga."

"Maybe that was it," Dame said. "You know, now that I think about it, I'm pretty sure the instructor's name started with an *R*. Rochelle maybe? Or Raquel?"

"Well, the owner of the studio is Rachel Suarez, but as far as I can see she hasn't taught evening classes in quite a while. She only teaches classes before noon."

"Oh. Okay. Well, I guess I'll just have to ask my friend again."

"Sorry I couldn't be more help! Have an Uplifting day!"

Dame hung up the phone. Rachel said she was teaching a *private* evening class the night Adam died. But what exactly did "private" mean? Was she making house calls? Or was she just lying to her? Maybe it was time to have a surprise visit with her old friend.

AT LUNCH, SHE called Aunty Bea and asked if she could feed Rosie and look after her until seven o'clock. Of *course* she could. She would be *delighted* to. It went without saying that she would charge time and a half for the extra two hours.

Later that afternoon, Dame left work late and took transit east on Dundas. She had debated about, and finally decided in favour of, wearing her raincoat that day. Now she was glad she had. Almost immediately after she stepped off the streetcar, a grey rain worked its way down from the sky. She pulled her hood over her head, and by the time she had hoofed it to North Riverdale, she was thoroughly drenched.

Dame was surprised, and more than a little disappointed, when she got to Rachel's house and discovered that no one was actually there. The SUV wasn't in the driveway, the lights weren't on, and no one answered the door. She had hoped that Rachel would come straight home from work and that, if she didn't, either Ben or even Zoe would be around to let her inside. After a good five minutes of knocking and discovering the limitations of her raincoat, she figured it was a lost cause.

Dame was just about to make a soggy run for it when she gave the door handle a try and found it unlocked.

Inside, Dame surveyed the living room. Had something happened here? An argument? A struggle? Had Adam and Rachel's modern romance ended in an old-fashioned crime of passion? There was nothing about Rachel's West 49 furniture or her bland HomeSense wall art that suggested villainy. But the old question came back to Dame: *Was anyone capable of murder?*

The truth was, she wasn't even sure what she was looking for. Sure, it would be peachy to open the front hall closet and find a yellow hoodie stained with Adam's blood, but investigations never seemed to work out that way.

Instead, Dame made her way into the kitchen. The first place she looked was the junk drawer. Dodge used to say the kitchen junk drawer was like the homeowner's subconscious: a place to hide the messy little parts of your life you couldn't leave lying around. Sure enough, Rachel's drawer featured the usual assortment of curiosities. Besides the flashlight, matches, screwdriver, duct tape, Lego pieces, lint roller, and pencils, she found a notepad with most of the pages ripped away. With one of the loose pencils, she used a trick so basic she'd learned it from television and not from Dodge. She shaded the blank page until the impression of the previous page revealed itself, a list of words that read: "*milk, eggs, bread, bananas, broccoli, yogurt, tortillas, salsa, eggplant.*"

Excellent. She'd uncovered the grocery list.

But then, overlapping and obscuring part of the list was a pair of slightly fainter words, something from an earlier note: "*Call Kristian.*"

Dame filed that away in her brain and continued snooping. At the bottom of the drawer she found a slim white envelope labelled "*Work Receipts.*" Inside were about thirty or so slips of paper detailing payments: clothes from Lululemon and Gymshark, meals from restaurants, protein powder, running shoes, and most substantially, car maintenance. Receipts for gas, oil changes, air filters, brake pads, and everything else. The Range Rover, Dame realized, must be a company vehicle.

She shoved the envelope in her back pocket and then looked around the kitchen. On the counter, between the recently purchased bread and bananas, she noticed the still-sealed vinyl bag with Adam's personal effects. Dame picked it up and felt the weight of it in her hands. Even though its contents had been listed on the coroner's report, it might be worth a look. And this might be her only chance. But before the thought could even finish crossing her mind, she heard a creak of the floorboards behind her and a voice say, "Stay right fucking there."

When she turned around, Dame discovered a small red dot on her chest. Rachel Suarez was standing on the other side of the kitchen, drenched in sweat, and pointing what looked like a taser right at her.

CHAPTER THIRTY

"Whoa! Easy! It's just me!"

"Polara?"

"Yeah." Dame pulled the hood of her raincoat down off her head.

Rachel lowered the taser. "What are you doing in my house?"

"The door was open. And it was raining. And — why the fuck do you have a *taser*?"

Rachel looked at the weapon as though she just realized it was in her hand. She put it down on the kitchen table. "A client gave it to me. He was worried about me taking transit home alone. After Adam died, I started carrying it with me."

"Do you even know how to use it?"

"Well," Rachel took a deep breath, "we were both about to find out."

They laughed. A little of the tension dissolved, but not all.

"What were you doing with Adam's stuff?"

"I was just looking at it." Dame took off her raincoat and hung it on a kitchen chair. "You haven't opened it yet."

Rachel shook her head.

"Why are you so sweaty?"

"I was in the basement. Running on the treadmill."

"You own a fitness studio and you work out when you come home?"

Rachel smiled. "I took the day off."

"But not from exercising."

"It helps. With everything."

Dame looked at her old friend's body. It had changed so much in the last few years. Whereas Dame's own body had survived pregnancy and more or less endured her brief, calisthenic attempts to revive some of its former glory, Rachel's body was a work of art. Every visible muscle seemed to be vying for attention.

"So, where is everybody?"

"Zoe's running an errand with Luka, and Ben's got the SUV. He's got a thing somewhere."

"He mentioned you've been letting him borrow the Range Rover."

"Sure. Every time he borrows it he brings it back with a full tank. Plus, he's had it detailed *three* times since he's moved in. Guy's a total neat freak."

"It's nice you two help each other out."

Rachel shrugged. "So, what are you doing here? Any updates?"

"Kind of. They replaced the lead detective on the case with a couple of bozos named Hall and Oates."

"Like the band?" Rachel frowned. "What happened to 'Call me Connie' Radovich?"

"No one's really sure. Seems like she just went off the grid."

"Huh. Did you find anything out about Adam's little gardener friend?"

"Yeah. She seems pretty harmless. Sounds like it was just a one-time thing."

"That tracks. He wasn't usually a repeat offender."

"Was there someone that Adam saw on a regular basis? Someone who maybe got a little too invested?" *Someone,* she wanted to ask, *who wore a yellow hoodie?*

Rachel considered the question. "There was this one woman a while back. Chelsea something or other. He'd see her Monday nights when I went to work. But as far as I know, it ended ages ago."

Dame considered asking Rachel about her Monday night work schedule but thought better of it. "Do you know anything else about her?"

"I creeped her on Instagram. She's thirtyish. All tits and tattoos."

"Could you find her profile for me?"

Rachel pulled out her phone. She flipped through a couple screens and then dialled in a name. "Here."

Dame looked at the photos. Rachel's assessment wasn't wrong. There were images of Chelsea laughing in a dimly lit dive, Chelsea hugging a leather-clad friend, Chelsea pounding a can of PBR, Chelsea flashing the middle finger.

"Nice place to visit," Dame said, "but you wouldn't want to live there."

"That's the impression I got."

Dame dragged her finger up the screen. One image showed the woman in front of countless liquor bottles, pushing a drink across a smooth oak surface.

"Looks like she's a bartender." Dame enlarged the photo with her thumb and forefinger. "I recognize that place. It's the Ice Haus."

"That shithole on Roncie?"

Dame nodded. "Dodge used to meet clients there, sometimes. He never let me use the bathroom."

"I can only imagine why."

"Might be worth stopping by. Maybe catch her at work."

Rachel shrugged. "You're the detective."

"So, how about you? Was there anyone you were seeing? Someone who might be jealous of Adam?"

Rachel looked out into the middle distance. "I — I wasn't really seeing anyone else."

"Why not?"

She sighed. "Because I have a four-year-old son and a twenty-four-hour fitness company and my husband disappeared and Jesus *Christ*, Polara, when am I supposed to find the time for a boyfriend? That's *why not*."

"Okay. I get it." Dame was quiet for a moment. "There was one other thing I wanted to ask you: When was the last time you saw Adam's Neil Young sculpture?"

"Come on, Polara. Not this again."

"You said you didn't want to spend your life staring at it. You said it belonged in the spare room."

"Yeah? So?"

"So, Ben said it hasn't been there for a couple weeks. He figured you threw it out."

"Polara, I would remember throwing it out. The thing weighs like thirty pounds."

"Yeah, and you lift weights for a living."

"Okay, fine. I'll prove it to you." She turned and headed up the stairs to the spare bedroom. Dame followed. When she got to the door, Rachel paused.

"What's wrong?" Dame asked.

"I haven't actually been in here since" — she cleared her throat — "you know."

Rachel pushed the door open and looked around at the band posters and the guitars on the wall. She went to a bookshelf stacked full of rock biographies and concert DVDs.

"It should be right here." She ran her fingers along the top shelf. It didn't take long for her eyes to well with tears. "Why isn't it here?"

"Don't feel too bad. I mean, the thing was pretty hideous."

Rachel laughed in spite of herself. "You know, I used to hear him in here once in a while, strumming on Suzanne. Muttering lyrics to himself. It was the only time that guy was quiet. When he was writing a song."

Dame nodded. "I remember."

"After Luka was born, he never seemed to have time for it. Making music, making *art*" — she laughed at the little word — "it just seemed so *unnecessary*. There were diapers to change and bottles to sterilize and everything else."

Dame resisted the urge to commiserate, to compare notes on motherhood. She wanted to tell her she knew all too well about "everything else."

"But now and then, I'd catch him singing these little songs to Luka. That's why I booked him into that studio. I thought maybe he could get some of those songs out of his head. And now —"

She sat down on the futon and wrapped her arms around herself. "Sometimes, I think it really is all my fault. All the things that happened — with us. If he stayed with you, maybe he'd still be alive."

"He was never going to stay with me." Dame sat down next to her on the futon. "Even if he had, you wouldn't have Luka and I wouldn't have Rosie."

"Even still. Sometimes, I just wish we could go back to when things were simpler." Rachel sighed. "Remember when we'd get high and watch *Supernatural* in your basement?"

Dame shook her head and smiled. "I can't believe how many episodes of that stupid show you made me watch."

"I did you a service, Polara. Dean Winchester is a *god*. Adam and I still use his code word at bad parties for '*Let's drop everything and run.*'" Rachel caught herself. "Or, at least, we did."

"What was the code word?"

Rachel cleared her throat. "Poughkeepsie."

"*Poughkeepsie?*" Dame laughed. "Well, on that note, I should probably —"

"Drop everything and run?"

"Something like that."

Rachel walked her down the stairs and went ahead to look out the front window. "It's still coming down pretty hard out there. Are you on foot?"

"Unfortunately."

Rachel opened up the oak cabinet beside the door. "Here. Take an umbrella. Otherwise, you're going to get soaked."

"You sure?"

"Yeah. I've got more than I need. I think they're multiplying in here."

It was then, when Dame reached for the umbrella, that she saw it. Hanging on a hook inside the wardrobe. It wasn't covered in bloodstains, but it was there. A French terry knit, full-zip, bright yellow hoodie.

CHAPTER THIRTY-ONE

"AND LOOK OVER here — you're going to love this — it's my favourite feature in the house." They followed the real estate agent into a room with vaulted ceilings and a stone accent wall. "Just look at those built-in bookshelves. Do you like to read?"

The detective nodded. "I do."

"Well, imagine: On a cold, rainy day like today, you could pull a book from the shelf, curl up on the sofa, and — check this out." Cheryl Weatherhead picked up a small device from the glass coffee table and pointed it at the fireplace. "Poof! Beautiful, contemporary, and natural gas. No muss no fuss. And that's solid marble, by the way."

The kid sat down on the couch and watched the orange and blue flames twist around one another. "I could get used to this."

The woman smiled at her briefly and then looked away. For the first time, the kid caught a glimpse of sadness under the cheerful veneer.

Real estate, the kid was starting to realize, was the business of selling people a possible future. How many families had Cheryl Weatherhead worked for since Jill died? How many futures had she imagined for other families, when she couldn't imagine one for her own?

"You know, for an open house" — the detective looked around — "I thought there might be more people here. Seems like we've got the place to ourselves."

"I think the rain scared some people off," she said, "and while I think the asking price is very reasonable, not everyone can afford a place like this."

"I'll say," the kid said.

Cheryl Weatherhead gave her a funny look. The small gold crucifix around her neck caught the light for a moment. "What was it you said you did, Mr. —?"

"I'm a private investigator."

"Oh. What an interesting line of work."

"Not as interesting as you might think."

"Well, you must be pretty successful if you're considering a home like this."

The detective cleared his throat. "To be perfectly honest, Mrs. Weatherhead, we didn't come here to talk about the house."

"You didn't?" The real estate agent's practised smile started to fade.

"Gabe Elliot hired me. Would you mind if I asked you a few questions?"

What was left of her smile vanished completely. "I'm sorry, but do you have any idea who my husband is?"

He nodded. "Staff Inspector Bruce Weatherhead."

"Then you should also know that whatever services you think you have to offer are completely redundant."

"Maybe," the detective said. "But I'd like to ask my questions all the same."

"Well, I have nothing to say to you. If you want to speak to me, you're welcome to make arrangements through my lawyer. And if you don't leave right now, I'm going to call the police."

"Mrs. Weatherhead, I —"

"I warned you." The woman turned on a heel and walked into the kitchen.

From where she stood, the kid could hear her punching buttons on the phone's keypad. "We should go."

"Mrs. Weatherhead," the detective called out, "did you know your daughter was pregnant when she died?"

There was silence for a moment, and then the girl heard the sound of the phone being replaced on the receiver.

Cheryl Weatherhead returned to the living room. "My daughter was only sixteen years old. I won't listen to you disrespect her memory with salacious accusations."

"It's not an accusation, Mrs. Weatherhead. It's just the truth. And I think you know it."

She started to say something but stopped. A couple in their early thirties had just walked in. They were well-groomed and wore expensive-looking coats.

"Feel free to look around," the real estate agent called over to them. "And please let me know if I can be of any help!"

She turned back to the detective, her features arranged in a perfect mask of professional tolerance. In her eyes, the kid could see something primal.

"What do you want?"

"I just have one other question for you," the detective said, "and then we'll be on our way."

The well-dressed woman ran her hand along the smooth marble fireplace.

"Did Jill know Gabe Elliot was her father?"

CHAPTER THIRTY-TWO

AS DAME EXPECTED, the Ice Haus wasn't a lot of laughs at four thirty on a Wednesday. It was a sad place, haunted by quiet, grey people who seemed to age right before her eyes. Not much had changed since she'd come here with her father. Same autographed photo of Dave Stieb hung over the bar. Same *Soup of the Day Is Whiskey* sign. Same spilled-beer-meets-urinal-puck smell.

An old-timer wearing a foam and mesh job on his head looked up from the sports page and noticed Rosie with his watery blue eyes. "Hope she brought ID." His laughter cut through the gummy works of his windpipe. Dame smiled politely and kept moving.

Chelsea Lodge wasn't working behind the bar when Dame sat down and hoisted Rosie up onto her lap. Instead, a large woman with short blond hair and ruddy, pockmarked skin hunkered over a clipboard.

"Help you?" It was the least inviting, most perfunctory offer of service Dame had ever heard.

"I'm looking for an employee named Chelsea Lodge."

The woman heaved a long sigh and looked up from her work. Her eyes widened a little when she saw the pigtailed two-year-old on Dame's lap. "Chelsea in trouble?"

"No, I just want to ask her a couple questions."

The woman nodded. She shouted for Chelsea in a voice that suggested multiple seasons in a slo-pitch beer league. When Chelsea herself materialized from another room, she was taller than Dame expected. Pale as porcelain and wearing dark red lipstick. She was young and pretty, but not as young and pretty as her Instagram profile would have the world believe. In person, there was something just slightly damaged about her, something a little asymmetrical under all the tattoos and mascara.

"What's up?"

The woman behind the bar tilted her head toward Dame.

"I was hoping I could ask you a couple questions about Adam Hoffman."

Chelsea looked her up and down. "Well, you're not his wife. That much I know."

"I'm his ex-wife. Dame."

"Okay. Sure. I heard about you. The detective."

"I work for City Hall."

"Oh yeah?" When she smiled, she revealed a significant gap between her front teeth. "Then what are you doing here?"

IN THE BOOTH, Rosie kept trying to crawl under the table and Dame kept dragging her back up to her seat.

"Sorry, we don't have any booster seats."

"That's okay. Never really was a family establishment."

Chelsea smiled again. "I read about how Adam disappeared in the news. Thought maybe he finally" — she jerked her thumb over her shoulder — "went out for a pack of smokes, you know? Ditched his old lady. But then, they found him."

"Did Adam talk about his relationship with Rachel?"

She shrugged. "He was always complaining about her. Said Rachel treated him like one of her employees."

"But she didn't seem to mind that you two had a relationship."

Rosie finally settled and put both her hands on Dame's face. "*Mama.*"

"I don't know if I'd call it a 'relationship.' I mean, he was funny, and hot, and we had a good time together. But yeah, as far as old ladies go, she was pretty chill about what we got up to. She had to be."

"What do you mean 'she had to be'?"

"Well, she had something going on too, right? Can't exactly go around calling the kettle black."

Rosie squished Dame's cheeks together. "*Mama!*"

"Rachel wush sheeing shomebody?"

"Yeah. Adam didn't say a whole lot about it, but I could tell that something about this guy rubbed him the wrong way. Adam would stop by the bar sometimes when she went out to meet him."

"Did he ever mention the guy's name?"

"Adam always called him Mister Frisky. He was apparently some old, rich Swedish guy. His real name was Frisk. Krispin Frisk, I think."

Dame thought of the grocery list in Rachel's kitchen junk drawer. *Call Kristian.* "Any chance it could be Kristian Frisk?"

Chelsea shrugged. "Sounds about right."

"Any idea how they met?"

"Actually, yeah. That's one of the things that pissed Adam off the most. Apparently Frisk was this real fitness nut, and they met at her studio, where she already spends most of her time."

Huh. "So, who looked after Luka when Rachel was with Frisk and Adam was with you?"

"His kid? I don't know. Probably that sketchy brother-in-law of his. He was always moping around the house."

"You think Ben is sketchy?"

"Well, yeah. I mean, he basically got fired from his job, and then right after that, his wife left him, and no one seems to know why."

"Adam told you that?"

"Yeah. Adam didn't exactly love that he was living with them, but what could he do? Guy was family, right?"

"Did Rachel feel that way?"

"Beats me. Sometimes it's hard to really see people when you're that close to them."

Rosie stood up and looked at the customers in the booth behind them. Dame could hear a gravelly voice say, "Well, hey there little fella …" She knew she was running out of time.

"You didn't happen to see Adam on Monday, July 30, did you?"

Chelsea shook her head. "He hadn't come in here for a few weeks, to be honest. There were never any expectations between us."

"Do you know if there was anybody around here who had beef with Adam? Jealous exes? That kind of thing?"

"Nah. When Adam started coming here, he mostly kept to himself. I think he was looking for a place where he could have a drink and be left alone." She smiled to herself. "Then I went and kind of ruined it for him."

"Sounds like you cared about him."

Chelsea sighed. "Yeah, but what am I supposed to do with that? I think about him once in a while. But honestly? Not that often."

DAME WAS RELIEVED that Rosie's stroller was still waiting for her in the entranceway of the Ice Haus. She wasn't sure what the patrons of the questionable establishment might do with a child's stroller, but seeing as she'd already had a tricycle swiped out of her own front yard, she wouldn't have been particularly surprised to see it gone.

After strapping her daughter in, Dame walked home along Queen. She might have taken one of the quieter, more residential streets, but there was a little stationery shop on the road more travelled that she wanted to visit.

Twenty minutes later, Dame backed her stroller through the front door of Tabula Rasa. The little boutique was a bit twee for her tastes, but besides browsing through countless beautiful notebooks she would never fill and a wide assortment of pop culture–themed puzzles (including a five-hundred-piece *Labyrinth* jigsaw featuring David Bowie and Jennifer Connelly), Dame wanted to have a brief chat with the store's proprietor.

"Fiona! Long time no see!"

The woman behind the counter jolted up in her seat. She was a slight, pale woman, unadorned by makeup, her straw-coloured hair tied back in a practical ponytail.

"Uh, hi." Clearly, Fiona had been deep in a novel and was having trouble making the transition back to reality. "Dame?"

"Got it on the first guess."

"Oh, wow." The woman got off her stool and came around the counter. "And who's this little one?"

"This is Rosie."

"Oh my gosh, she's beautiful. Look at those big green eyes. How old is she?"

"She's already two. Guess it's been a little while since I've stopped by."

"Clearly, you've been busy."

"Honestly, I don't know where the time goes. Especially when every day feels like a decade."

"Gretchen Rubin says, '*The days are long but the years are short.*'"

"Yeah. That about sums it up." Dame looked around. "The store looks fantastic, by the way."

"Mama, pretty picture," Rosie said, pointing at a wall of handmade greeting cards.

"There's a lot of pretty things in Mrs. Suarez's store, isn't there?"

"Actually, it's Ms. Wallace now," Fiona said.

"Oh, that's right" — Dame feigned realization — "you and Ben are separated. Sorry — old habits."

"Not a problem."

"So, what ever happened with you two? I always thought you were such a great couple."

A momentary darkness passed over Fiona's face, before she pulled her lips back into a smile. "We just" — she cleared her throat — "grew apart. It happens, you know? People change."

"Yeah, I hear that," Dame said.

"God, I was so sorry to hear about *Adam*. I know your relationship with him was complicated, but still — sometimes that can be worse."

Dame nodded. "You know, in spite of everything, I'm really just worried about Rachel. The bad luck those two Suarez kids have had, right? First their parents, and now Adam. Plus, I heard" — Dame sculpted a mask of sombre concern — "that Ben lost his job recently. Do you know what happened there?"

"Uh, no. Not really." Fiona suddenly seemed very interested in her watch. "You know Dame, I hate to do this, but I should really start closing up the shop. If I don't do it now, someone's going to come in right at five thirty and I won't get out of here until seven o'clock."

"Of course," Dame said. "I get it. I didn't have a specific shopping agenda, anyway. Nice to see you!"

She navigated the stroller down the narrow aisle toward the door. There was a story there, and Dame knew she wasn't getting all of it.

CHAPTER THIRTY-THREE

DAME SAT DOWN on the couch and put her head in her hands. She rubbed her temples with her fingers and tried to put the pieces together.

"Mama sad?" Rosie was lying under the coffee table and Panda was walking across its underside, defying gravity.

"I'm okay, partner. Just tired."

What it came down to, basically, was a shortage of reliable sources. Chelsea's insights into Rachel and Adam's relationship were interesting, but inconclusive. And Fiona seemed unable or unwilling to confirm anything about Ben. *If* she could believe Houseboat Harry (a big, rickety *if*), the narrative went like this: Adam took the ferry home. When he got there, Luka and Ben were already asleep. Rachel — in her bright yellow hoodie — and Adam — in his Expos hat — loaded something heavy into the back of the Range Rover. Rachel went back to the house, while Adam drove to Christine's Auto Repair. Once he got there, he dumped his beloved guitar and — apparently — some or all of a twenty-five-year-old bust of Neil Young. After that, he drove off toward the Port Lands, where his body was found five days later. But who drove the Range Rover back that night? And why did Adam text Rachel if they were both in the same house at the same time?

None of it made any fucking sense.

Dame stood up and walked toward Rosie. "Okay, partner" — she bent down to pick up her daughter — "it's sleepy time."

"No! Not sleepy time!" Rosie's body went limp in a form of wet noodle protest. It was an ingenious strategy. Eventually, Dame hoisted her onto the change table for what she hoped would be the final time that day. As she worked at the diaper, she thought through what Chelsea Lodge had told her. Rachel's alibi was obviously fishy. But why would she lie about where she was that night? And who was this Kristian Frisk guy she so conveniently neglected to mention?

She stuffed her daughter's chubby arms and legs into her Paw Patrol pyjamas and carried her over to the little bookshelf in her nursery. After knocking a selection of books onto the floor, Rosie eventually picked out a Jon Klassen story. They settled into the second-hand rocking chair Dodge and Fatima had bought them, and Rosie listened as Dame impersonated a bear interrogating various woodland creatures about his lost hat. When they arrived at page four, Rosie's eyes went wide and she pointed at the illustration.

"What do you see, partner?"

"Hat!"

"Whose hat?"

"*Bear's* hat."

"And who has Bear's hat?"

"Rabbit. Rabbit *stole* Bear's hat."

"He sure did! What a sneaky —"

Dame felt the sudden zap of minor epiphany: What if Houseboat Harry was wrong? What if the guy driving the Range Rover wasn't Adam? What if it was somebody else *wearing* Adam's Expos cap? Somebody like Kristian Frisk?

For the next hour and a half, Dame waded through a tar pit of storybooks and *night nights* and *one more hugs*, but when Rosie finally drifted off into her fragile sleep, Dame crept over the creaky floorboards, sat down at the kitchen table, and lifted the lid of her laptop. She Googled Kristian Frisk's name, scoured Rachel's social media sites for him, and came up with exactly nothing useful. There was Kristian Frisk the Swedish hockey player, Kristian Frisk the military history scholar, and Kristian Frisk the Danish hedge-fund manager. None of them seemed like viable contenders to be Rachel's side piece.

Which meant, of course, Dame would have to move on to Plan B.

"A SPIN CLASS?" Meera yanked on the laces of her runners. "You know I have underdeveloped quads, right? My mom used to write me notes to get out of phys. ed."

"What happened to all that hot yoga you were doing?"

Meera shrugged. "They replaced the hot yoga instructor with one that was not-so-hot. I just wasn't as motivated after that."

Dame had expected the change room of Uplift Fitness to be overrun by impossibly buff and beautiful women — a veritable horde of Rachels — stretching and flexing, flaunting their toned bodies between workouts. Instead, it contained the same percentage of pale flab, cellulite, and regrettable tattoo choices as any women's change room. One significant aesthetic difference was that painted across the change room walls, in aggressively cheerful fonts, were motivational quotations from surprising sources. Mark Twain advised that *"The secret to getting ahead is getting started!"* while Aristotle enthused that *"Excellence is not an act but a habit!"* Dame assumed the exclamation marks were editorial.

"How did you find out when this Frisk guy's class was?"

Dame pulled on a pair of Meera's pink Adidas shorts. She

didn't own a pair of her own. "I told the receptionist that we were old friends and we wanted to surprise him."

"Rachel needs to work on respecting her clients' confidentiality." Meera closed the door to her locker. "You don't think we're going to run into her?"

Dame shrugged. "She apparently only teaches morning classes. We should be okay."

They locked up their civvies and headed toward the exit.

"Did you have to buy a membership or anything?" Meera asked.

"First workout is free. I had to fill out an online questionnaire and give them an email address."

"You know they're going to spam the shit out of you, right?"

"Nope." Dame pushed open the door. "They're going to spam the shit out of Lewis."

They hurried up a spiral metal staircase, past a wilting plant wall, and down a long hallway lined with glass doors that were labelled with names like "*Brave,*" "*Strong,*" and "*Joyful.*" Finally, they came to their door.

"This is us," Dame said.

"'*Fierce*'?" Meera sighed. "I want to go back to '*Joyful.*' Maybe they're all just hanging out on beanbag chairs, eating Cinnabons."

"Unlikely."

Dame pushed opened the door and immediately they were assaulted by urgent, pulsing pop music that they were way too old to recognize. There were about a dozen bikes in the room, and almost all of them were already occupied with the exception of two near the back.

Dame took a deep breath and threw one leg over the seat. The LED screen in front of her was crowded with numbers and graphs, none of which made any sense to her. In the rows ahead of her, clients were already pedalling to the beat of the music, and she tried her best to do the same. A wall-sized mirror at the front of the room reflected everyone's faces back at her, and she tried to pick out which one most looked like — according to Chelsea Lodge's description — an old, rich Swedish guy. There were, in fact, only two men in the class. They were both in their early fifties, slight and slim with greying blond hair. They both wore simple white workout gear juxtaposed with incredibly gaudy running shoes. But whereas one sported a well-manicured beard along his jaw, the other was clean shaven and wore dark-rimmed glasses, secured behind his head with a fluorescent green strap.

"So, who's our guy?" Meera whispered. "Beard or Glasses?"

"Not sure," Dame said. She was about to elaborate when the instructor finally materialized. She was tall and toned and armed with a smile full of dangerous-looking teeth. She wore a black tank top with the Uplift logo scrawled across her chest and a wireless mic clipped to one ear.

"All right, people," she said, climbing onto her bike. "We're not messing around today. We're going to do a double Tabata, which means two back-to-back rounds of high-intensity interval training. So, I hope everybody got a good night's sleep."

The room sounded with what could only be the false cheer of Stockholm Syndrome.

"Folks, we're going to torch some calories today. This room is a calorie crematorium, you got that?"

More laboured enthusiasm from the crowd.

"Guess she doesn't really like calories," Meera said.

"Looks like we got some fresh meat in the crowd." The instructor glared in Dame and Meera's direction. "You two — back row. Thought you could hide back there, huh?"

Dame felt all the eyes in the room on her — including four that belonged to the potential Swedes.

"Did you move up from Annabeth's intermediate class?"

"Uh, yes?" Dame said.

"And Annabeth thought you were ready for *my* class?"

"Uh, sure."

"Well, fair warning: You're in Lorraine's House of Pain, now. And this is going to be a baptism by fire. This is going to be a fresh meat *barbecue*."

The room sounded with nervous, knowing laughter.

"All right folks. Buckle up. We're going to start off at one hundred and ten rpm. Use your cadence sensors to follow along —"

"Our what?" Meera asked Dame.

"— and hey, fresh meat?"

Dame and Meera looked at the instructor.

"Try to keep up."

CHAPTER THIRTY-FOUR

APPROXIMATELY FORTY-SIX MINUTES later, Meera was throwing up into a recycling bin located between "*Joyful*" and "*Fierce*."

"I think that's supposed to go into compost," Dame said, collapsing against a bench on the other side of the hallway.

Meera lifted her face from the bin. "I hate you."

"That's valid."

Meera took a pull from her water bottle and spat into the recycling bin. She slid down the wall and looked at Dame. "Are you still going to try and follow the Swedish dude?"

"Beard or Glasses? I'm not even sure which dude is the Swedish dude."

The glass door of their cardio torture chamber opened and a number of clients began filling the hall, wrinkling their noses and avoiding eye contact as they passed by Meera and Dame. One of them was the man with the glasses. But just as Dame was about to admit defeat, someone sat down beside her on the bench. It was Beard.

"Is your friend all right?"

Dame looked over at Meera, whose face was buried in her arms. "She'll be fine. She's just a little melodramatic."

Without looking up, Meera extended her middle finger in Dame's general direction.

"I promise it gets easier," Beard said. "Not a lot easier, mind you, but easier. Lorraine is quite a taskmaster, but the results are — well, I might not be the best exemplar — but I'd say, quite extraordinary."

There was certainly something a little *Ikeaesque* about his very slight, very controlled accent, but Dame couldn't be sure he was Swedish. "I'll keep that in mind."

"There are many who drop out after the first experience, but I hope you'll come back."

"Thanks." Dame flashed her most saccharine smile.

"You know," the man said, "I run a small business here in the city." He reached into his fanny pack and produced a card. "I have a feeling you and your friend would find it very interesting. You should come by sometime for a screen test."

"A screen test?"

Beard stood up. "Hopefully, I'll see you both soon."

As he walked away, Dame looked at the card.

"What does it say?" Meera asked.

"'*Michael Issakson's Lascivious Film Productions.*'" Dame flicked the card across the hall. It landed next to Meera where she picked it up.

"MILF *Productions*? Gross." Meera got to her feet and tossed the card into the recycling bin. "So, Glasses?"

Dame nodded. "Glasses."

RACHEL — OR AT least, Rachel's real estate agent — had done a bang-up job of finding a location for her small business. Uplift Fitness was on Eastwood Road, carved out of what was once a spacious two-storey dog food cannery. It was just close enough to the Beaches that the studio's faux Zen spirituality and sadistic discipline would attract both hippie boomers and financial analysts re-evaluating their life choices. Dame could see why Ben would think Rachel was struggling with the rent.

Besides its location and square footage, another advantage of the fitness studio was its impressive thirty-car parking lot, which it shared with a Dollar Tree next door. Wedged between a Porsche and a Volkswagen Beetle reissue, Dame and Meera waited in Meera's Jeep.

"I'm not sure where your stench ends and mine begins," Meera said. "Why couldn't we take showers?"

"I didn't want to miss Frisk on his way out of the building."

"That guy's probably enjoying an hour-long sauna. You know Swedes. All they do is sit in the sauna."

"I think that's Finns."

"Could we just agree that many Nordic people enjoy overheating in small, cedar rooms?"

"Sure."

"This vantage point kind of sucks, by the way. All we can see is the front door. What if he goes out the back?"

"The back door is staff only."

"Maybe Rachel granted him special privileges. That is, if they really are in some kind of romantic relationship."

"What do you mean?" Dame asked.

"I just mean that he doesn't seem like Rachel's type, does he? She always went for big, tall, loud guys. She and Adam always made sense to me."

"Meera —"

"But Glasses? I don't get it. He's quiet, thin, and definitely doesn't crack five ten. Plus, he's a little on the old side for her."

"Maybe he gives her something that Adam couldn't."

"Like what? A senior's discount?"

Just then, the quiet, thin Swede in question walked out the front doors of the fitness studio and toward a recently waxed Audi hatchback.

"I feel like he should be driving a Volvo," Meera said. "Or maybe a Saab."

Dame shushed her. Frisk got into his car and turned on the engine. For nearly two minutes, he sat in the driver's seat looking at his phone.

"He shouldn't just let the car idle like that," Meera said. "I thought Swedish people were supposed to be environmentally friendly."

Dame was about to shush her friend a second time when she saw Rachel hurrying out of the fitness studio.

"Get down," she hissed.

Hunched into her seat, Dame watched Rachel make a beeline to the Audi. She opened the passenger door and sat down beside Frisk. Without a word, the Swede put the car into gear and they drove out of the lot.

Dame and Meera followed the hatchback for the better part of twenty minutes. They took Gerrard to Sherbourne and then headed north. Eventually they found themselves in one of Toronto's most exclusive neighbourhoods.

"Rosedale?" Meera asked.

"Guess this guy really is loaded."

They navigated the quiet, twisty avenues of the suburb, until the Audi in front of them turned into the paved driveway of a boxy, hyper-modern monster that looked oddly out of place between a pair of neo-Gothic gingerbread houses.

"That's quite the renovation," Meera said.

"Park just up the street."

As Meera pulled the Jeep to the side of the road, Dame commandeered the rear-view mirror. Frisk got out and made his way up the carefully landscaped front walk. He opened the door and waited for Rachel. As she walked past him, he patted her on the bum and then shut the door behind them.

"So, what do we do, now?" Meera asked. "Go peek in the window?"

"I don't think there's any need for that."

"What if there's something we're not seeing here? Like, what if he's an investor for the fitness studio, and this is some kind of business meeting."

"I have no doubt they're engaged in some kind of business."

"Well, maybe we should wait around and see what happens. Maybe she just ran in to use the washroom or something."

"Come on. Be realistic." Dame looked at her watch. "We should probably get going."

Meera sighed and put the car into gear. An old Jesse Maracle song drifted out of the radio.

"I'm just having a hard time believing that Rachel would have anything to do with Adam's death," Meera said. "We're talking about *Rachel* — who would catch-and-release centipedes because squashing them was cruel — who famously drove her car into a telephone pole to avoid hitting a squirrel."

"Meera —"

"You seriously believe she bashed Adam over the head and let some old Swedish guy dump his body in Lake Ontario."

"It's not about belief, Meera." Dame stared at the traffic ahead. "She lied about where she was, she lied about who she was with, and an eyewitness saw her doing some pretty shady shit right around the time Adam died."

"You said that motive and opportunity make a suspect, right?"

"Right."

"Well, I'm not hearing a lot of motive. Maybe Rachel was sleeping around. But so was Adam. That's how open marriages work. They had rules."

"Yeah, but I'm guessing statutory rape wasn't on the list of approved activities."

"What do you mean?"

Dame sighed. "I think Adam may have knocked up their fourteen-year-old babysitter."

"I'm sorry, he *what*?"

The car swerved momentarily into the other lane before Meera regained control.

"Zoe — their babysitter — she's pregnant."

"And Adam's the *father*? Christ, I would've killed him myself. Do you have any proof?"

"Not yet."

Meera looked over at her. "Do you really think Adam could've done something like that?"

"I — I'm not sure." Dame could feel the heat of tears behind her eyes. "I'm starting to wonder if I ever knew Adam at all."

CHAPTER THIRTY-FIVE

WHEN DAME LET herself into her father's apartment, she found her daughter asleep on the couch, and Fatima gone. Dodge was sitting at the kitchen table, head in his scarred hands, staring at what looked like a thousand-piece jigsaw puzzle. He was more than halfway finished, but the picture was still a confusion of colour.

"What's this supposed to be?"

The old man shrugged. "*Famous p-painting.*"

Dame picked up the box. "Jackson Pollock? Jesus, Dodge, you sure don't make it easy on yourself." She sat down beside her father. "And since when do you do jigsaw puzzles?"

"*F-Fatima's.*"

"Well, it looks like you're doing okay without her. Where is Fatima?"

"*Err-errands.*" Dodge stood up and went to the fridge. He slid two cans of Fifty out of the door and put one in front of his daughter. "*Thirsty?*"

Dame looked down at her clothes and realized she was still in her sweat-stained workout gear.

"Yeah. Guess I am." She cracked the beer and took a sip. "I can't believe Rosie's asleep. She barely ever naps anymore."

"*Busy d-day,*" Dodge said, sitting back down.

"That makes two of us."

"*How's the c-case?*"

Dame took a pull of her beer. "How do you always know?"

He put his hand to his chest. "*Detective.*"

"You never have trouble with that word, do you?"

Dodge smiled. "*So?*"

"So, the case is a mess." Dame picked up a paint-splattered tile and tossed it back onto the table. "It's like I have all these puzzle pieces, but I'm not sure how they fit together. Or even what the picture's supposed to look like."

"*You need an ed-ed —*"

"A what?"

Dodge picked up a puzzle piece and ran his finger along its one flat side. "*Edge piece.*"

"What do you mean?"

The old man cleared his throat. "*Everything starts at the ed-ed-ed —*"

"Okay. I get it. Everything starts at the edge," Dame said. "But I don't need to know how everything starts, Dodge. I need to know how it ends."

The old man looked down at the puzzle. He took the edge piece in his hand and snapped it into place. Then he picked up another piece and fit it snugly into the previous one. And then another piece. And another.

"*Find the ed-edge.*" Dodge coughed into his fist. "*Rest makes sense.*"

"Right. I just need to find the one thing that makes all the other things make sense." Dame stared at the chaos of the jigsaw puzzle. "That shouldn't be too hard."

AS DAME PUSHED Rosie in her stroller down Queen, the sun was low in the sky and the sidewalks were full of people. A group of monks in orange robes argued outside an electronics repair shop. Shirtless men rolled dice on a concrete stoop. Two girls in hijabs rumbled by on skateboards. Even as the Caribbean and Mexican restaurants were forced out of business, even as huge, international real estate firms bought up churches and community centres, Dame still wanted to believe her neighbourhood was a place where everything that would be, could be. Some days it was easier to believe than others.

Despite the kaleidoscopic commotion, there was something missing from the whole scene. Dame hadn't really thought about Mr. Kirby since she'd seen him hightailing it through the evening pedestrian traffic and gabbing on a cell phone. But as she pushed Rosie's stroller past his usual haunt, she was a little surprised to notice that the bus shelter outside of the LCBO was empty. No rumpled suit. No sunglasses. No bottle wrapped in a brown paper bag. Dame wondered if maybe she had seen the last of the old man.

Eventually, she made it to O'Hara and, soon after, her apartment. She scooped Rosie up with one arm and dragged the stroller up the steps with the other. She snagged the handful of envelopes and flyers from the mailbox and barely managed to get the whole mess inside before Rosie woke up and decided she was furious with the universe. As Dame bounced her on one hip and tried to work the cap off a plastic pouch of strawberry-flavoured squash puree, she couldn't help but notice that one of the envelopes she had chucked on the kitchen table had the now-familiar Penetanguishene return address. Once her daughter was in her high chair, cheerfully sucking back the pinkish goo, Dame put the letter with the others in the little cabinet above her fridge. That was a problem for another day.

As usual, the apartment was a disaster — dirty dishes in the sink, toys scattered all over the floor, an overflowing basket of laundry on the couch, a week's worth of domestic labour gone unfinished — but there was also a new development in neglect: Her once-vibrant houseplants were looking faded and brittle. Peggy Beckers' old monstera, in particular, was brown and wizened. She filled a glass with tap water and gave them all a round on the house. It didn't make any sense. Ignoring them had worked so well before. Why wasn't it working now? How Peggy had kept these things alive, she'd never understand.

IT WAS ALMOST Rosie's bedtime when Dame got a call from her lawyer.

"I've got some bad news."

Something in the pit of Dame's stomach braced for impact. "What is it?"

"Connie Radovich is dead," he told her.

Dame looked over at the tortoiseshell sunglasses on her coffee table. "Wait, what? What do you mean she's *dead*?"

On the other end, Hargrove put down his beverage with a *clawk*. "I just talked to my buddy in Homicide. He said they found her body a couple days ago, but they've been trying to keep it quiet. Looks like someone hit her over the head pretty good with a chunk of cinder block. No witnesses yet."

"Jesus."

"Dame, they found her on Cunningham, in a grove of trees by the overpass."

"Cunningham? Christ, that's —"

"Just a couple blocks from your house. I know." Hargrove cleared his throat. "Look, I'm going to be honest with you. You're a person of interest in a murder case, and the original detective on that case was just murdered in your neighbourhood. There's no way they're not going to bring you in on this."

Dame looked at Rosie. The little girl was forcing her stuffed raccoon to complete a nauseating series of somersaults. "How long do I have until then?"

"I don't know. Not long. Those shitbirds they put on your case didn't seem particularly motivated, but now that they've got a dead cop on their hands, all that's going to change."

"Any legal advice?"

"Yeah. Find out who killed your ex-husband."

"And how do you propose I do that?"

"I don't know. What would Dodge do?"

Dame sighed. "Dodge would've solved the case by now."

CHAPTER THIRTY-SIX

THE VEHICLE HAD been following them for a good ten minutes. It was a shiny black Grand Cherokee, and while its windows were tinted, both the kid and the detective had a pretty good idea of who was behind the wheel.

"Mrs. Weatherhead was pretty angry," the kid said.

"Yep. She was."

"Do you think it's true? Was Mr. Elliot Jill's father?"

"To be honest, I wasn't completely sure. But after the way Cheryl Weatherhead reacted, I'd be willing to bet a few bucks on it."

"But that would mean" — her voice was quiet with mild horror — "Spencer and Jill were brother and sister."

When they reached the deep lawns of Kenilworth Avenue, the detective slowed down. When they neared the Elliots' sprawling Edwardian, he pulled to the curb. Behind them, the driver of the black Jeep did the same.

"Well" — the detective sighed — "might as well get this over with."

The kid started to open the door.

"Nope." He tousled her hair. "Sit this one out."

"But —"

"Not this time, kid."

A moment after the detective stepped out of his car, the Grand Cherokee's driver knocked him to the pavement.

The detective pushed himself to his feet and rubbed his jaw. "Afternoon, Staff Inspector."

The kid watched as Bruce Weatherhead grabbed her father, twisted his arm behind his back, and pushed him up against the Buick. Through the glass, she caught his eye. With a nod of his head, he gestured toward the Elliots' house. She turned around in her seat to see Spencer Elliot on the front porch, watching the scene unfold.

"Is this an official part of your investigation?" The detective was trying and failing to disguise his pain.

The burly police officer slammed him against the hood of the car. "You come to my wife's place of business. Make crazy accusations about our family. Our daughter's barely in the ground, you piece of shit."

"Just trying to do my job," the detective grunted.

"You ever talk to my wife again, you'll be doing your job with two broken arms. You got that?" The staff inspector looked up at the Elliots' house.

The boy on the porch watched them in silence.

Weatherhead abruptly let go of the detective and walked toward his Jeep. The kid watched her father's body slide down the windshield and disappear from sight. She opened the door, ran around the car, and found him slumped against the tire.

"Are you okay?"

"Been better."

The Grand Cherokee peeled off down the street.

"Hey" — the detective smiled at his daughter — "think you could ask our friend Spencer for a little help?"

The kid stood up and called over to the boy. "Can you give me a hand over here?"

Spencer turned and grabbed the doorknob. For a moment, it looked like he was going to go back inside.

"Come on, Spencer. Help us out."

Another moment passed before the boy finally trudged across his yard. With minimal fuss, the two kids put the man on his feet.

"Nice neighbour you got there," the detective said, bending his elbow and rotating his shoulder.

"Look, if you want to talk to my parents, they're not home right now."

The detective leaned against the car and dusted his pants. "Actually, Spencer, we wanted to talk to you."

"Yeah, well" — he put his hands in his pockets and took a couple steps back — "I'm not feeling all that chatty."

"Look, son" — the detective's voice was gentle — "if there's anything you're not telling us — anything that might —"

"Like I said — I've got nothing to say."

"We're on your side here. Your father hired us to get you out of a bind, but right now we could really use your help."

"Yeah, that's not my problem." He turned and started walking toward the house. "Maybe you should try being better at your job. You're detectives. Go detect something."

The kid slammed her hand down on the hood of the Buick. "We know Jill was pregnant."

For a moment, Spencer stopped walking.

"And we know she was your sister. If she wanted the baby and you didn't, a lot of people might call that motive."

The boy shook his head and continued into the house. He closed the door behind him.

"Dammit." The kid kicked at the car tire. She took a deep breath and tried to compose herself. "I screwed it up."

"I wouldn't be so sure of that."

When the kid looked up, Spencer was standing on his front porch.

"I found this in Jill's typewriter the night she died." There was a piece of paper in his hand. "It's — it's her suicide note."

CHAPTER THIRTY-SEVEN

IT WAS ROSIE that kept her out of jail that Friday.

Just before lunch, Aunty Bea called with some distressing news about Dame's daughter: "Her little tummy must be upset because she's gone through all my diapers. Any chance you could drop off some fresh supplies on your lunch break?"

"Sure thing, Aunty Bea."

Dame knew better than to ask Meera for a ride that afternoon. Her boss already had a series of meetings with lawyers and architects, and her hair was decidedly up in a bun. Still, she did the math and figured that, if she grabbed some diapers at the Shoppers Drug Mart on Bay and then caught the 501 on Queen, she'd have just enough time to run them over to Aunty Bea's and catch the streetcar back. In theory, Dame would be sitting at her desk by one o'clock, maybe even with a few minutes to spare.

That afternoon, she executed the plan beautifully. But just as she was lugging a package of Pampers up the front steps, Aunty Bea came out onto the porch.

"I have some more bad news, I'm afraid. Rosie just threw up macaroni and peas all over the kitchen floor."

As if to confirm, Rosie toddled to the door and clung to Aunty Bea's leg. The little girl looked tired and pale.

"She's running a bit of a fever, and I don't want to risk getting the other kids sick. Do you think you'd be able to take her home?"

Dame smiled and picked the little girl up. "I guess I don't have much of a choice, do I, partner?"

After Rosie tried unsuccessfully to pull the glasses off Dame's face, her arms flopped to her sides. "Don't feel good, Mama."

"I know, partner. We're going home."

"Here's her diaper bag," Aunty Bea said, "and her drawing of Grandpa, and oops, we can't forget her raccoon, can we?"

"Panda." The little girl reached out and grabbed the stuffed raccoon.

"Thanks. Hope everyone stays healthy."

"Yeah" — Aunty Bea gave a weary smile — "you and me both."

AS DAME PUSHED her daughter's stroller down Dunn Avenue, she wondered if there would ever be a time in her life when she wasn't dealing with other people's shit. It was entirely possible — she acknowledged — that by the time Rosie was out of diapers, Dodge would be in them. And what about her own shit? When was she supposed to deal with that? Today was another perfect example: She should be out looking for hard evidence so she wouldn't be charged with a murder she didn't commit, but instead she was delivering diapers. She loved Rosie more than anyone or anything she had ever loved before, but that little girl sure made it hard to get things done.

She called Meera to let her know she'd need the rest of the day off, but when she got her on the phone, she sounded a little strange.

"Dame? Sorry, she's gone."

"No — Meera, it's me. Rosie's not feeling well, so I'm going to have to take the rest of the day off."

"Say it isn't so."

"Do you still need me to stop by the office and pick up those Marinetti files?"

"Uh, I can't go for that."

"Meera, what are you talking about?" She stuck a finger in one ear so she could hear better. "I'm just leaving daycare now, but if you need me to —"

"*Look*," Meera interrupted, "you're out of touch. And, unfortunately, I'm out of time. Got it?"

"Oh shit." The penny dropped. "Private eyes are watching you, watching you, aren't they?"

"Some things are better left unsaid."

"Okay. Thanks for the heads-up. I'll be in touch soon, okay?"

"You make my dreams come true."

She ended the call and put her phone in her pocket. *Fuck*. If those two morons were looking for her at work, it meant they'd be heading to her apartment soon.

Dame smiled down at her daughter. Rosie's poor face had taken on a greenish tinge, and if she was being honest, Dame wasn't feeling so great herself. She swallowed down the panic that was rising in her guts and dialled Dodge's phone. Fatima answered.

"I have to ask for a pretty big favour," she told her father's girlfriend.

BEFORE SHE DROPPED Rosie off with Dodge and Fatima, Dame was going to have to make a pit stop at home. Grab a few things. Pack a bag for her and one for Rosie. And she had to do it before the cops showed up.

As she turned down O'Hara, she thought about who she could stay with. If Dodge and Fatima were looking after Rosie, and the cops were already onto Meera, who else was there? Aki, her landlord? Terrence from work? God, how did she not have any friends anymore?

A little voice drifted up from the stroller. "*Tummy hurts* ..."

"We'll be home soon, partner."

She thought about hopping on a Greyhound, but how was she going to fix this mess from a different city? And who would look after Rosie? Fatima and Dodge could handle her for a few days — *maybe* a week — but any longer was unfathomable. Dame also wondered what would happen to Rosie if they arrested her. Child services would probably take one look at her frail, disfigured father and put her daughter right into foster care.

She took a couple deep breaths and shook the nerves out of her fingers. Dame knew she had to keep her shit together. Considering downtown traffic, she probably had half an hour before the cops showed up. *Step One*: Drop Rosie off with Dodge and Fatima. *Step Two*: Pound a stiff drink. *Step Three*: Figure out step four. There. She had a plan. She was fine. Rosie was fine. They were all going to be fine.

But when Dame arrived at her apartment, she once again found her door unlocked. *Goddammit*. Had Hall and Oates already found her? No, that didn't make any sense. Cops didn't waste time picking locks. So, who was it then?

She lifted Rosie out of the stroller and, with the little girl in one arm, pushed the door open. As she made her way toward the kitchen, she noticed a strange smell — some odd combination of mothballs, sweat, and aftershave. She could also hear the sound of her kettle just starting to whistle.

"Hello?"

Sitting at the table was a man. But it wasn't Hall and it wasn't Oates. At first, in the dim light of the kitchen, Dame didn't recognize him without his sunglasses. His eyes were larger than she expected — almost cartoonishly large — and while one was dark brown, the other was a strange milky-blue colour. Nevertheless, the grey hair and rumpled linen suit quickly brought him into focus.

"*Kuh-bee!*" Rosie confirmed. "*Pee-ew!*"

"Mr. Kirby?" Dame was dumbfounded.

"Hello, my lovelies," the old man said. "We've been waiting for you."

"We?"

The kettle's whistle turned into a shriek as a woman with silver curls stepped into the room.

"Oh, hon," Peggy Beckers said. "It's been far too long."

CHAPTER THIRTY-EIGHT

"WOULD YOU LIKE a cup of tea?" Peggy said, lifting the kettle off the stovetop. "You don't seem to have a lot of options here, but I'm sure we can make do."

Dame took a step back.

"I'd stay put for now, hon." Peggy seemed to read her mind. "Kirby's getting on in years, but he's still quicker than he looks."

Dame took a slow breath and addressed the woman who had once tried to burn her alive. When it came, her voice was barely a whisper. "What are you doing here?"

"You don't have anything by way of a teapot, do you?" Peggy sighed. "No, I suppose not."

She took two cups off the shelf and dropped a tea bag into each. She poured boiling water and then went to the fridge. "I assume you still take milk." She opened the carton and gave it a sniff. "A little close to the expiry date, but I think we'll be okay."

"Peggy" — Dame's voice was louder now — "what are you doing here?"

The silver-haired woman poured a little milk into each of the cups and put the container back in the fridge. "We'll get to that in just a bit. We have so much to catch up on."

Peggy put one cup on the kitchen table and cradled the other in her hands. She looked around the cluttered apartment. "Not much of a housekeeper, are you, hon? And the state of your plants. My old monstera, in particular. If we hadn't been attending to them every Thursday, I'm sure they'd all be dead by now."

"You were breaking into my apartment?"

"Well, Kirby was. But after his run-in with that unpleasant lady detective, he couldn't really risk it anymore, could he?"

"Oh my God." Dame looked at the man seated at her kitchen table. "You killed Connie Radovich."

"A clear-cut case of self-defence," Peggy said. "When she found him in your apartment, she tried to *apprehend* him. And I'd be lost without my Kirby, wouldn't I? Absolutely lost." She put a hand on his shoulder and he patted it. "Aren't you going to drink your tea, hon?"

Dame shook her head.

"She never really loved tea," the woman said to Kirby, "but she stopped drinking coffee when she was trying to get pregnant. Which reminds me" — she walked around the table toward Dame — "I believe some congratulations are in order."

Dame took another step back and held Rosie tighter in her arms.

"Look at those *cheeks*! And those bright green eyes! She looks a little pale, though." Peggy reached for the child. "Is she eating enough?"

"Don't you touch her."

"Kirby tells me you named her Rosie." Peggy crouched down and smiled in the little girl's face. "Did you know you were named after my friend? My very *best* friend?"

"The best friend that you murdered," Dame said.

"Well, technically *I* didn't murder her. I mean, there's no sense splitting hairs, but you should always give credit where credit is due. Shouldn't you, Kirby?"

A familiar high-voltage hum started burning though Dame's brain. What had Anton Felski said about her mother's murderer? *Kind of strange looking. Has two different-coloured eyes.*

"It was you," Dame said, vibrating on the strange frequency. "Behind the wheel of that white Chevy. You killed my mother." Slowly, she eased her phone out of her pocket. She squeezed the top two buttons together so that the SOS display appeared on the screen.

"Oh, hon." Peggy frowned. "Kirby? Could you —?"

In one swift motion, Kirby tore the phone out of Dame's hand and threw it against the wall. It exploded on impact, the screen separating from its casing, metal and plastic shrapnel scattering across the small kitchen. Rosie scowled and put her hands over her ears.

"Dame, the police are going to arrive any minute as it is," Peggy said. "I think it's in all of our best interests that we conclude our business before they do."

"Then tell me," Dame seethed, "what you fucking want."

"Now, now, my lovely," Kirby said. "Watch your language in front of the little one."

"Don't call me 'lovely,' you piece of shit!"

Rosie started to cry.

"See?" Peggy sat down at the table and shook her head, seemingly exasperated. "This is exactly what I'm talking about. When I was younger, mothers always put their children first, but these days, we expect so much from women. Look at you: A divorced parent, already busy with a full-time job, and here you are, solving little mysteries on the side. No wonder you don't have time to wash your dishes. To water your plants. To be a good mother."

"I'm a *great* mother," Dame said.

Rosie squirmed and sobbed in her arms.

"Do you even see yourself?" Peggy asked. "Do you see the

state you've put your child in? I'm sorry, hon, but you're out of your depth. Something's got to give."

It took all of Dame's energy to stay calm. "Peggy, I'm going to ask you one more time. *What do you want?*"

Peggy sighed. "I just want to relieve you of one of your many burdens."

Dame bounced a mewling Rosie in her arms. "What are you talking about?"

"All this Marinetti business at City Hall — they've got you running around in circles. Memorizing useless facts and figures. I just want you to forget about it. That's all."

"What do you mean, 'forget about it'?"

"I mean, at the end of the month, when you stand trial against our old friend Phillip Marinetti, I want you to forget everything you know about him and his business: zoning violations, unsanctioned demolitions, money laundering, arson. Forget all of it. Like it never happened."

"You want me to lie under oath? For you? What makes you think I would ever do that?"

"Just look at this place. This sad, little apartment. It's a mess. *You're* a mess. Don't you want something more? If not for yourself, then for your daughter? I can help you."

"Help me? Jesus Christ. Three years ago you tried to kill me."

Peggy took a deep breath. "I know. I made a terrible mistake. And truthfully, I feel absolutely horrid about it." She stood up from her chair. "So let me make it up to you. Let me give you the life you deserve."

"And if I refuse?"

"Well, if you don't drop all this trial nonsense" — she walked across the room and tousled Rosie's curls — "I'm sure we can find another way to lighten your load."

"Get out of my house," Dame whispered.

"Oh, hon. Don't think that we —"

"*Get out of my house!*"

Peggy cleared her throat. "All right. Let's go, Kirby. We don't need to stay where we're not wanted."

When the door slammed shut, Rosie looked up at her mother with bright green eyes, and proceeded to vomit the rest of her macaroni and peas all over Dame's sweater.

CHAPTER THIRTY-NINE

DIAPERS, WIPES, CHANGE of clothes, children's ibuprofen, and what else? *What else?*

As quickly as she could, Dame stuffed a duffle bag full of things Dodge and Fatima might need to look after Rosie that weekend. God forbid she forget Rosie's favourite blanket. Or her stuffed raccoon. As she packed, Dame's brain cycled through the ways in which Dodge and Fatima might get it wrong. What if they didn't read the right books? Or say *night night* to all the stuffed animals? Or sing the right songs in the right order? Worse, what if Rosie wouldn't stop vomiting?

And of course, every time she heard anything that vaguely resembled a siren, her brain would short-circuit, and she'd have to start from the beginning again: diapers, wipes, change of clothes, children's ibuprofen, *what else*? Meanwhile, Rosie sat in her high chair and built geometric monstrosities out of Magna-Tiles, dark circles lurking under her eyes.

Dame had packed her own bag with far less care. Flashlight? Sure. Dodge's old lockpick kit? Why not? There were two particular things, though, she was certain she'd need later. Two things that she carefully placed in the zippered pocket of her backpack.

Dame checked her watch. It was almost two o'clock. She managed a droopy daughter, an umbrella stroller, and a couple of bags down the front steps. She strapped Rosie in and started covering ground. When she got a block away, Dame couldn't remember if she'd locked the front door — even thought about going back to check — until she realized the cops would probably kick it down anyway.

"ARE YOU SURE you shouldn't just turn yourself in?" Fatima asked. "If you run away, the police might get the wrong idea."

Dame turned to Dodge for a second opinion. He knew cops. He knew the way they thought. The old man just shook his head.

"Go."

"Do you know what you're going to do? Where you're going to stay?" Fatima asked.

"I've got a couple ideas." She crouched down next to Rosie, who was busying herself with the old Fisher-Price play farm. "How's your tummy feeling?"

"Good."

"I'm glad."

Rosie put a little brown dog on top of a yellow tractor.

"Listen, partner" — Dame sniffed and wiped away the tears welling in her eyes — "Mama's going to go away for a little while, okay?"

"Doggie drive tractor."

"Yeah, partner. I see." Dame forced a smile to her face. "So, Rosie, I'm going to need you to be really good for Grandpa and Fatima, okay? Just for a little while. Just until —"

The dam burst and renegade tears spilled down Dame's face. "*Shit.* I'm sorry," she said. "I'm so sorry."

Rosie reached up and rested her little hand on Dame's cheek. "Mama?"

"Yes, sweet girl?"

"Doggie drive tractor."

Dame laughed a little in spite of her tears. She turned and looked at her father. "Dodge, I — I saw her."

The old man's face asked: *Who?*

"Peggy. I saw Peggy Beckers. She was waiting for me. In my apartment. She said if I testified against Marinetti, she'd —" Dame couldn't bring herself to say it out loud.

"She'd what?" Fatima finally asked.

Dame kissed the top of Rosie's head and took a deep breath. "When this is all over and done with, I'm telling the cops about Peggy. And her psychopath boyfriend. If they're out of hiding, they can't be that hard to find."

Fatima frowned. "Psychopath?"

"She had some guy — some guy named Kirby — scoping us out for weeks. I thought he was just some old drunk."

Dame's father looked at her again. His eyes were hard and unblinking, like pieces of polished ice.

"I think" — Dame eyes once again filled with tears — "I think he's the one who —"

For a moment, the old man looked unsteady on his feet. He reached behind him and stumbled backward onto the couch. Fatima hurried to sit down beside him and took his hand. Dame surveyed the chaos she'd created.

"I can't leave." She slid the backpack off her shoulder. "Not like this."

Dodge looked up at her and pointed one shaky finger toward the door. "*Go.*"

DAME SAT WITH a tequila soda at the back of Lath & Plaster. She didn't want to sit at the bar and look at herself in the old mirror behind it. She didn't want to see how red-eyed and haggard she already looked at two thirty in the afternoon.

When she first walked in, she had the place to herself. But now there were others: two dudes debating the saddest song of all time. One of the dudes had his money on "The River" by Bruce Springsteen.

"It starts with all the promise and possibility of youth," he was saying, "and by the end, he's stuck in a loveless marriage, saddled with a kid, and working some dead-end job. What's worse than that?"

"Definitely a bummer," the other dude said, "but there's something a little too *optimistic* about Springsteen, you know? Too American Dream. If you really want a song about oppressive domesticity, 'Love Will Tear Us Apart' wins, hands down. With those cold-ass synthesizers? And that voice? I mean, Ian Curtis *killed himself* a month before the song was released. Now *that's* fucking *sad*."

Dame smiled a little to herself. Their conversation sounded so much like the endless debates Adam used to have with his buddies. And she realized that she'd almost forgotten about Adam these past few days. Not his death, of course — his death had become some kind of strange, all-consuming riddle — but the man Adam was. Or, at least, the man she thought she knew. The little mark on his earlobe from that silly-looking stud he got as a teenager. The way he always smelled like Speed Stick deodorant, even when he wasn't wearing it. The way his beard grew a little too high on his face and he had to trim it just below his cheekbones.

Had that man really slept with a fourteen-year-old girl? Had that man's wife really killed him?

"What about 'Wicked Game' by Chris Isaak," one of the dudes was saying. "Now *that's* a sad song."

"Oh yeah. Good call. Do you remember how *hot* Helena Christensen was in that video? God, if she broke up with me, I'd be devastated."

Dame had to admit she missed her old problems — betrayals, breakups, unrequited love — and she missed all the sad songs that could soothe her little heartaches. Where were the songs about miscarriages, postpartum depression, and 4 a.m. diaper changes? Where were the songs about abandoning your child so you could more effectively evade the police?

It was only after the server brought her a second tequila soda that Dame hoisted her backpack onto the chair next to her and took out the two things that she, even in her haste, had taken care to pack.

The first thing was Neil Young's terracotta nose. She put it on the table in front of her and stared at it awhile. Dodge had once described an old Russian story in which a man is separated from his nose. The nose in the story makes quite a go of it — even becomes a state councillor — before reuniting with its face. Old Neil's nose didn't seem like it was going to be quite so successful.

But just how did this particular nose come to be separated from the rest of the sculpture? Did the Neil Young bust get busted in a struggle? The rest of the sculpture would've been about twenty inches tall and twelve inches wide. And as Rachel herself estimated, it would've weighed a good thirty pounds. Not quite a lead pipe or a baseball bat, but definitely solid enough to fracture an occipital bone. Dame considered the nose a final time before putting it back in her bag.

The second thing she took out of her backpack was the envelope Dame had stolen from Rachel's kitchen junk drawer. An envelope labelled "*Work Receipts.*" One by one, Dame took little slips of paper out of the envelope and piled them on the table in front of her. Two receipts she put aside. Both had been issued by a company called Lux Interiors — a car detailing place near the corner of Gerrard and Coxwell.

Dame brought her backpack and her empty glass up to the bar.

"Want another?" the bartender asked.

Dame shook her head. "Any chance you guys have a landline I could borrow?"

The man heaved an ancient rotary phone from behind the bar. "Not sure why we still have this. You might be the last person to ever use it."

"Thanks." Dame dialled one of the very few numbers she still had memorized.

"Holy shit are you okay?" Meera asked.

"Yeah, but listen" — Dame cleared her throat — "I need to get to the other end of town, and I don't want to risk transit. I know you're busy this afternoon, but do you think you could give me a ride?"

"Of course. Where are you?"

"You remember the alley where Lewis threw up eggplant Parmesan all over his new Stan Smiths?"

"Of course I do."

"Meet me there in twenty minutes."

Dame ended the call and started heading for the door. As she did, she passed by the two dudes.

"'Little Green,'" she said to them.

"Sorry?"

"'Little Green' by Joni Mitchell. That's the saddest song of all time."

She pushed through the exit and started making her way east.

DAME DID HER best to stay off the main arteries and, in doing so, found herself walking once more down Seaforth Avenue. It had been a week since she'd encountered the cruel fence that cordoned off her old house, and she'd avoided the street so she wouldn't have to watch Phillip Marinetti's version of progress make a ruin of her childhood memories.

But as she hurried down the sidewalk, she could sense the change before she really saw it. A shift in the light. Too much sky. She braced for the desolate rubble, the teeth of the excavator, the shattered glass of a bedroom window. Instead, there was nothing. Only a cruel and quiet emptiness. A dimple in a field of dirt and a few muddy tire tracks on the surrounding asphalt. Marinetti's demolition crew had worked quickly. Even the metal fence was gone. All that remained was the sign that read "*Coming Soon.*" It was as much warning as it was advertisment. *Don't slow down*, it cautioned, *the future is on its way.*

Dame adjusted her glasses and kept moving.

CHAPTER FORTY

"OUR BEST DEAL right now is probably the Gold Package," the man in the pale blue jumpsuit was saying. "It's regularly one-eighty, but we have a special this weekend for one-fifty. It includes full interior cleanup, vacuum, and shampoo, plus exterior hand wash and dry."

"Wow," Meera said, "that actually sounds pretty good."

"We can do it while you wait, or you can book an appointment for later."

"Let me think about it a bit," Meera said. "My friend had a couple questions, too."

"Actually, I kind of need a favour." Dame tried on her best I'm-sorry-and-thank-you smile.

The man adjusted his hairnet. "How can I help?"

"Well, my brother's brought my Range Rover here a few times, and he always gives me the receipt so I can claim it for taxes."

"Black Sport model, right?"

"Uh, yeah."

"Sure. I know that vehicle." He looked Dame up and down. "So, you're the owner of Uplift Fitness?"

"Uh, yep. That's me."

"Huh."

"She's all core," Meera explained. "Doesn't bother with any of those glamour muscles."

Dame resisted the urge to scowl at her friend. "In any case, I lost the receipt for the last time he was in here. Any chance I could get another copy?"

"Do you have his credit card number?"

"I don't."

The man sucked his teeth a little. "Well, I guess that won't really be a problem. Just give me a sec." He clacked at his computer screen for a moment. "What's your brother's name?"

"Ben," Dame said. "Ben Suarez."

"*Suarez, Suarez ...*" The man scanned the screen. "Here it is."

A strip of white paper curled out of the little printer. The man tore it off and handed it to Dame.

"Are you sure about this date?" she asked.

"If that's what it says, then that's when it was."

"Okay. And — just out of curiosity — why did this cleaning cost more than the previous ones?"

"Looks like he got the Platinum Package that time. Costs a little extra, but the boys go over everything with a fine-tooth comb. We give you back that new car smell. That's the Platinum Package guarantee. Plus, we don't charge extra for spot cleans."

"Spot cleans?"

"Yeah, like if there's some kind of hard-to-remove stain — you know, like coffee, or grape juice, or —"

"— or blood?"

"Sure. We do vomit, urine, feces, and yeah" — he grinned — "sometimes we do blood."

"Okay," Dame said. "Good to know."

A FEW MINUTES later, they were sitting in Meera's Jeep. The sky had started to cloud over, and Dame watched the first drops of rain explode on the windshield.

"That guy was good," Meera said. "He talked me into the Diamond Package and it wasn't even on sale."

"Sorry about that."

"No, it's cool. I'm going to bring the Jeep in on Sunday. I've actually been meaning to get it cleaned for ages. You would not *believe* how much Elwy Yost sheds."

Dame brushed some white hairs off her jeans. "I have an idea."

There was a low rumble of thunder and the rain started pattering on the top of the Jeep.

"So? Are you going to tell me what that was all about?"

"It was just a hunch. Rachel said Ben had her SUV detailed *three* times, but when I looked through her files, there were only receipts for *two*."

"Well, maybe Ben's more into cleanliness than record-keeping. That's not a crime."

"Yeah, but look at the date on this receipt."

"It says July 31."

"At *nine thirty* in the morning. Like he'd made a big mess the night before and was just waiting for them to open."

"So?"

"So that's the *morning after* Adam disappeared."

Meera sighed. "Now you think Ben was involved, too."

"It makes sense. Wouldn't you help your sister if she was in trouble?"

"I don't have a sister."

"Okay, but if Lewis killed somebody, wouldn't you help him bury the body?"

"On occasion, when Elwy Yost brings me a dead chipmunk, I'll put on a pair of old gardening gloves and throw the corpse in my neighbour's trash bin. Honestly, though? That's where I draw the line."

"But you know you're currently helping a wanted fugitive evade the police, right?"

"That's different. You're innocent. Just don't ask me to hold your hand and drive the Jeep off a cliff."

Dame laughed.

"So, where to next?" Meera put her key in the ignition. "Have you figured out where you're going to stay tonight?"

"I think so. There's a cheap hotel in the east end I'm going to try. I should have enough cash to avoid using my credit card."

"You want me to drop you off?"

Dame looked at her watch. "Actually, I had something else in mind."

CHAPTER FORTY-ONE

THE WEATHER OUTSIDE had gone from bad to worse, as though summer had decided to pack up and call it quits a few weeks early. And just as they started heading north on Jones Avenue, the sky opened up and pissed down a bladderful of bad news. Visibility was instantaneously shit, and it continued to be shit when they arrived at their destination and sat in the shelter of the Jeep.

"Range Rover's not there," Meera said.

"Ben usually borrows it. Rachel takes transit."

"It's after four o'clock. Think anyone's home?"

"Only one way to find out."

Meera squinted through the windshield. "Didn't you already break into Rachel's house? And didn't she almost taser you for doing it?"

"The door was open. So technically, it wasn't breaking. Just entering."

"Is that what you'll tell the cops this time?"

Dame turned back to the window and watched beads of water collect and disappear down the glass. Little wet comets blazing into nothingness. "Right now, the cops think I murdered two people. This might be my last chance to prove them wrong."

"There's also a pretty good chance you'll get caught."

Dame sighed. "I just need an edge piece."

"An edge piece?"

"Yeah. The one thing that makes everything else make sense. If this is actually where Adam died, then this is where I should've started in the first place. There's got to be something here I missed."

WHEN DAME STEPPED out of the Jeep, she was immediately drenched. The small, cinched aperture of her hood kept just enough water out of her eyes to find the front steps. When she knocked on the door, no one answered. When she tried peeking through the window, she couldn't see anybody. When she tried the handle, it was locked.

Okay. Go time.

Dame gave Meera a thumbs-up and watched the Jeep pull away. Even with the lousy weather, Dame was too exposed on the street to pick the front lock. She hurried down the narrow corridor between Rachel's house and the one next door, keeping an eye out for nosy neighbours and noisy watchdogs. When she got herself under the gable roof of the back porch, the coast looked relatively clear. But before she could fish Dodge's lockpick kit out of her backpack, she encountered a new, unexpected problem: There wasn't a lock to pick. It seemed that Adam and Rachel had decided to install an electronic keypad on their door and Dame, for all intents and purposes, was shit out of luck.

Or maybe not. She took a closer look. The thing was an Armstrong SmartCode Deadbolt, the same kind of lock she'd helped Meera install last summer. If memory served, you could program it with a six-digit code. If you messed up the code three times, it would lock you out for a solid hour (apparently, this had happened to Lewis no less than three times).

Dame tried to do the math in her head. Six digits meant how many possible combinations? A million? Jesus, could that be right?

She bent down to get a better look. Some of the numbers were a little more faded than the others, but only four: 2, 3, 4, and 6. She figured that some of the numbers had been used more than once.

Dame racked her brain. Birthdays and anniversaries didn't work. The house number was seventy-seven, so that didn't work either. But what about phone numbers? Instinctively, Dame reached for her own phone and then remembered it was currently on the floor of her apartment in about one hundred pieces.

Growing up, Dame's head had been a veritable Yellow Pages, but these days, thanks to the invention of smart phones, she only knew three numbers by heart: Dodge's, Meera's, and her own.

But that wasn't entirely true, was it?

She closed her eyes and held out her hand. Into an imaginary keypad, she could dial her mother's phone number at the *Toronto Star*, the number of the pizza place on King Street that closed in 2014, and her boyfriend's number — before he was her husband, before he was Rachel's husband, and before he was dead. If she dropped the area code and the last digit at the end, it might work. Dame stabbed the six numbers into the keypad. The mechanism flashed red and made an angry-sounding noise. *Shit.*

She looked at her watch. It was nearly four thirty. Ben would probably be home in the next half hour or so. She had to hurry.

Dame tried to remember all the music Adam liked that had something to do with numbers. There was that Tommy Tutone song with the chorus "867-5309." Nope. There was that old Toots and the Maytals song he liked, "54-46 Was My Number," but that wouldn't work either. What was that AC/DC song his band used to cover? There was some weird six-digit Australian phone number in it: 3 — 6 — 2 — 4 — 3 — 6. She looked at the faded digits on the keypad. That *had* to be it. She punched in the lyrics to "Dirty Deeds Done Dirt Cheap" and the machine flashed red again. *Shit.* Strike two.

She tried to think of the things that Adam loved besides music. Disc golf? Smoking weed? The *Expos*. Adam's father had indoctrinated him into Expos fandom from an early age, and even after the player's strike in '94 and the team's eventual collapse ten years later, he remained a true believer in their mythology. But Adam's favourite sport was a vast quagmire of statistics, dates, and percentages. She might have better luck just guessing at random than pulling a number out of that world. Still, it was worth a shot. And she wouldn't have to look up the names of his favourite players — the ones he never shut up about — they were long since burned into her brain: Andre Dawson was Number Twenty-Four. Tim Raines was Number Thirty-Two. So far so good. But Vladimir Guerrero was Number Twenty-Seven, and Pedro Martínez — his favourite pitcher — was Number Forty-Five. It just didn't fit.

But then, Dame remembered Joe Siddall — a catcher for the Expos, and a Canadian guy from Windsor. Adam had managed to get his autograph when he was just a kid, and he was psyched when Siddall resurfaced as a broadcaster for the Jays. Joe Siddall, Dame remembered, was Number Twenty-Six.

Okay. Bottom of the ninth. Two outs. Two strikes. She punched the numbers in chronological order: 2 — 4 — 3 — 2 — 2 — 6.

Lo and behold, the machine flashed green.

CHAPTER FORTY-TWO

DAME STARTED IN Rachel and Adam's room. In the dresser, she found all of Rachel's fancy, lacy things in the top drawer, and all of the practical athletic stuff in the bottom, but nothing damning. Everything was just beautiful and new. Adam's drawer, on the other hand, was like some strange time capsule dug up from the dirt. She recognized so many of the old T-shirts and hoodies. There was underwear that had to be more than a decade old. God, how did these two ever make sense as a couple?

Next, she looked through the shirts and pants hanging in the closet. For someone struggling financially, her old friend had a pretty impressive wardrobe: Givenchy, Louis Vuitton, and a pricey-looking Hermès shoulder bag. Rachel was certainly doing her best to keep up appearances.

The ragged jeans and corduroys were obviously Adam's, but there were also some dress shirts Dame had never seen before, some expensive-looking slacks, a navy blue Burberry suit, a tie with little guitars all over it. And next to the closet door, there was a framed photo of the two of them — a selfie Adam had taken. They were strapped into a rollercoaster, grinning anxiously, waiting for the ride to begin.

Eventually, Dame started to see it. The ways in which Rachel and Adam overlapped. The ways in which they had wanted to move forward together. It wasn't just Luka or — as the worst parts of Dame suspected — some twisted desire to hurt her that kept them together. It was love. They had loved each other. Rachel hadn't ruined his life. She just helped him make a new one.

So why then, would she murder him?

Dame tried Ben's bedroom next — the room that had once been Adam's studio. If Rachel was guilty, then so was Ben — but to what degree, Dame wasn't sure. Was he there when Adam died? Had he helped move the body? Rachel was the only real family Ben had left. Dame thought of Dodge and Rosie. How far would she go to protect them?

The room was still spotless. A curated museum of all things Adam: the guitars on the wall, the amp on the ground, the rock show posters, the tower of CDs no one would ever listen to anymore. She looked in the tiny closet, wondering if maybe she'd uncover a noseless Old Neil, but found instead a few old boxes of unsold seven-inch records and Long Walks on the Beach T-shirts. This room, Dame understood, was where rock 'n' roll dreams went to die.

She searched through the dresser where Ben kept his clothes. Everything was modest, clean, fairly vanilla — a few more cardigans than the average dude, but overall, nothing unusual. All of his socks matched. Even his underwear was folded.

She looked at the futon, crisply made with military corners. The one part of the room that was so conspicuously Ben's. When she lay down and put her head on the pillow, Dame was surprised to find a familiar smell there. Sweet and spicy. Almost savoury. She couldn't quite place it, but as smell often can, it brought her back to very specific feelings: anticipation, anxiety, optimism, dread. What was it? The more she chased the memory, the more it receded.

It was then that she heard a door slam downstairs.

"Hello?" a voice called.

Shit. The babysitter.

"We got rained out at the park."

Dame's heart started racing, but her head talked it down a few BPMS. If she gave the kid some kind of reasonable explanation, Dame could be long gone before Rachel or Ben showed up. She started down the stairs.

"Hi, Zoe!" She held her hand up in a friendly wave.

The teenage girl was in the living room tending to a slightly soggy Luka. "Uh, hi?"

"Didn't mean to startle you," she said. "I just forgot something here the other day and Rachel said I could stop by and grab it."

"How did you get in?" Clearly, the teenager's bullshit detector was on high alert.

"Back door." Dame gestured behind her. "Rachel gave me the code."

The babysitter shrugged. "Okay. I was just about to set Luka up with his tablet."

"No problem. I'll let myself out."

As the girl turned to help Luka, Dame heaved her bag over one shoulder and made her way across the kitchen toward the back exit. But before she pushed her way out, she noticed something that hadn't been there earlier. Hanging on a hook by the door was the yellow hoodie, wet with rain.

"Huh."

When she picked it up, Dame noticed there was a smell coming from it. Sweet and spicy. Almost savoury. It was the same smell that she'd noticed in Ben's bedroom. Dame realized why she knew that smell. It was the smell of her first trimester, just after the morning sickness kicked in.

Dame reached into the pocket of the hoodie and pulled out a

package of ginger-flavoured gum. Her head swam with sudden realization. *Edge piece.* She had it all wrong before, but now, it made perfect sense.

"This" — Dame said to herself — "this isn't Rachel's hoodie."

"No. It's mine."

Dame turned to face Zoe, standing in the kitchen, her arms wrapped around her body.

"I'm sorry," the babysitter said.

From behind her, Dame heard the back door swing open. Before she could turn to see who was there, she felt a flash of cold agony at the base of her skull. Everything went white. And then everything went black.

CHAPTER FORTY-THREE

THE THREE OF *them sat down at the table in the Elliots' kitchen. Spencer handed the piece of paper to the detective. He scanned it and then handed it over to his daughter.*

It was carefully typed. Short and to the point. It told Spencer not to blame himself. That she couldn't live with the truth. That she couldn't live with ending their baby's life. That the only option was ending both of their lives.

They waited for Spencer to speak. Eventually he did, fighting to keep his voice even.

"At first, we were excited about the baby. Jill wasn't scared or anything. We knew it would be hard, but it felt kind of — I don't know — kind of right."

The detective nodded, and Spencer continued.

"But then, one night I was poking around my dad's studio looking for his stash — he's a total pothead — and I found" — *his face creased in disgust* — "these love letters from Jill's mom. I showed them to Jill and she kind of put two and two together."

"How'd she take it?"

"How do you think?"

"Okay," *the detective said.* "Then what happened?"

"Well, about a week later — just before Jill died — we had this huge fight. That's what Mrs. Schulz heard. Nosy bitch. I wanted Jill to get an abortion, but she said she wouldn't do it. Her family's like, super religious. She said it was 'God's will.'"

"You didn't want the baby anymore?" the detective said.

"Are you nuts? That kid would've been an obscenity. God's will. Fuck that." He shook his head. "And if people found out the truth — Jesus — I would've been a fucking joke. My whole life would've been over."

The detective took the suicide note from his daughter's hands. "Is that why you didn't show this to anybody?"

Spencer nodded. "It seemed pretty obvious at the time that Jill did this to herself. At least until Bruce Weatherhead went all Charles Bronson on everyone's ass."

"Did you tell anybody else about Mrs. Weatherhead's letters?"

"I showed them to my mom. I thought for sure she was going to leave my dad over it — asshole deserved it — but I don't know if she even talked to him about it. Nothing happened, in any case."

The detective looked down at the letter again. "Spencer, if you want me to clear your name, you're going to have to let me have this letter."

The boy's cruel, proud face finally crumpled, and his eyes shone with tears. "Fine."

When the detective stood up, he put a hand on Spencer's shoulder. "Son, I don't know if I'm the right person to tell you this, but none of this is your fault."

Spencer wiped a trail of snot across his sleeve and squinted up at the detective. "No shit, Sherlock."

On the car ride home, the kid reread the typed note.

"I'm almost disappointed he didn't do it."

The detective gripped the steering wheel. "Just because you're innocent of a crime doesn't mean you're a good person."

The kid nodded to herself. "You know, Spencer could have saved us all some time by handing this letter over earlier."

"Maybe."

"I guess if it walks like a duck and talks like a duck, it's a suicide."

The detective looked over at his daughter. "You really think that poor girl killed herself?"

"Well, yeah. I'm holding the evidence in my hands as we speak."

"That's evidence, all right." The detective turned on his blinker and hung a right on Lansdowne Avenue. "But not evidence that Jill Weatherhead committed suicide."

CHAPTER FORTY-FOUR

AS DAME OPENED her eyes and struggled to unkink her neck, it became quickly apparent that her wrists and ankles had been duct-taped to one of Rachel's kitchen chairs. When she tried to call out, she realized there was tape over her mouth as well.

Through the window, Dame could see that most of the blue had been washed out of the sky, and that the afternoon was fading into evening. Her glasses were missing. Her skull throbbed, and she imagined if she could feel the back of her head, there'd already be a sizable goose egg growing out of it.

Dame looked for some means of escape. There weren't a lot of options in the immediate vicinity. A number of scrawly child's drawings were spread haphazardly across the table. A big box of crayons stood open next to a rubber triceratops and an Iron Man action figure. She scanned the rest of the kitchen. Maybe, if she could scooch the chair over to the cutlery drawer, wiggle out a knife somehow, she could cut herself loose. But before she could implement her half-baked plan, Dame heard the sudden thunder of footsteps on the stairs. A moment later, Ben Suarez was searching through the liquor cabinet above the refrigerator.

"God, it's as if Rachel's taste in booze crystallized after second year university," he was saying. "Silent Sam. Malibu rum. There's like, seven different flavours of liqueur and not a single decent bottle of bourbon. Oh. Wait. Here we go. This'll do."

He brought down the cheap tequila she and Rachel drank the week prior. He poured himself a glass. "Sorry, I can't really offer you anything right now."

Ben replaced the bottle in the cabinet. When he sat down across from Dame, he had the drink in one hand, and a child's wooden baseball bat in the other. He put the bat on top of the table. It was painted fluorescent green and featured a little cartoon man hitting one out of the park. Dame found it hard to believe that something so silly-looking had just caused her so much pain.

"Now" — he took a sip of the tequila — "I'm going to take the tape off your mouth, but if you get noisy, I'm going to have to give you another whack, okay?"

Dame glared at the man.

"Okay?" he asked again.

Dame forced herself to nod her head.

"By the way," he slugged back the rest of the tequila, "did you know the *police* are looking for you? And not just about Adam. They think you killed some cop, too. I just saw it on CP24."

Ben reached across the table and pinched the corner of the duct tape over Dame's mouth. "Seems like you've got yourself into quite the predicament, haven't you?" He ripped the tape from her face and Dame let out a strangled scream.

"You fucking killed Adam," she spat.

"Whoa, easy there, Veronica Mars. I'd lay off the wild accusations if I were you."

"Adam came home early from the island. He went to hang up his guitar in the spare bedroom, and he caught you with — Jesus, Ben, she's only fourteen years old — and you" — she pulled uselessly against the kitchen chair — "you fucking killed him."

"No. You're wrong." Zoe walked into the room. "I killed him."

Dame felt all the oxygen leave her body.

"I mean, to be fair, it was mostly Adam's fault," Ben said.

"He was going to call my parents." There was something vacant, almost rehearsed to her words. "He was going to ruin everything. Ben tried to explain that we loved each other. But he wouldn't listen. And then they were wrestling and knocking things over and Adam kept hitting him and hitting him." She started to cry. "So I picked up that — thing — and I —"

"She saved me," Ben said, standing up and putting his arm around Zoe. "In more ways than one."

Dame's skin crawled.

"Anyway," Ben said with a sigh, "you probably figured out the rest. We put Adam in the back of the Range Rover. I got rid of his stuff, and then I took his body down to the water."

"Were you the one who called me from Adam's phone?"

"Me?" Ben smiled. "Can't say that was me. I did text Rachel from Adam's phone. Guess I screwed that one up. God, who texts in all caps? But don't worry, I won't be making any more mistakes. We've got one more mess to clean up, and then things can go back to the way they were."

"You're going to have a lot more than one mess to clean up when that baby arrives in April," Dame said.

"Baby?" Ben smiled. "God, you really don't miss a trick, do you, Polara?"

"She'll start showing in a month or two. How do you think she's going to explain that?"

"Well, after Zoe's little appointment next week, she won't have to explain anything to anybody."

"Are you sure about that?" Dame looked at Zoe. "Women terminating a pregnancy don't usually take folic acid to prevent birth defects."

Ben turned to Zoe. "Is there something you want to tell me?"

The girl stood hugging herself. When she spoke, her voice was barely audible. "I — I don't think I can do this," she said. "I don't want to hurt anybody, anymore. Not her. Not this baby. I just want us to be a family."

"We *are* a family." Ben put his hands on Zoe's shoulders. "But do you know what would happen if you had that baby? They'd put me in jail. There'd be no 'us.' No family. You'd be all alone. Is that what you want?"

Zoe shook her head. Tears fell down her cheeks.

"The same thing goes for her." He jerked a thumb in Dame's direction. "Are we going to let her ruin our future? The way Adam tried to ruin it?"

"But, couldn't we just —"

"Let me handle this, okay? I've got it all figured out."

"I know, but what if we —"

"*Uncle Be-e-en!*" a voice called from upstairs.

Ben groaned and looked up to the ceiling. "Jesus, Zoe. You were supposed to give him melatonin."

"I — I thought I did, but —"

"You *thought* you did?" Ben's voice had turned a shade uglier. "You obviously didn't, because he's still awake."

She looked at Ben and then at Dame.

"Well, don't just stand there. Go see what he wants."

"You're not listening to me," Zoe said quietly. "You never listen anymore."

The young woman jammed her hands in her pockets and hurried out of the kitchen.

Ben watched her leave and then turned toward Dame. "Oh, come on, Polara. Don't look at me like that. Fifty years ago, no one would've thought twice about our age difference. Maybe in another fifty years people will get over themselves. I mean, come on. Who can put an age limit on love?"

"The Criminal Code of Canada?"

Ben ignored her. "And of course, Adam just had to get involved, didn't he? That douchebag's out there fucking the Greater Toronto Area, and he has the *audacity* to try and destroy something pure and honest and — "

"Illegal?" Dame offered. "Exploitive? Abusive? Predatory?"

Ben sighed. "It seems like our dialogue has come to an impasse." He stood up and dragged a hand through his floppy hair. "I'm going upstairs to try and repair some of the damage you've caused, but if I hear one peep out of you, it'll be nighty-night. And I won't be using melatonin. Got it?"

He didn't wait for an answer and made his way out of the kitchen. Dame struggled against the tape, but it was no use. Eventually, she put her cheek down against the cool of the table. For a few minutes, she listened to the tick of the kitchen clock and wondered just what the fuck she was going to do.

"Are you a bad guy?"

When Dame raised her head, Luka stood in front of her, wearing Pull-Ups and an Expos T-shirt. She hadn't even heard him come down the stairs.

"No, I'm not a bad guy. I'm a friend of your mom's. Remember?"

The boy shrugged.

"Shouldn't you be in bed?" Dame asked.

"Can't sleep. Uncle Ben and Zoe are fighting." The boy scratched his elbow and seemed to consider her for a moment. "Why are you all taped up like that?"

"Well, your uncle and I, we're just" — Dame looked down at her wrists — "playing a game."

"Oh." The boy looked unconvinced.

"Do you want to help me win the game?"

"I guess."

"Could you go into the cutlery drawer and get me a pair of scissors?"

Luka shook his head. "I'm not allowed to go in that drawer. Too many ouchies."

"Too many ouchies." Dame disguised her disappointment. "Right. Can't argue with that."

The little boy sat down across the table from Dame. He picked up a crayon and started scribbling on a piece of paper. "Are you sure you're a friend of my mom's?"

"Very sure. Your mom and I have known each other a long time." And just then, an idea presented itself to Dame. "In fact, once, your mom taught me a magic word."

Luka stopped drawing and gave her a skeptical look. "How is it a *magic* word?"

"Well, it's so magic that, if you spell it right, we'll both win the game. But it's kind of a tricky word. Are you good at spelling?"

"My teacher says I need improvement."

"Well, how about I *tell* you how to spell it and you write it out on that piece of paper you've got there?"

Luka shrugged again. "Okay."

Dame's heart raced as the little boy crayoned out twelve letters with agonizing care. When he finally finished, Dame read it over.

"Perfect! Now go stick it to the fridge with a magnet, so your mom will see it later."

The little boy did as he was told. "What's next?"

"Next, you have to sneak back upstairs, the way you snuck downstairs. And you can't let Zoe or Uncle Ben see you, okay?"

Luka nodded his head. He started toward the stairs and stopped. "What's your name again?"

"Dame."

"Dame?" The boy thought about it for a moment. "That's a weird name."

"Tell me about it, kid."

THERE WAS AN unscratchable itch under Dame's left eye and it was making each minute feel like an eternity. In a strange way, the discomfort was comforting. The longer Ben and Zoe spent planning their next move, the longer Dame stayed alive. Occasionally, she could hear snatches of her captors' conversation. Zoe's voice in particular seemed to carry ("— *don't want to do this again — not her fault she —*") but it wasn't enough to know what came next. Soon though, Dame heard the inevitable footsteps on the stairs and Ben materialized in the kitchen.

"Well, unfortunately, Dame, our time is up."

"Where's Zoe? Trouble in paradise?"

"She'll come around. She always does."

"So what's the rush, then? Is Rachel on her way home?"

"Rachel works pretty late, these days." Ben opened the junk drawer. "But she'll be here sooner or later, and I'd like to have this little problem resolved by the time she gets back."

When he took the roll of duct tape from the drawer, Dame's heart sank. "Ben. Come on. Don't do this."

He stretched out a length of tape and tore it from the roll.

"Ben, listen —"

"You know, Dame, all day long, people want me to listen. To their ideas. To their problems. To their stupid little stories. Everybody always has one more thing they just *need* to tell me. But the fact is, at this particular moment in time" — he fixed the tape over her mouth — "I'm done listening."

CHAPTER FORTY-FIVE

"PRETTY NICE BACK there, isn't it?" Ben asked from the driver's seat. "Those Lux Interiors guys do a decent job. You should have seen what it looked like before. It was a *mess*."

Dame watched the street lights slide past the windows. They'd been heading southwest for a good twenty minutes now. Her wrists and ankles were bound with tape, and she had a pretty good idea of where Ben was taking her.

"Don't waste your time trying to get someone's attention, by the way. The tint on these windows is pretty intense."

It was dark and the rain had stopped. They were driving past a series of aluminum portables in wide asphalt lots, secured with barbed wire fences, and concealed by vinyl advertisements for construction companies. Mountains of crushed rock and gravel rose up beside the squat buildings, while below, the curbs crumbled into the street. Clumps of uncut grass and weeds burst from the broken pavement. In the haze of the city light, Dame could make out smokestacks and power towers in the distance.

"Shame what this city did to its waterfront, isn't it? On the west side, the only people who can see the lake live in towers that block it from the rest of us." He was reflected in the rear-view, staring ahead, his face blank. "And on the east side, you have this: Desolation Row."

Eventually, Ben took a left on Cherry Street, and they rumbled across the imposing steel bascule bridge, its massive counterweights looking down at Dame like the two heads of some mutant dinosaur. They took another left and drove for fifteen minutes or so, past impound lots, shipping containers, and brown fields. The industry gave way to greenery, and the road was soon hemmed in by sprawling bushes on either side. "There's actually some nice walking trails around here. But it's nowhere you'd want to go after dark."

They thumped up onto another bridge, and in the rear-view, Ben smiled a little to himself.

"That canal below us is actually a cooling channel," he said. "Not really sure how it works, but some big company uses it to produce air conditioning. It's pretty deep. And it leads right out into Lake Ontario."

When they reached the other side of the bridge, Ben pulled the SUV over. Through the back window, Dame could see a metal gate, almost completely obscured by scrub brush. Inside the tangle of foliage, a sign read *"No Trespassing."*

Ben stepped out and pulled on a pair of yellow dishwashing gloves. As Dame watched, he pushed the gate open. He got back in the driver's seat, put the engine into gear, and crept forward up the gravel driveway. A few moments later they parked, and the headlights shone ahead into a vacant lot.

"I just happened to read about this place a few months ago. There used to be an old shipping warehouse here, right on the channel. Some hippie collective bought it and tried to turn it into an industrial arts studio, but — unsurprisingly — they ran out of money. Eventually, the city took it over, knocked it down, and it's just been this secluded, empty place for a couple years."

Ben stepped out of the Range Rover and walked around to the back. He opened the rear door and leaned against the bumper. From below, the tail lights gave his face a strange, cheerful glow.

"I used to bring Zoe here sometimes, so we could be alone. God, if I had the money, I'd build us a little house, right here on the channel."

He was quiet for a moment. "Do you hear that? Just frogs and crickets and the rustle of leaves in the wind. No one talking at me all day. No one asking me endless questions: *Dr. Suarez, why am I sad all the time? Dr. Suarez, why doesn't my daddy love me?*"

Ben took a deep breath. "I used to go home every evening and my wife would tell me about some dumb thing a customer said to her, or the plot of some book she'd been reading. Honestly, is there anything worse than that? If I wanted to read the book, I'd read the book. I don't want your shitty Coles Notes. Jesus."

He turned to Dame. "You probably think we split up because of Zoe, right? Or maybe Zoe's the reason I got fired?" He shook his head. "Officially, it was the bourbon that got me canned. Not that I have a problem, mind you. I just found myself unable to sit through another tedious appointment without knocking back a slug of something first. And then, a little later, I couldn't go home to Fiona without stopping by the bar. For some reason, the only person I could really stand was Zoe. Some sessions, we didn't even talk. We'd just sit there in silence."

As if to demonstrate, he spent a few seconds listening to the sounds of the night.

"But now Zoe's talking about keeping this fucking baby. Well, that's not going to happen. God, who in their right mind would *choose* to have a baby? All that piss and shit and noise? No thank you."

Ben let out a long sigh.

"So anyway, there's a little trail just down there. Takes you right to the channel." Ben pointed the bat toward a thicket of brush. "That's where I put Adam into the water. I guess that's where I'll put you in, too. It's kind of poetic, if you think about it."

Dame cursed him through the tape.

"Yeah" — Ben laughed — "I bet you'd have a whole lot to say right now if I took that tape off." He tapped the bat against the side of his shoe. "How about I tell you a little secret, okay? Just between us? When I brought Adam down here, he actually woke up for a little while. He wasn't completely coherent — I mean, Zoe gave him a pretty decent whack — but God, he was loud. *Where am I? What the hell are you doing?* Thought for sure he was going to get us caught. Luckily, nobody's all that noisy when they're underwater."

Dame stared at Ben. Through her tears, his face blurred and twisted into something unfamiliar.

"I didn't mention that particular detail to Zoe. She doesn't need to know. Zoe's very mature for her age, but I'm still the one who has to make the difficult decisions. The way I figure things — she started the job, and I just helped her finish it. Speaking of which" — he looked at his watch — "we better wrap this up. I want to get home before Rachel wonders where I am."

Ben stood up and leaned the bat against the tire. "Okay, Veronica Mars. Let's get you out of there."

He reached into the back of the vehicle and grabbed Dame by her duct-taped wrists. She struggled against him, but he was strong — stronger than he looked — and he eventually managed to haul her out and drop her on the rocky ground below. She landed face first and felt the cartilage give way in her nose. Blood ran warm down her chin. Dame cursed again.

"Look, I know things aren't going according to plan," Ben said, picking up the bat, "but think of what a relief this'll be, right? No more project deadlines. No more late-night diaper changes. Isn't that what you wanted?"

Ben grabbed her ankle and started dragging her across the ground. She could feel every sharp twig and stone stab at her body. Could hear the water lapping against the shore.

"You were always so smart, Dame," he was saying, "so *gifted*. But God, to walk around every day with the weight of what you did — to Adam, and to that poor police officer — it would've been a terrible burden to bear. I think people will understand that you couldn't live with yourself. Maybe in time, they'll even learn to forgive you."

They'd come to a clearing and a dark ribbon of water stretched out in front of them. Ben pulled her to the edge of an old metal embankment. With a gesture that was almost tender, he crouched down and zipped her raincoat up to her chin. A moment later, he started filling the coat pockets with stones.

Dame's skull pounded where the bat had already connected. Panic was blooming in her lungs like carcinogenic flowers. She tried to imagine what Dodge would tell her to do in this situation. Tried to listen for his voice inside her head. There was only a blank and terrifying silence.

But then, she heard a different voice. A louder voice. *Slow your heart rate*, it said, *keep your movements to a minimum, and don't think about the time.*

Dame looked out at the black channel before her. She knew what she had to do.

CHAPTER FORTY-SIX

"THERE ARE WORSE ways to go, believe me," Ben was saying. "They figure my parents were still conscious when their car caught fire. But you? A little headache, a little cold water, and then nothing but peace and quiet."

Dame heard Adam's voice inside her head again: *Slow your heart rate.*

Through her swollen nose, she took a few measured breaths.

"And don't you worry," Ben continued. "I'll make it look real natural." He picked the bat up off the ground. "Like it was your idea all along."

When he raised his weapon in the air, Dame made her move. She rolled over the stones and the weeds and flung herself off the edge of the embankment.

"*Dame!*"

She fell through the air for what felt like a surprisingly long time. Long enough, in fact, to hear Ben Suarez curse her name. When she finally hit the water, a sudden cold contracted every muscle in her body. Dame struggled against the terrible gravity before remembering Adam's second edict: *Keep your movements to a minimum.*

Against every impulse, she let the stones in her pockets pull her down into the darkness. She didn't know how deep the channel went, but she knew that thrashing around would just use up what little oxygen she had left. Instead, she ripped the gag from her mouth and, with her teeth newly exposed, gnawed at the tape around her wrists.

The water gripped her body like a fist, dragging her deeper and deeper. Soon, the blackness was total, and the surface was a distant sky. As the seconds ticked by, Dame could feel her lungs boiling inside her body. She knew she wouldn't last much longer.

Don't think about the time.

Adam's final piece of advice proved the easiest to follow. Already, a new vertigo had started to blur the edges of Dame's thinking. As she struggled to stay focused, her mind reeled through all the things she stood to miss: Rosie's first day of school, Rosie's first bike ride, Rosie's first crush. People talk about their life flashing before their eyes, but Dame didn't see her life. She saw her daughter's.

It was in that moment that Dame's hands tore free of the tape. She unzipped her raincoat and let it fall into the abyss below. With everything she had left, she clawed her way back up.

Her first breath was a miracle. By her second, Dame spotted Ben pacing along the shore, scanning the surface. As far as she could tell, he hadn't seen her. Quietly, she swam alongside the embankment. Twenty feet away, the skeletal remains of an ancient dock jutted out of the channel. She made her way toward it and, after navigating the treacherous slime of the rotting wood, heaved herself up onto land. Dame sat down and ripped away the remaining tape that bound her ankles. She stayed low and waited until Ben started walking back toward the Range Rover. When she lost sight of him, she stood up and started to run.

She almost made it out to the road when something swept her legs from underneath her. Dame fell forward and smashed her head against the unforgiving ground. She felt dizzy. Had trouble seeing straight. She pushed herself up on all fours, but a swift boot to the ribs put her back down.

"That was a nice trick, Veronica Mars" — Ben stood over her, the bright green bat hanging loose in one hand — "but now we're right back where we started." He raised the bat once again. "All that effort didn't amount to much, did it?"

But then, Dame noticed something — a familiar red dot on Ben's chest.

"You're wrong," she said. "It bought me just enough time."

There was a loud bang and Ben clenched his teeth. He dropped the bat behind his head and fell to the ground, writhing and twitching.

Rachel walked past Dame and stood over Ben's body. The long wires of the taser hung slack, connecting the weapon in her hand to the silver darts in her brother's chest.

A moment later, Meera was crouched at Dame's side. "Oh my God! Are you okay?"

Dame nodded. "How —?"

"The babysitter," Meera said.

Rachel sat down in the weeds next to her brother. "I got home early and Zoe seemed upset," she said. "Then I saw your message on the fridge. '*Poughkeepsie.*'"

"'*Drop everything and run*,'" Meera said.

Rachel and Dame looked at her.

"What? Dean Winchester is a god."

"I knew something was up, and when I confronted Zoe" — Rachel wiped tears out of her eyes and took a deep breath — "she told me everything. I called Meera as quick as I could."

"How did you know where to find me?" Dame asked.

"Zoe knew. She said Ben" — Rachel looked out at the water — "came here before."

The man moaned and curled into the fetal position.

"Jesus Christ, Ben." Rachel put her head in her hands. "What did you do?"

CHAPTER FORTY-SEVEN

THEY SAT WAITING *in the little office. On the desk in front of them, the kid stared at the backs of picture frames. On the other side, she imagined there were photos of a dead daughter and an unfaithful wife.*

When Staff Inspector Weatherhead finally entered the room, the kid noticed he was dressed in the white shirt sleeves and black tie of his uniform. He looked very different from the man who had only yesterday walloped her father.

He paused when he saw them, then slowly sat down in his chair. "You have one minute before I think up some plausible reason to arrest you."

The detective pushed a piece of paper across the staff inspector's desk. "Spencer Elliot found this in Jill's typewriter after he found her body."

Weatherhead picked up the piece of paper like it was soaked in poison. He took his time reading it. Finally, he spoke. "My daughter didn't write this."

"No. Your daughter's typewriter is a Hermes Rocket. The typeface on this letter is from a 1942 Smith-Corona Sterling." The detective stood up and the kid stood beside him. "You shouldn't have to look too far to find one of those."

The staff inspector glanced down at the paper again. It was hard to read the expression on his face. The kid and the detective made their way toward the door.

"You probably think I owe you an apology," Bruce Weatherhead said.

The detective paused. "Honestly" — he put his hand on the kid's shoulder — "I don't know what I'd do if someone took my daughter from me."

A few minutes later, they sat in the Buick and waited for the traffic on College Street to thin out.

"It was Mrs. Elliot, wasn't it?" the kid said. "When Spencer told her the truth about everything, she wanted to protect him."

"How do you know?"

"She wrote the note. She was the only one with a key to the cabinet — the one they kept the fancy typewriter in."

The detective nodded his head. "How did she do it?"

The kid thought for a minute. "The night she died, Jill had a bad headache and Mrs. Elliot gave her some Tylenol. Except it wasn't Tylenol, was it? She gave Jill the pain meds for Mr. Elliot's broken leg."

"That would explain the opioids in her system."

"A few hours later, Jill would have been half asleep in the bathtub. All Mrs. Elliot had to do was let herself in with Spencer's house key and push Jill under the water."

"And that would explain the bruises on Jill's chest. Nicely done, partner."

"She didn't seem the type, did she?"

"Nope. She didn't."

The kid was quiet for a moment. "Do you think anyone is capable of murder?"

The detective checked the rear-view. "I'm not sure about that.

But one thing I am sure about — every mother I've ever met would do anything to protect her child."

"Is that what Mom was like?"

"Yeah, partner. That's what she was like." He put the car into gear. "Come on. Let's go home."

CHAPTER FORTY-EIGHT

"AND TO YOUR knowledge, Ms. Polara, how many units had Mr. Marinetti sold before he had legal clearance to demolish the existing heritage structure on site?"

Dame leaned forward. Despite the fact that most of the seats were empty, and the judge looked half asleep, she still felt small in the big room. "Mr. Marinetti had already sold off almost seventy per cent of the units."

Meera, sitting in the front row, gave her two thumbs-up.

"Seventy per cent?" The Crown Attorney turned to the jury and raised his eyebrows. "That's quite impressive."

The courtroom, Dame had observed, was one of the last great venues for live theatre in this city.

"Ms. Polara, was this the first time Marinetti Developments misrepresented the availability of its properties to the public?"

"Uh, no. It was not."

Dame snuck a glance at the defendant. Phillip Marinetti was in his late sixties but sported the thick hair and slim build of a man half his age. There might not be a fountain of youth, but sometimes a sizable bank account is just as good.

"Would you care to elaborate?"

"They pulled the same trick with a number of properties

listed on the Heritage Register: the Blakely House in 2008, the Edinburgh Hotel in 2010, Baldwin Hall in 2011, Saint-Boniface Church *and* the old post office on Leslie Street in 2013 — I could keep going if you'd like."

"That won't be necessary, Ms. Polara. What you're saying — if I understand you correctly — is that Marinetti Developments has not just committed the occasional infraction but has engaged in a clear pattern of illegal activity."

"Yeah. That's been their go-to move for a while now."

The Crown Attorney took a few steps toward the witness stand. "Ms. Polara, what might make a heritage property attractive to a developer?"

"Heritage properties usually *aren't* attractive to developers."

"And why's that?"

"Well, even though these properties have a lot of historical and cultural value, they're always tied up in red tape. Even if you own the property, you still have to apply for permits anytime you want to make any significant structural changes. And to have one of these properties demolished" — Dame let out a low whistle — "you need some friends in high places."

"And what," the lawyer asked, "would happen if you had friends in high places?"

"You'd be able to corner a very specific and very profitable market of property development."

"I see." The Crown Attorney laced his fingers behind his back and took a little stroll past the jurors. "So, why then," he pondered, "do you think Mr. Marinetti was so *confident* that he would receive permission to demolish all of these historical buildings?"

"*Objection*," Marinetti's lawyer shouted. "Calls for speculation."

"Sustained," the judge said.

It was a nice move. The defence could object all they wanted, but the idea was firmly implanted in the jury's mind.

"I'll ask another question: Ms. Polara, could you describe your professional relationship with Ms. Peggy Beckers?"

Dame nodded. "Ms. Beckers was the team leader of the Heritage Planning Department for the City of Toronto. She was my boss, essentially."

"And to your knowledge, did Ms. Beckers — your boss — ever use her position as team leader to assist Mr. Marinetti's developments?"

"Yes. Ms. Beckers would — would —" She paused. At the back of the courtroom, an old man in a shabby linen suit was finding his seat.

"Ms. Polara?"

The old man stared at her with two different-coloured eyes. Dame took off her glasses and rubbed the lenses with a Kleenex. When she put them back on, the man had vanished.

"Ms. Polara?"

"Sorry. Yes. Ms. Beckers would secure special permits and corporate exemptions to circumvent established designations."

"Do you know of any other means by which Ms. Beckers assisted Mr. Marinetti in his efforts to develop properties in the city?"

"Yes. Ms. Beckers coerced Sharon Fischer — a member of the Municipal Review Board — to approve a number of Mr. Marinetti's development projects, regardless of their historical designation."

"*Objection*," Marinetti's lawyer called. "Hearsay. As of this date, Peggy Beckers has not been convicted of any crime related to her affiliation with Mr. Marinetti or Ms. Fischer."

"Your honour," the Crown argued, "Ms. Beckers has not been convicted of a crime because Ms. Beckers has been evading arrest for nearly three years."

"Sustained. Counsel, you know better than that."

"Let me keep it simple then. Ms. Polara, do you *believe* that Ms. Beckers created opportunities for Marinetti Developments to illegally develop heritage properties?"

"Yes, I do."

"And do you *believe* that Marinetti Developments paid Ms. Beckers to facilitate these opportunities?"

"Yes, I do."

"And *why* do you believe that Marinetti Developments and Peggy Beckers were engaged in this illegal arrangement?"

"Because Peggy Beckers told me they were."

"*Objection!*"

The judge sighed. "Sustained."

"Thank you, Ms. Polara. No further questions."

"HOLY SHIT," MEERA said, throwing her arms around Dame. "You were amazing!"

"Thanks, boss."

"Did you see Marinetti sitting there?" Lewis asked. "It was like the guy got smaller and smaller with every word that came out of your mouth."

Waves of men and women in expensive-looking suits rolled past them, carrying briefcases, leaning in to talk to one another, staring blankly at their phones. Dame's mother had wanted her to be a lawyer, but Dame figured she'd never like cigars or golf enough to be a legal professional.

"You should be feeling pretty good right now, Dame," Meera said. "Your testimony is going to help nail a guy who destroyed decades of history in this city."

"It better."

"*And*," Lewis added, "you're no longer a person of interest in a homicide investigation."

"Which is always nice."

Meera squinted at her. "So why aren't you more excited?"

"I am," Dame said. "I'm just exhausted. And hungry. Do we have time to go to Lotsa Tacos for lunch?"

"Time?" Meera smiled. "We're taking the rest of the day off, my friends. And the margaritas are on me."

As they walked toward the exit, another crowd of lawyers walked toward them. A grim palette of cobalt and navy. But amid all the sleek tailoring, Dame thought she caught a glimpse of an old man wearing something light and linen and rumpled. When she turned to look again, the old man was gone.

CHAPTER FORTY-NINE

FOR A FEW days after the trial, Dame had trouble sleeping. The idea of Peggy Beckers and her pet psychopath breaking into her apartment had infiltrated her dreams, and on more than one occasion, she woke up gasping, sweating, rushing into her daughter's room. She'd started stacking pots and pans in front of the doors as a kind of DIY alarm system. It wasn't like she was going to do any cooking with them, anyway.

That night, however, Dame was enjoying the irresitible gravity of her living room couch. Rosie was safe and asleep in her crib, the television screen was black, and the book she had started to read was boring. It seemed in her best interests to close her eyes and let her subconscious do the driving for a while.

That, of course, was when her phone started buzzing.

Nope. She didn't even bother to see who was calling. She switched it off and dropped it back onto the coffee table. The knocking started almost immediately after the buzzing stopped.

Goddammit. Dame got up off the couch and pushed the cookware aside with her foot. She opened her front door a crack.

"Hey, Polara. Can I come in?"

FOR THE SECOND time in nearly a month, Rachel Suarez sat at Dame's kitchen table, drinking a mug of tea. This time, she brought her own little Tupperware container of almond milk.

You're lucky I found those glasses," she was saying. "They were halfway under the fridge. Guess you got hit pretty hard.

Dame sat down across from her. "Have you heard what's going to happen with —"

Rachel shook her head. "Not yet."

They drank their tea in silence for a few moments. There was so much history between them, it was difficult to know where to start.

"So, listen, Polara. I need your help." Rachel leaned over and took a grey vinyl bag out of her purse.

"Are those Adam's personal effects?"

She nodded.

"You still haven't opened them yet?"

She shook her head. "I — I thought maybe we could open them together."

"Wait." Dame adjusted her glasses. "Are you messing with me?"

"No. Why would I —"

"Because of what you're wearing around your neck."

Rachel's fingers went to her collar. "Adam's wedding ring?"

"Yeah. If you haven't opened the bag, how could you have it?"

"He gave it to me before he left for Toronto Island. You know what he was like. He didn't like to play guitar with a ring on his finger. He wanted me to look after it while he was recording."

"But why then" — Dame reached across the table and took the vinyl bag in her hands — "did the coroner's report list his wedding ring as one of his personal effects?"

"What do you mean?"

"I mean, if you've got your wedding ring on your finger, and his around your neck, then whose ring is in this bag?"

They looked at each other for a moment. It was Rachel who stood up and started opening drawers.

"Cutlery's on the left," Dame said.

She returned a moment later with a pair of kitchen scissors. She cut the top off the bag and dumped the contents on the table. His wallet was there, the leather ruined by water. And a cheap watch — a stainless steel Casio that no longer kept the time. There were a few plastic guitar picks, a few loose coins. And there was a wedding ring.

Dame's wedding ring.

She picked it up and turned it over in her fingers. The familiar inscription read: *"Forget your perfect offering."*

And then Dame remembered.

"Did you say Adam wore a jacket the night he left for Toronto Island?"

Rachel nodded.

"Was it an old hunting jacket? Maybe a little small on him?"

"Yeah," Rachel said. "I'd never seen him wear it before. He pulled it out of the back of the closet. But why —"

"We used to share that jacket. Kept it on a hook by the door at our old place. The day I found out about" — Dame took a deep breath — "about you and Adam, I grabbed it on my way out of the house. I wasn't really sure where I was going, but I wound up in High Park by the duck ponds. I took my wedding ring off — I was going to throw it in the water —"

"Very theatrical."

"Yeah, well, instead I just shoved it into the inside pocket of that jacket. And that was the last time I saw it."

"Maybe that's why he called you," Rachel said. "The night that he died. He found your ring in his pocket. And he called to tell you."

"Maybe." Dame put the ring down on the table. "Guess we'll never know for sure."

"He missed you, Dame. We both did."

Dame was quiet for a moment. "Can I ask you a question?"

"Sure."

"Why did you lie about your alibi?"

"My alibi?"

"Yeah. You told the cops — you told me — you were working the night Adam died, but when I called Uplift Fitness to confirm, they said you weren't there."

"I — I don't work at the studio on Monday nights. I told you. I teach a private class."

"Where?"

"At a private residence."

"You make house calls?"

Rachel took a sip of her tea. "Sometimes."

"Okay, but when I talked to Chelsea Lodge, she figured you were seeing your boyfriend — some guy named Kristian Frisk. And later, when we were still figuring things out, Meera and I followed you to his place in Rosedale."

"Kristian isn't my boyfriend, Polara. He's a client." Rachel put her mug down on the table. "The one who gave me the taser, actually."

"But, we saw —"

Rachel sighed. "Okay look, I became friends with this wealthy older guy from one of my yoga classes. He wanted me to come to his house twice a week and offered to pay me under the table. The studio was losing money, we'd already asked the bank for an extension on our mortgage payments, and things being what they were, I couldn't really say no, could I?"

"What exactly was he paying you for?"

"You're the detective, Polara. You figure it out."

"Oh."

"It's safe, it's clean, and I'm in control. Plus, the money's good. Really good. I've always used my body to make a living. I've been a model, a landscaper, and a fitness instructor. Work is work, right?"

"Did Adam know?"

Rachel was quiet. "I think he had a pretty good idea."

Dame nodded.

"Don't look at me like that, Polara. Adam was the one who wanted to have an open marriage. Adam was the one who made up the rules. At least when I fucked around, I did it to help our family."

Dame picked up her old wedding ring and read the inscription on it. "You know, Adam and I were always such a disaster — with the miscarriages and the infidelity and everything else. I always figured he found some kind of — I don't know — some kind of stability with you. I was jealous of that. Of what I thought you had. But you two were just as fucked up as we were."

Rachel shrugged. "Love is complicated, Polara. Trying to keep a family together isn't easy. It didn't mean we didn't love each other. And as messed up as things were between us, I'd give anything to have him back. I miss him so much."

"I miss him, too."

"Yeah," Rachel said, "but at least you've had some practice."

Dame laughed. "Fuck you."

AFTER RACHEL LEFT, Dame went to the cabinet and took down the stack of unopened envelopes she'd kept there. There were eleven altogether, each with the same return address: Central North Correctional Centre, Penetanguishene, Ontario.

She brought them over to the kitchen table, sat down, and tore open the oldest one first.

Dear Dame, it started, *I'm not really sure why I'm writing this letter. I can't imagine you'll be all that excited to receive it. Maybe you'll throw it straight into the trash. Or maybe — sentimentalist that you are — you'll file it away somewhere and read it ages from now.*

Dame laughed a little at this.

How are you? How's your father doing? I guess I'm settling in here — as much as someone settles into a twelve-year sentence. It's a lot better here than at Toronto South, in any case. The food's okay, and no one's really trying to mess with me. I've been reading a lot lately.

Last winter, after everything that happened at the Sainte-Marie Hotel, you came to see me. You said you wanted to know what kind of person I really was. I told you I wasn't sure. I guess I'm still not sure.

I know we were only together for a short while, and I know you've probably moved on with your life, but I thought, maybe, if I wrote to you now and then, you'd be able to decide for yourself what kind of person I was. And that, maybe, one of these days, you might even write back.

Hope you're well,

Gus

One by one, she read through the letters. He talked about what kind of food they served him, how the other prisoners treated him, how his mother refused to visit him, but would accept his collect calls every Wednesday night (*"She still calls me Goose."*).

And, letter by letter, a picture came into focus. A picture of a man she knew and did not know. A man who did terrible things under drastic circumstances. A man who accepted the consequences of his actions. A man that, maybe, she wanted to know a little better.

And when she finished the last letter, she stood up and found a pen and notepad in the junk drawer. She sat back down at the table and stared at the blank page. God, how long had it been since she'd written an actual letter? She smoothed the paper with her hand, uncapped the pen, and waited for the words to come.

It was time to tell Gus Morrow about his daughter.

CHAPTER FIFTY

AFTER A THANKFULLY uneventful Tuesday, Dame caught the 504 and stared out the window as it passed by the Union Building, the Royal Alex, and the countless grey condos that cast their shadows across King Street.

Earlier that afternoon, Dame had learned that Phillip Marinetti was expected to serve six years in prison, pay a number of exorbitant fines, and step down as CEO of Marinetti Developments. Somehow, as the streetcar rumbled and screeched toward her neighbourhood, all the glass and steel towers she passed seemed a little smaller, a little less imposing.

It was amazing, Dame was coming to realize, how quickly life could return to some semblance of normalcy. Already, people at work had stopped asking her about her near-death experience and started focusing on whether or not the Blue Jays would make the playoffs. Rosie had switched from diapers to Pull-Ups. Terrence had dashed Meera's matchmaking hopes by moving in with a young man from the Accounting Department. And, with an almost perfectly articulated question, Dodge had asked Fatima to marry him.

Things felt strangely steady, but she knew it wouldn't last. Andrew Hall and Carl Oates had recently requested a *formal debrief* about her *informal investigation* (Hall had stressed these words in his email). Both Ben Suarez and Zoe Marsland were serving time in detention centres and preparing to face prosecution in the spring. Dame knew it was only a matter of time before they subpoenaed her again. But for now, she felt like she had found some kind of balance.

Maybe the most daunting change on the horizon — as far as Dame was concerned — was that after more than two years on the planet, Rosie was finally going to meet her father. That Friday, Dame was taking her daughter up to Penetanguishene for the long weekend. Their first Thanksgiving together. She wasn't sure how to feel about it, but at the very least, it felt right.

Dame got off the streetcar at Dufferin and walked the rest of the way to the large Victorian on Dunn Avenue that housed Sunny Day Childcare. September had been unexpectedly hot, but the weather was cooling, and the leaves were starting to reveal their October orange.

As she neared the house, she could see Aunty Bea and the two boys playing in the front yard. One of the boys wore a blanket tied around his neck like a cape. When the caregiver spotted her, she came and stood at the fence, a quizzical smile on her face.

"Uh-oh. Did you forget about our plan for today?" she asked.

Dame paused. *Had she?* It wouldn't have been the first time she walked all the way here before realizing it was a Thursday. But no, it was a Tuesday. And Rosie should be here, waiting for her, like any other Tuesday.

"I don't think so," Dame said.

"You messaged me this morning to say that Rosie's grandpa was going to pick her up. They left about half an hour ago."

"Wait. Dodge was here?"

"And it was so nice to finally meet him. He's really quite the charmer. I can see where Rosie gets it from."

"Huh. I wonder if —"

"Snazzy dresser, too. But he should really take better care of that suit."

"Suit?" Dame couldn't remember the last time Dodge wore a suit. For that matter, she couldn't remember if Dodge even *owned* a suit.

"Linen wrinkles so easily. He should really get someone to iron it for him."

"Sorry — a linen suit?" Fear and dread started pushing themselves through every vein in her body. "Was he wearing dark glasses?"

"He was, actually. And when he took them off, I was a little surprised." She walked over to her front steps and picked up something in a plastic grocery bag. "You never told me your father had heterochromia. I read about that in nursing school."

"Hetero —"

"You know — two different-coloured eyes."

A spiderweb of ice wrapped itself around Dame's heart. Time slowed, and she fought off the blank, stupid madness of panic.

"Anyway, it's a good thing you stopped by. Rosie left this."

Aunty Bea handed her the plastic bag. Inside was Rosie's raccoon.

"Bea?" Dame's voice was barely a whisper. "Could you call 911 for me please? That man — that man was not my father."

A darkness crept over the woman's face. Silently, she turned and hurried into the house. Dame held on to the fence to keep her balance. She could hear a dog barking in the distance. Two people arguing in a language she didn't speak. Somewhere, music fell out of an open window. Peggy Beckers had made good on her threat. Dame's daughter was gone.

ACKNOWLEDGEMENTS

First and foremost, thanks to my partner Sarah Wyche for her continued support.

Thanks to Walter and Ezra, my parents, Sam Hiyate, and all my early readers, including Elyse Friedman, Mark Rhyno, and Leanne Toshiko Simpson.

Thanks to Marc Côté, Sarah Cooper, Fei Dong, Marijke Friesen, Sarah Jensen, Barry Jowett, and the incomparable squad at Cormorant Books.

The following people have also helped me keep this mystery train on the tracks: Justin Armstrong, Kityan Au, Catherine Bush, Fraser Calderwood, Kerry Clare, Jeff Dupuis, Andrew Ekblad, Hollay Ghadery, Sahar Golshan, J.E. Hewitt, Jeremy Luke Hill, Andrew Hood, Amy Jones, Grady Kelneck, Kelvin Kong, Nina Lynn, Cara MacMillan, Mathew McCarthy, Ben Minett, Dale Morningstar, Aefa Mulholland, Bryan Muscat, Lee Puddephatt, Deepa Rajagopalan, Christina Ray, Elizabeth Renzetti, Sam Shelstad, Russell Smith, Jamie Tennant, Vocamus Writers Community, Emily A. Weedon, Karmen Wells, Damian Weston, Nathan Whitlock, the Wyches, and the incredible staff at Guelph Collegiate Vocational Institute.

Thank you to the Bookshelf and to independent bookstores across Canada.

Thanks also to the North Writers Group: Chris Bailey, Diana Biacora, Kris Bone, John Currie, Simone Dalton, Radha Menon, Walter Palmer, Ashish Seth, and Aaron Tang.

And, as always, thanks to the 2019 graduating class of U of G's MFA program: Claire Freeman-Fawcett, Alexandra Mae Jones, Rebecca Kelly, Hajer Mirwali, Stephen Near, Marilo Nunez, Oubah Osman, Kaitlin Ruether, Leanne Toshiko Simpson (yep, twice), Bardia Sinaee, Zack Standing, and Ambika Thompson. No final hangouts!

(No thanks to Mayday Chungus Tessa Rhyno Wyche for eating my eyeglasses.)

The title *Who By Water* is a reference to the lyrics of Leonard Cohen's song "Who By Fire" featured on his 1974 album *New Skin for the Old Ceremony*. Cohen's song echoes the Jewish liturgical poem *Unetaneh Tokef*. I borrow this sacred language with the utmost respect for Jewish people, culture, and faith.

We acknowledge the sacred land on which Cormorant Books operates. It has been a site of human activity for 15,000 years. This land is the territory of the Huron-Wendat and Petun First Nations, the Seneca, and most recently, the Mississaugas of the Credit River. The territory was the subject of the Dish With One Spoon Wampum Belt Covenant, an agreement between the Iroquois Confederacy and Confederacy of the Ojibway and allied nations to peaceably share and steward the resources around the Great Lakes. Today, the meeting place of Toronto is still home to many Indigenous people from across Turtle Island. We are grateful to have the opportunity to work in the community, on this territory.

We are also mindful of broken covenants and the need to strive to make right with all our relations.